This Farewell Symphony

This Farewell Symphony

Edmund Bealby-Wright

First Published 2011
by Impress Books Ltd
Innovation Centre, Rennes Drive,
University of Exeter Campus, Exeter Ex4 4RN

© Edmund Bealby-Wright 2010

The right of the author to be identified as the originator of this
work has been asserted in accordance with the
Copyright, Designs and Patents Act 1988.

The stories, characters and incidents portrayed in this book are
entirely fictitious. Any similarities to persons or organizations,
actual or not, living or dead, are purely coincidental and unintentional.

Typeset in 11/13 Garamond by Swales & Willis Ltd, Exeter, Devon

Printed and bound in England by imprint academic.com

All Rights Reserved. No part of this book may be reprinted
or produced or utilized in any form or by any electronic,
mechanical, or other means, now known or hereafter invented,
including photocopying and recording, or in any information
storage or retrieval system, without permission in writing from
the publishers.

British Library Cataloguing in Publication Data
A catalogue record for this book is available from the British Library

ISBN: 978 1 907605 109

In fond rememberance of P
an inspiring friend

Acknowledgements

This book owes its existence to the endurance of my beautiful wife Nedra. Bits of it have benefited from critical assessment and encouragement from Dr Anthony Mellors, Professor Fiona Robertson, and Ian Marchant, Jackie Gay and Nicola Monaghan, who have all taught me at the National Academy of Writing. Other passages were workshopped by my fellow students; Robert Ronsson, Bruce Johns, Fiona Joseph, Federay Holmes, Geoff Mills, Roger Noble, Nick Le Mesurier, and Bobbie Darbyshire. Thank you all for encouraging and tolerating me. Three fellow tyros have been especially valuable – Tina Freeth, Rena Brannan and Sophie Ward. My family have of course been unable to avoid reading duties too.

Lastly, having masterclassed an excerpt, the Director of the National Academy of Writing Richard Beard read the entire ragged opus and with his superfine mind helped me form it into a presentable final draft. Did I say presentable? I meant prize-winning.

There can be no better proof of how much need there was for all this help than a glance at my age cross-referenced with the words 'New Writer'.

Many thanks are also due to Richard and Julie Willis, Colin Morgan and all at Impress Books, together with everyone at Exeter University who has been involved in organizing the Impress Prize For New Writers and the publication of this book.

Finally to the curious reader: I hope we meet again.

No one is truly dead until they are no longer loved.
Théophile Gautier, *The Tourist*

. . . it is not too fanciful to suggest that at this period the symphony was expected to represent the whole of man. The first movement is his intellect, the second his sensuality, the third his manners, and the finale his sense of fun.
Antony Hopkins, *Talking about Symphonies*

The Programme

First Movement – Head	1
Allegro Assai	3
Second Movement – Senses	69
Adagio	71
Third Movement – Manners	103
Menuetto	105
Trio	130
Menuetto da Capo – Senza Ritornello	145
Fourth Movement – Fun	157
Presto	159
Adagio	167

I
HEAD

Allegro Assai

You are about to read a story that begins with the line *The coach left Vienna for the long drive to the Prince's summer palace*, but don't take anything for granted, this historical romance belongs in the present, as does the coach. Along its dark green flank are the words *Euphony Escorted Tours* in gold letters, and instead of a royal crest, it bears the tour company's insignia in the form of an enormous treble clef. It is a Mercedes Travego, with tinted windows, air con, drop-down video screens, and rear toilets. Euphony Escorted Tours invites you to climb on board this, the most luxurious landlocked vessel ever to be found cruising the autobahns of the Austro-Hungarian Empire.

The coach was not quite ready to leave Vienna – and so the story had not yet begun. First it had to gather its passengers, a select group of the most cultured people that money could buy. Not that such people were for sale, of course. On the contrary, everything else was offered to them at an exclusive price. And where would the robust roadcruiser find these high-class passengers? Answer: by prior arrangement, standing outside five star hotels, of course.

That is why Carl, the well-rehearsed driver, spun the steering-wheel in his deft fingers and arced the tour-bus into the empty space in front of the Steigenberger Hotel, where a group of smartly dressed people casually loitered in the early morning sunshine. They all seemed to know each other already and appeared to be absurdly perked by their breakfast of coffee, ham and cakes. They gambolled up the metal steps into the Travego, nodded at Carl and received an officious greeting from a woman who introduced herself as their tour guide. They were all Germans, and had expected the coach to come for them first. So, when they saw the elderly couple sitting in the midst of the cabin, a look of puzzlement crossed their faces. They passed along the aisle in an amicably informal shuffle to take their seats, confirming the impression that they were all well acquainted. Checking that his passengers were safely seated and belted, Carl engaged the gear and set off in the direction of the Hotel Intercontinental.

Although they were obliged to spend a lot of time on this coach, the Germans were in high spirits, exchanging cheery remarks in anticipation of their day. They knew that they had some of the best roads in Europe spread before them, and once they had got their seat backs adjusted comfortably, and twiddled with the little ventilation nozzles until the airflow was just right, what could prevent them from being happy? And if melancholy should happen to strike, there would be time to watch a film or gaze out through the polarised windows at the magnificent glare-free landscapes of lower Austria; some of them were even looking forward to passing the time taking a leisurely onboard dump. With so many amusing diversions, the kilometres would literally *fly* past.

Carl pulled up in the forecourt of the Intercontinental, where two women had already formed the smallest queue that is numerically achievable. They were two young women of Indian extraction travelling together; the first wore a silk salwar and kameez (with thermal undergarments) and struck the driver as his ideal of an exotic beauty; the second was more unusually clad in what looked like a frock coat, but might, the driver assumed, be some item of Asiatic wear. He was wrong about this but it wouldn't have bothered him since he took no interest in plain women. Although they both came from India, for one of them this trip was a spiritual homecoming. The tall, slim one passed down the coach fluttering her draperies and settled into a window seat, while her squat companion waddled after her, flipping up the tail of her coat to nest herself into the aisle seat. Carl was about to whisk them away but the tour guide, consulting her passenger manifest, told him that they were expecting two more from this hotel.

After a while a couple approached. From a distance you would say they were dapper pensioners recreating their salad days, but once they got closer it was clear that only the style of their clothes was vintage. Wearing a buttermilk blazer, the young man escorted his wife in her lilac lambs-wool cardigan to the coach and carefully assisted her to mount its steps, instructing her to hold on to the handrail. He followed her down the aisle with a solicitude that conveyed to the continentals (and the Intercontinentals) an English gentleman at his gentlest, and lowered her into the seat by the window as though putting a porcelain vase into a tea chest. After placing a small bag overhead, he seated himself beside her with such care there was no measurable impact of his mass on the upholstery; his buttocks were apparently weightless.

Towards the rear of the coach, the two Indian women had been regarding the onset of the delicate English couple and slyly making comments in Hindi and in whispers, either of which would have sufficed to veil their thoughts.

'Do you think he is keeping her a virgin?'

The penguin-shaped one suppressed a deep-toned laugh. 'They are trying for a baby,' she said.

'How do you know that?' asked her friend in a gasp.

'I know because I just know some things, Anjali.'

Anjali glanced out of the window, conscious that she was too literal for her friend sometimes. Satma was a prodigious psychic. There was no end to the things she could discover with her second-sense. Hadn't she found out all about *her* before she even knew herself? In return Satma felt sorry for her friend who did not have her gifts and confessed that on this occasion her knowledge was not of occult origin. 'I met him at breakfast, he was taking all the pomegranate seeds from the fruit salad, and when he saw me standing next to him he told me they were for his wife, and that pomegranates had something in them.'

'Seeds.'

'Exactly! He thinks he can get his wife knocked up by feeding her pomegranate seeds.'

'How uneducated! What is she going to give birth to, a pumpkin?'

Pondering the possibilities of pomegranate impregnation, Anjali began to giggle and soon the two friends were speculating about the other passengers who were all calling across to one another in high spirits.

'Those Germans seem very good friends. They must be on a group tour.'

As usual, Satma knew more than this. 'They are more than good friends . . .,' she said.

'What do you mean?'

'Wife-swappers!'

Anjali muffled her delighted shriek with her hand and furtively looked at the Germans, then wrinkled her nose. 'Are you sure, Sati?'

'It's so obvious – look at them!'

'I can't now, not without thinking of that.'

'They are nudists, too, usually.'

'Oh stop it Sati!'

The Germans were unaware that they were the cause of the barely suppressed hilarity emanating from the back of the coach.

Carl had experienced passengers in all states of drunkenness and elation, returning from victorious football matches or beer festivals, but he had never known such a buoyant mood so early in the day. It was a beautiful morning and with a whistle he pulled away from the hotel's forecourt, steering the wheel of the coach as though panning for gold, his pink fingertips protruding round its perforated leather grip. Indeed, he had sensuous hands and was perfectly adapted for his situation in life; his squatness was proportioned so that his feet reached the pedals and his arms the gear stick at a comfortable stretch. A taller man would have been all knees and elbows. Similarly, though his neck was extremely thick, he could turn his head sufficiently to get the rearward views in the wardrobe-sized mirrors that descended from the Travego's pelmet, and his belly, which had been softly growing over the years, had stopped just short of jeopardising passenger safety by rubbing against the wheel and impeding its free rotation. His greatest pleasure in life – apart from begetting children – consisted of expressing his personality through driving the Travego. However, it was an unwieldy instrument of expression for such an artist. He was akin to a tuba virtuoso waiting for someone to write a concerto for his chosen instrument, ignoring its sorrowful clumsiness. Now, as they arrived at the Hotel Imperial, the final stop before they could set forth, Carl was minded to sound the horn, but, remembering that this was a classical music trip and not a football excursion, he restrained himself.

Waiting at the entrance was an Englishwoman upon whom the force of gravity was merciless: she propped her excess bulk partly on sticks clasped in swollen hands, like an old mulberry tree whose limbs had to be supported. When she saw the coach arriving she got herself into motion, but she was so slow that before she reached the doors she had been overtaken by a little Asian man who clambered on board, agile despite being at least sixty years of age. He either did not hear, or pretended not to hear the comment she passed on his inadvertent rudeness. In a moment he was at the back of the coach and curled up in his seat.

'Tamil?' speculated Anjali, in a confidential whisper, after he had passed them.

'Or orang-utan?' suggested Satma outrageously. She believed her gifts also entitled her unlimited licence to shock. The target of this comment did not hear it, but if he had, he would have enjoyed the joke. Lakshman was a theoretical physicist of international renown, equally celebrated for his good humour. Anjali was almost right – he was a Malaysian of Tamil origin, and he did not put much price on his dignity since, with his small curved stature, he was practically a hunchback.

The stout female had reached the step of the coach and was preparing to ascend. She swore at every inconvenience, which in her rheumatoid condition appeared with such frequency she could barely keep up in swearwords. To spare the blushes of my readers I shall substitute alliterative alternatives wherever possible.

'Blast this *ferrous* step,' she began, 'why do you make it so *ferociously* high?' Transferring her annoyance to the *fumbling* handrail that was in her opinion covered in *futuristic* grease, she suddenly found herself being hoisted aloft by invisible hands. This was the first kindly act of our hero, who had arrived on the scene just in time. Without thinking what he was doing he laid both his palms on her backside and thrust her upwards to enable her ascension into the coach. He was not sure if the response he received from the front end of the hefty female was a thanks or a curse.

'Why did you feel that lady's bum, Daddy?' inquired a small voice.

'I didn't, Sally, I was helping her on board,' said our hero, astonished at his own behaviour. It was not a crime – what would you call it? Inadvisably imprudent. This was the sort of phrase he might have adopted to describe such an action to any of his banking colleagues when they conspired to inflate some unwieldy stock to unfeasible heights. But he knew he would be called to account in one of his own final audits: *You may not have meant any harm by your actions, old chum, but that fat lady's arse has got your fingerprints all over it.* Such self-administered scolding was always delivered in the wide-boy accent of the young bank traders who affected a mocking attitude towards his type of banker.

The grand lady obstructed the view down the coach as she made her majestic way to her seat and earned further speculative comments from the two young Indian women.

'So, what do you think of that? She must be a duchess or something,' said Anjali.

'Hardly! Look at her luggage!' scoffed Satma.

This reference to luggage was deliberately inaccurate for satirical effect. Once settled into her seat, considerably less well upholstered than herself, the stately personage had placed onto the empty seat beside her a green plastic bag on which the word Poundland was printed in large letters. She pulled from this plastic portmanteau a banana, which she proceeded to eat whilst she stared loftily out of the window.

'Funny kind of duchess, don't you think?'

'Perhaps she's the Duchess of Poundland.'

Finally, the last of the passengers mounted the steps to board the coach. A boy of about twelve and a girl of seven or eight were propelled down the aisle by a series of nudges delivered by an enormous holdall wielded by a man draped in misshapen brown corduroy. This was the late arrival into view of Edward, our hero, but his entrance was marred by the hugeness of his bag, to which the driver objected in gruff German monosyllables. The tour guide politely explained to the client in English that his case was too large to be carried on board. 'It will have to go in the hold,' she explained.

It was an unusually large bag to be taking on a day-trip; but it was full to capacity with spare and warm and waterproof clothing, to combat chill and spills and showers of rain. It also contained colouring materials, a sketchbook and reading books to combat boredom, and an assortment of toys – an electronic one belonging to Hamish and Sally's most beloved companion, a gingham duck with a yellow bonnet. Enough indeed for an entire window display at a charity shop, all assembled in an effort to keep two children occupied so that they didn't drive their lone parent absolutely mad.

Edward allowed the driver to take his bag away and put it in the storage compartment, realising too late that being deprived of access to these pass-times when they needed them most – on the coach – made bringing them at all somewhat pointless. He prodded his children down the aisle, looking for empty seats. The Germans had assorted themselves throughout the middle section of the coach, but there were some empty rows towards the rear. Edward could not help scanning back over the row containing the Indian woman. She was so beautiful, her face stood out like an opened flower in a field of closed buds. He can be forgiven for the double-take, since perfection is so unusual, but he tore his eyes away guiltily as though invisibly admonished.

Our hero seated himself across the aisle from his children. What can we say of him? He is a man with bottom, mentally as well as physically. He looks good in corduroy. He has a public school haircut; presumably, then, he went to a public school. His children were well behaved and they showed no sign of excitement to be going on this trip. The boy began to fiddle idly with the reclining button and his little sister frowned out of the window.

'Is there going to be a film, Dad?' asked the boy, spotting the overhead screens.

'I don't suppose so.'

'This is so lame.'

Edward had to be careful dealing with Hamish. What sometimes came out as inflexibility or rudeness could be the only way he dared to show his deeper feelings. Or alternatively he could just be a stubbornly annoying little boy. 'Hamish, this is going to be wonderful, I promise,' said Edward, willing himself the strength to stay chirpy. 'You will never forget this day.'

Sally turned round. 'We're going to meet Mummy aren't we, Daddy?'

Hamish immediately retaliated to this by straightening his seat back so that it banged her elbow, and when she whined he maintained, rather plausibly, that it was an accident.

Sally transferred her whine across the aisle: 'But Daddy, you said . . .'

Edward leaned across the aisle and lowered his voice almost to a whisper, but a harsh one, that conveyed his anxiety; 'I said we would get to know Mummy better, by finding out more about her – this is what she did. You would like to know what Mummy did, wouldn't you?'

What mummy 'did' was music; she played the violin. Edward's banking colleagues, who mostly had to resort to coupling with other bankers, could not explain how he had found the time to meet a glamorous classical musician given the incompatible working hours. For Edward, it had been as if he had been given a free pass to another universe co-existing in London. On the way back to Putney he sometimes crossed platforms with Pamela's friends carrying musical instrument cases on their way to the South Bank.

'What are you up to tonight?' he would cry out.

They would say 'Dick Shit', meaning the Dixit Dominus.

Once in a while a rare serendipity would strike their transitions and he would bump into his outgoing wife on his way through the connecting tunnels, and they would speak under the suppression of painfully amplified music by Gerry Rafferty and shake their heads with perplexed love.

They were Orpheus and Eurydice in the underground. Edward and Pamela worked in different worlds and by different timetables.

Their domestic life coordinated well – at least in terms of childcare, the sole responsibility for which had now become Edward's. He was used to handling Sally and recognised the signs that she was about to curdle; this could become a sulk, or even tears.

'I want Jemima!' she screeched, loud enough to be heard by the Indian women, who exchanged significant looks. 'She wants her mother.'

Edward immediately took to pleading in a falsetto voice: 'Sally, darling, you know I had to put her in the boot.'

Hamish resumed his destruction-testing of the seat recliner by pushing his feet against the seat in front, thus irritating his immediate neighbours fore and aft. Edward asked himself whether he had not undertaken an impossible task – to restore in one day the yawning absence from their lives.

Introductory remarks, having gone round in German, came round again in English. This was their tour escort; not Frau, certainly not Fraulein, but, as she preferred to be acknowledged, Doctor Dietrich. Hush, she is about to speak.

'Welcome on board, everyone, I hope you enjoyed a good breakfast and with apologies for the late start, we will see if our driver can make up for lost time by driving *molto allegro con fuoco, ma non troppo!*'

Some of the passengers responded with muffled laughter, others wondered why she had just added Italian to her already multilingual burden when most of the anticipatory chatter heard so far had been in German and the silences could be presumed to be in English. If there were any Italians on board, they were uncharacteristically taciturn.

This excursion was alluringly dubbed the *Esterházy Experience* and Dr Dietrich was certainly not going to sell it cheap. Sure, she knew that it was one of the less popular day trips that competed for tourists staying in Vienna. Everyone went on the Mozart trail, or the Johann Strauss boat trip down the not-so-blue Danube. Not that Haydn was at the bottom of the league – you didn't even need to hire a coach for the Alban Berg tour, it was sufficient to hail a minicab. Being a professional, Dr Dietrich described this particular excursion as a magical journey into the musical past. Places associated with Haydn were built up into hagio-musical shrines, so she took care not to mention that the Palace of Esterházy had not been fully restored, that the gala performance would be an under-rehearsed thrashing of the Farewell Symphony by third-rate musicians, and that the catering was to be an all-you-can-eat buffet dinner. In Austria the phrase 'all you can eat' is seldom used; for most visitors *all you can stand* covers it.

Dr Dietrich was the conductor of the tour, but she was more a bus conductor than a conductor on a concert platform. True, she was the only one standing up and facing backwards, but her backward-facing posture did no more than verify her confidence that the driver knew the way. If we widen the philosophical viewpoint we can infer that she comfortably assumed that the future was as reliable as the past, and being a proficient explorer of the past she anticipated that the future would succumb to the same assumptions. She loved history; it was so fixed, nailed down by facts. She did not care for music at all, but this was Austria, you couldn't get away from it.

Whilst the Mercedes Travego was steaming into the sunlit future towards its first destination, her job was to interpret the experiences they were about to share. For safety reasons she chose not to do this by waving her arms about in that narcissistic puppetry practised by the symphonic breed of conductors. She guided her band of travellers through the musical landscape with her voice alone, aided by a microphone that descended from the ceiling on a length of pliable armature.

Proud linguist that she was, Dr Dietrich felt obliged to say everything twice, since the group was bisected by language into the Anglophones and the Deutsche-Spreckers. The absence of French passengers was a blessing, but still, Dr Dietrich had a lot of facts to get through, and she had to get through them in duplicate, so she packed at least five into each rapidly fired-off sentence. Out of mercy I have removed all but the most essential facts and dates from the torrential hailstorm of Dr Dietrich's guidance.

'I hope you have all got your passports because today we shall be going over the border into Hungary, but we will also be travelling back in time to the summer residence of Prince Nikolaus Esterházy where we will be enjoying a wonderful performance of Haydn's symphony No. 45, the *Abschieds*, or 'Farewell' Symphony – and we will hear it being performed just as Prince Nikolaus himself would have heard it – in the very same chamber, and with the musicians in the costumes of the day – and for such time travel, no passports will be required. The Hungarian border guards are not so lenient.'

To choose the median between the age she admitted to and the age she looked, Dr Dietrich must have been fifty-seven and a half. The other thing about her was that she had absolutely no bottom: she was all thorax; her pinstripe slacks fell from her back straight down unbuttocked, which only exacerbated her top-heaviness and made her job more perilous, especially as the coach swung round a turning off the Ringstrasse. Whilst the driver was performing this manoeuvre as if trying to prove that Fiat Cinquecentos didn't have all the fun, she never lost her hold on the nearest headrest, nor did she relax the grip with which her elbow clutched her handbag. She held onto her bag with iron resolution and frequently dipped into it for the tools of her tirade: throat pastilles, nicotine gum, caffeine pills and – most imperatively after that lot – breath fresheners.

One of the passengers was getting up out of his seat, despite the fact that the Travego was in motion. Edward was staggering down the aisle bellowing like a corduroy cow being taken to slaughter.

'I'm terribly sorry,' – a traditional English gambit: the apologetic opening before the command – 'we have to go back, I'm afraid. I haven't got our passports with us.'

'Have you checked your pockets?' asked Dr Dietrich sternly.

Whilst such a question would have provoked fury in some, Edward merely flapped his jacket like a flightless bird. The stench of caffeine and tobacco on Dr Dietrich's breath restored his spinal rigidity and he assured her that they were in his hotel safe.

Dr Dietrich sighed, and said to the coach driver: 'Da capo, subito!' Carl was not a musical man, and so she explained it to him in German without gimmicks.

Carl took special delight in swinging round the vehicle to go back to the Hotel Imperial. With the expertise of a mahout he about-faced the elephantine vehicle and set off at a charge. As he drove the coach back into the centre of the city, Dr Dietrich said in German that they were getting a free tour of Vienna thrown in, which made the jolly Germans laugh, but not enough to encourage her to repeat the same quip in English.

When the coach stopped outside the Hotel Imperial Edward jumped from the step as the doors were still parting and sprinted in to the reception to get his room key. Hamish and Sally watched their absconding father and wondered if they should get off the coach too.

'We should probably stay here . . . for a bit,' said Hamish.

'What if he doesn't come back?'

'He will come back, stupid.'

'What if he doesn't?'

They decided that they would keep a look out and if he didn't come back in five minutes, they would start to scream.

Having ascended to his room and opened the empty safe, Edward returned to the front desk ready to accuse just about anyone of stealing the passports. It did not help that the receptionist was a master of the supercilious arts. He was the same fellow who had greeted Edward into the hotel with the solicitous inquiry: 'Are you here for the clown conference?' Edward had been too tired from the journey to respond coherently to this comment. He was admittedly holding a bag with the face of a cow sown onto it in pink felt, which had picked up some dust since Sally had started dragging it on the airport terminal floor. Since at the time both the children were out of sight – Sally collapsed across some lobby seating; Hamish dangling his fingers in the waters of a kitsch indoor fountain – Edward could see how the Ermintrude bag might be enough to wrong-foot the receptionist. For myself, I believe that Edward was innocent snake-feed to the boredom of that arch maître of the lobby, but then I happen to know that there was no clown conference booked for that week.

'Perhaps, sir, you packed the passports in your bag,' suggested the receptionist.

Edward had forgotten about the bag. He dashed back to the coach where Dr Dietrich was drawing the exhaust from a cigarette.

'So, we may go now?'

'No, they weren't there – can I get my bag please?'

Dr Dietrich stepped on her half-finished cigarette and called Carl down from the driver's seat to retrieve the bag from the storage hold. Once Carl had grudgingly performed this labour Edward unzipped the holdall and began to rifle through its contents. Kneeling on the ground, he pulled out everything: the spare clothes, the cuddly duck, the colouring books, an electronic game, and endless other requirements of juvenile travel. He spread them all out on the tarmac until the bag was empty, but the relevant documentation wasn't there. He checked his jacket pockets again, a sure sign of desperation, and in doing so looked up, and what he saw struck him like a heavy blow to the back of the neck.

In the tinted window of the coach was that beautiful face of the Indian woman. She was looking down at him and smiling. Was she smiling? Yes. And laughing? Yes, he saw in her eyes the amusement, the perfect teeth displayed, and though he could not hear it, he knew she was laughing. The next time he looked up he saw the other face had appeared beside her beautiful one. Edward had no choice but to carry on searching the outer pockets of the bag knowing that he looked utterly ridiculous.

Meanwhile, Hamish had stepped off the coach to find out what his father was doing. Stockily built like his dad, though shrunk to scale without keeping the proportions exact, taking more off the height than the width, Hamish looked like a boy made out of bricks. There was hope that at puberty he would show some signs of his mother's willowiness, but at twelve that was not evident.

'Dad, what are you doing?' he asked in a monotone.

'Hamish!' gasped Edward. 'You had them, didn't you? I saw you looking at the photos – what did you do with them?'

'With what?'

'The passports.'

'That was two days ago, Dad – at the airport.'

'Where did you put them?'

'I gave them back to you, Dad.'

'Did you? I don't remember – I know what you're like – always fidgeting with things and then losing them.'

'That's so unfair!' Hamish resented the unjust accusation, and Sally appeared at the step of the Travego, alarmed at the unhinged behaviour of her parent.

'What are you doing with Jemima, Daddy?'

'Nothing.'

'Yes you are, you're hurting her, give her to me.'

Crouching so that he could direct his intensity directly into their faces, Edward subjected both his children to a brief but harsh interrogation. The power of his bombast only succeeded in making Hamish very angry and making little Sally cry and making Edward himself ever more flustered and confused. And, throughout, he felt the presence of that face looking down at him from the panoramic window of the coach. He glanced up and despite the polarised and tinted windows, and the relative darkness within the coach, he could clearly see her face again – long, symmetrical and laughing.

The mockery from above was hard to bear, especially since he was making a fool of himself in precisely the sort of area in which he was supposedly most competent. If he had fallen off a horse he could have laughed off the pain and brushed off the dirt, knowing that he had never been a horsey type anyway. The care of valuables, however, was his trade, and he had shown himself incapable of looking after three important documents and, what was worse, he had also lost his temper. He was beneath ridiculous, he was unprofessional.

There was a cough and the uniformed hotel receptionist was back at his side holding the passports and unsuccessfully repressing a smirk. Edward's demeanour instantly changed, he was so flooded with relief he no longer felt the eyes of laughter on his back. Looking up at the slim and immaculately attired figure, he practically blubbed.

'You found them! Where were they?'

'The maid discovered them quite easily when she stripped the bed. They were under the pillow, sir.'

Instantaneously Edward remembered that he had put them under his pillow last thing at night so that he wouldn't forget them. He could even recall feeling the corners of them beneath his head as he tried to sleep, and more than once in the night he had been roused by the discomfort of their presence, and yet a moment ago his mind was fabricating all sorts of alternative theories that included theft and espionage rather than direct recourse to memory.

What's the use of recalling these vivid images and sensations now, Chum? Edward's silent auditor challenged. *Your memory is playing tricks on you, I should watch myself mate; you know where this leads.*

He had been hampered by dreaming of Pamela. Last night in his room at the Imperial, he had encountered her again in a dream. Their house in Putney was being redecorated (would his therapist interpret this as rubbing her memory out or just the subconscious reaction to sleeping in a strange bedroom?), when Pamela came home unexpectedly (with some of her orchestral friends? Possibly, but anyway they quickly dissolved). Perhaps one is better prepared for the unexpected in sleep because although Edward was thrilled to see her again, he was not astonished.

To get away from the smell of paint they walked around the small back garden together, where they struggled to have a natural conversation, as though they were strangers who had only just met. Circling the trampoline, he said apologetically: 'The garden's all gone to ruin since you left.'

'That peony will come back,' she said.

It was this dream that had caused him to oversleep and forget where he had put the passports. He knew from previous dreams that this one would keep coming back to disturb him all day.

Edward fumbled in his jacket pockets this time for some change to tip the receptionist, who accepted it circumspectly, unable to conceal his contempt. Edward was pitifully grateful for having been granted this pardon and knew that he was the flunky now.

As he repacked his bag, Edward could once more sense the mocking smile of that dark, lovely face looking down from the coach window onto his back. When he stole an upward glance he saw that she had pulled the gauze curtain across to spare both of them further embarrassment. No amount of gauze could bandage Edward's wounded dignity. He followed his angry children back onto the coach, past the angry driver and the angry tour-guide. He risked smiling apologetically at the other passengers, the briefest apology, so that they could restart their daytrip promptly. After causing such a long delay, he could at least return to his seat and not strain their patience with unreturned grins.

'Got them!' he said, patting the breast pocket of his jacket, which only reminded him that he was now damp with sweat. Negotiating his way down the narrow aisle, he took his place opposite his two children who he could see were snubbing him whilst beaming hatred in his direction. Sally held Jemima protectively, and Hamish was thumbing furiously at the little arrows on his game pad.

Edward knew that of course he would eventually be back on good terms with his children, but he felt that everyone else on the coach must be fuming with hatred for him and winning them round would be a tougher job. An incomplete survey left him simultaneously disappointed and grateful that he was sitting alone. The Germans seemed a high-spirited bunch; they were sharing jokes, no doubt about him. Further forward there was that grandiose dame with arthritis and an empty seat (or nearly half of one) beside her. Edward could see her between the headrests, eating a hotel croissant out of her Poundland bag, which she held up to catch the falling crumbs, her face grim but calm. A few rows ahead of her, the fretful young Englishman in the cream blazer was long-windedly comforting his silent wife for the late start, reassuring her that soon everything would be all right. From other rows Edward imagined he could discern the voices of Austro-German disdain and disapproval.

The sweat resulting from coffee and panic was uncomfortably confined in his shirt. He pulled on the Travego's air vent as the tour escort recommenced her outline of the day's itinerary. He realised at once that the only derision that wounded him was that of the Indian beauty who had mocked him with her eyes. The two Indian women were sharing something privately between themselves, he could hear their voices in an attractive mixture of Hindi and giggles and he felt sure they were discussing him, and in this case at least he was right: they were speculating about the probable causes for the absence of wife and mother from the truncated family.

'What do you think has happened to her, Sati? Do you think she's pretending to be ill so she can spend the day lazing around the hotel?'

'No, they have had a row.'

'How do you know?'

'I can just tell. She's gone shopping to spend his money, leaving him to look after the kids.'

'Do you think she hid the passports too?'

'No doubt – that would be the first thing I would do.'

Anjali's laughter skimmed across the seatbacks.

Hearing her laughter was a torment to Edward, and he determined to redeem himself by making an impression that was strong enough to eradicate the ridiculous one he had just made. He would be extremely witty, or excessively generous, so that she would forget his misdemeanours under a shower of laughter and gifts. He would win her good opinion – possibly even her love. Or perhaps he should try the route of rectitude and play the English gentleman, which, from this angle, looked like a less arduous climb. He might win some respect, but it would cost him any pleasure he might otherwise get from the daytrip.

In the dream last night he had been convinced he could make his wife stay if he had only found the happy phrase and nonchalant air. Now he was searching for the gambit to win over this other woman.

Apprehensive at the task he set himself, Edward turned to point out something (anything) of interest out of the window to his children, by way of an olive-branch, and for the first time he spotted Lakshman grinning, the Malaysian physicist and queue-jumper whose body was curled up in his seat three rows back. Edward did not know that the smiling man was a physics professor with an international reputation for good humour, but he recognised instantly that he had been educated by an outreach arm of the English public school system and therefore they shared the same repertoire of evasion. Lakshman's grin instantly dropped into the look of a schoolboy being set detention. Edward sat back and closed his eyes, with a brief conspiratorial smirk, reassured that he should not abandon all hope of making at least one friend.

Carl, the inspirational coach-driver, had with practised virtuosity circled the incoming traffic and resumed the journey eastwards from the city. They were, as Dr Dietrich pointed out, *dadurch hatte der Bus Verspätung,* or if you prefer; a little behind schedule. Somewhere between the Ringstrasse and the Autobahn she began detailing their itinerary in English. 'If no one else has any other reasons to delay the onset of our journey we will be making a pilgrimage to the birthplace of Haydn, the little town of Rohrau.'

The croaky guidance of Dr Dietrich had a self-generated fascination – because she would never impart any fact without first awarding it a little ribbon, telling them beforehand that it was going to be both historically accurate and of abiding interest.

'It is a most interesting fact that, among all his castles, not one gave Nikolaus Esterházy satisfaction after he had seen the one at Versailles.'

Half-attentively, Edward frowned at the Palace of Versailles being described as a castle; the word she chose sounded almost rustic. He should talk, as a man who sometimes wore brown corduroy in town, among his other sloppy misdemeanours. He dressed this way because his role had always been to be unexcitable. If we had unlimited space it might be possible to go back to his school days and see the boy who calmed fights and settled things with irate masters. If instead we were inclined to investigate his professional career, we would find that his role at the merchant bank was to act as ballast when the Young Turks rocked the boat, but most amazing of all, and of more interest to us, he had captured as his wife a beautiful headstrong girl who must have been attracted to him as another kind of anchor. With his business suit he seemed an established figure when she was still climbing her way up, and his reliable salary allowed her to be picky about accepting jobs, and to launch herself into a higher level of the musical world, which sadly is prone to treat young musicians as no better than itinerant buskers.

She had flown away now, to put it poetically, and he was heavier for it.

He could barely make out the two Indian women speaking privately. Since it is of material consequence in setting forth the events of this day, I shall once more breach their confidences by divulging to you the following dialogue, translated from the Hindi whispers:

'I have a really terribly bad feeling about this daytrip,' began Satma.

'What is it? – you mean a premonition?' asked Anjali.

'Could be – it's still too vague to say but I just feel something is going to go really badly wrong with this little excursion.'

'How badly?'

'There is the presence of death here somehow among us,' concluded Satma ominously.

What her vague premonitions of this particular morning reveal we shall have to wait and see, but I assure you that these forebodings arose genuinely from Satma's beliefs. She lived in a psychically active universe, at the centre of which was her self-generated conviction that she was the modern manifestation of Mozart reincarnated into her body. Once you have ingested an idea like that you are an irrevocably changed person. She was never simply Satma, she would always be Satma inhabited by the soul of Mozart. Of course she believed that everyone else had to be reincarnated from someone, but she was unusual for her sensitive insight and also in the distinction of the person from whom her soul had relocated. She showed no astonishment that her previous life was so illustrious, a phenomenon that has frequently been observed among enthusiasts of reincarnation.

Her present perturbations tell us much about the mind of Satma herself, a mind which was entirely in thrall to thoughts of this kind; a mind that had learned to use these ideas to manipulate others and to make something more of herself. A mind from which we must now skip three rows ahead on the Mercedes Travego and re-enter that of our hero, Edward, who was dozily imagining that he was suffering the discomfort of a hospital armchair as his head became heavy and needed support. He would never forgive himself for falling asleep. If he was not to be lost in them, Edward had to push away his thoughts. Visiting time was over. Looking up he tried to find his place in the narrative of Dr Dietrich.

'This is how Prince Nikolaus Esterházy earned for himself the name *Magnificent*,' she was saying. 'He gave order for a magnificent castle to be erected in the marshy grounds about Lake Neusiedl.' She intoned 'Neusiedl' deliciously. While Edward would probably never learn to pronounce (or spell) that word, she invoked a magical realm. It was a word that was probably easier to say whilst chewing nicotine gum.

'Within a few years this bold idea had taken shape. The beautiful castle was called Esterházy, the fairyland of Prince Nikolaus. Here he built his own private opera house and a puppet theatre in a fantastic grotto. Every evening there were concerts such as the one we shall hear tonight at which Nikolaus wore a jacket sown with diamonds.'

But it wasn't a castle it was a palace. In fact, as Edward knew, because he had spent some time researching rococo palaces with musical connections when he should have been working, it was the opposite of wearing brown in town – it was a pinstripe suit in the country. Like the rival Bourbon Bank in Versailles it was a Head Office of a financial institution that for some reason had found itself transplanted to a swamp.

'You may be expecting the sort of edifice with turrets and towers, built on the summit of a promontory so that it may not be captured.

But you would be wrong. Such castles were outmoded by Prince Nikolaus's day and their fortifications were looked upon as more of a sign of insecurity than strength. Relocating to the plain demonstrated that the fight for power had been won. Prince Nikolaus had no need of a suit of armour now that he had a jacket sown with diamonds, making himself invulnerable not by strength but by fabulous wealth.'

How wrong they were, with the revolutionary year of 1793 approaching, thought Edward. And how like his own bank that had been collecting wealth – any wealth, even phoney wealth – purely to make their destruction more calamitous, more unthinkable and in the end more absolutely inevitable.

These thoughts had taken Edward away from the route demarcated by Dr Dietrich's script; their paths had diverged, and for a while her voice was no more consciously audible than the 16-valve engine of the Travego. He was roused from his thoughts only when her voice changed gear. She had been speaking German for some time and now she suddenly made an announcement in English. She changed her tongue to introduce another speaker: 'Ladies and Gentlemen, Euphony Escorted Tours are proud to have on board, to tell us about the music we shall hear in tonight's royal performance, Professor Maximillian Kirchel from the Vienna Society of the Friends of Music.'

A man in his early seventies, the one who (to the puzzlement of the Germans) had been sitting next to his wife even before the first five-star hotel was reached, stood as upright as the low headroom allowed and made his way to the front of the coach, stooping to protect the stiff ribbons of autumnal hair that crested his head like an assemblage of peeled bark from silver birches. He was tall, especially for his age, and still handsome. Professor Kirchel was one of those fortunate men who somehow avoid male pattern baldness. They usually celebrate their triumph by keeping their hair long, and it looked suspiciously as though the professor put a permanent wave in his hair, or at least used some sort of product to keep it in shape, since his streaky grey forelock was as stiff as the carved scroll on a cello and his careful avoidance of the roof of the cabin betrayed his narcissism.

'Thank you, Dr Dietrich for all the information about Prince Nikolaus Esterházy. Of course, Haydn is an incomparably more important person than his employer, Prince Nikolaus,' he asserted, counterbalancing Dr Dietrich's monarchist snobbery with his own based on elitism. 'We know Haydn from the things he made, and we know Nikolaus only from the things he bought, and those things were standard luxuries of the day. His palace is unoriginal, his diamond jacket and private opera house show flair – but only as a consumer.'

'He bought Haydn, didn't he?' said Dr Dietrich irritably from her seat.

'Not really. Haydn was actually a hand-me-down. Like his title, Nikolaus inherited the one thing for which he is most widely remembered.'

Dr Dietrich chewed her nicotine gum peevishly.

Now that his larynx had warmed up, Max Kirchel hardly had need of the microphone as he resonated on the musical banquet that awaited their arrival. He was very concerned to right a wrong done to Haydn, who had the misfortune to be born before the emancipation of artists, when, if they were not to be itinerant strollers, were obliged to become flunkies. 'Today we may imagine the artist as a free spirit,' Professor Kirchel went on, 'but for Haydn the creative life was one of servitude. Indeed, Haydn's life had none of the characteristics we commonly associate with the word *artist*.'

Edward shuddered at the common associations of the word *banker* and felt that his life also fell short. The reality of banking was far more austere than the public assumed. In the acquisition of endless wealth the initiates spent much of their lives in rooms without natural light, furnished only with electronic apparatus and living on junk food and caffeine, sleeping on bunk beds, sometimes, when necessity demanded that they catch the HK market when it opened, having seen off the NASDAQ when it closed.

They were engaged in materialising billions, but the process often demanded that they should deny themselves all happiness, all pleasure and all rest. The life of a banker was almost monastic; they were a brotherhood devoted to wealth. They piled up the sort of sums that could gratify any desire, but in doing so lost the ability to experience desires, or the time to indulge them.

Meanwhile, Professor Kirchel rumbled on like an empty stomach. Contrasting with the striking facts of Dr Dietrich his tone was lyrical (if a little gastric) when describing the delicious 'Farewell' Symphony, or *Abschieds-Sinfonie,* ('des Adieux'). He went one better than the trilingual Dr Dietrich as he found himself unable to express the importance of the work in fewer than four languages at the same time. The resolute and virile atmosphere of the first movement he described as 'an *allegro assai* typifying the au courant *Sturm und Drang* style'. He sang the theme whilst thwacking his thigh to show how brusque and militaristic it was supposed to be. It was, he explained, a musical portrait of the Prince. Then he introduced the second theme as though he was introducing Haydn himself, explaining that the reason for the extreme change from strident to winsome was part of the story, for the second subject was intended to represent a courtier beseeching the Prince to grant a small favour. He illustrated his point with hummed sycophancy. 'The second theme simpers – Haydn's tactic is to soft-soap his august employer.'

This remarkable insight was not entirely understood by the audience but he assured them that it would become clear when they heard the symphony later having seen the interplay between the superb actors playing the roles of the magnificent Prince and his lowly Kapell-master.

Dr Dietrich had to interrupt to remind the professor that one of the actors was indisposed and would not be performing tonight. 'There has been a substitution.' She withdrew a note from her bag unfolded it and began to read: 'Sadly, due to illness, Herman Fraenkl will not be able to appear tonight as Prince Esterházy and his role will be played by an understudy.' She put the paper away in the bag and attempted a chortle. 'But don't worry people, I am sure the stand in – whoever he is – will be very good, and anyway he really hasn't anything very much to do.'

'Quite,' agreed Kirchel. 'He is, after all, a prince. We have come to pay homage to a genius not to an aristocrat.'

Dr Dietrich assured the travellers that in this respect they would not be disappointed, such was the thespian genius of Bernhardt Croek, the veteran of many Viennese theatres, who had taken the trouble to learn the very words of Joseph Haydn. Words that had been drawn from various letters preserved in numerous bureaux and collated by scholars such as Professor Kirchel, and finally memorised by the great Bernhardt Croek with the astonishing capacity that is the mystery of the acting profession. So astonishing was this great actor's ability to inhabit a role, they would be able to ask him any questions and he would answer them with such veracity that they would believe they were speaking to Franz Joseph Haydn himself. Indeed, she asserted, if Haydn's beloved Mozart were to reappear he would not be able to discern between our Bernhardt and his dear friend.

'We'll soon see about that,' said Satma, loud enough to be heard at the front.

Dr Dietrich never thought that her claim would be challenged, but then, she hadn't observed what Satma was wearing.

Professor Kirchel began running through his revolutionary analysis of the 45th symphony for the German speakers. When he sang the strident theme of the first movement, with its slashing downward strokes, they joined in, singing rumbustiously. As they sang the theme, Kirchel slashed his arm as though flogging a peasant, and to be fair, the action matched the tune very well.

After this convincing performance he went on to express the slimy phrases of the symphony's contrasting second theme and, as they knew this tune as well, they all continued to perform in pantomime and song. Kirchel cowered as he bleated out the craven notes. He was the humblest petitioner for an audience with the most terrible of princes. And most remarkably of all, the curls on his head were unmoved.

The resumption of the 'Thwacking as Usual' theme was belted out fortissimo by the Germans to prove how ineffective a direct appeal to the clemency of an absolutist prince would have been. Professor Kirchel decided it was time for him to retire from the microphone, but his triumph turned to awkwardness, as his wife provided a comment that attributed his enthusiasm for rapid solo arm movements to solitary spanking sessions. Thankfully it was untranslatable. Kirchel recovered himself sufficiently to say: 'Tonight we shall meet Haydn and the Prince. The status that they enjoy in our memories is the reverse of that which existed when they were alive. Like a marriage between a quiet man and a noisy wife.'

This simile was accidentally offensive to Dr Dietrich, but it was intended exclusively for his wife. She always accompanied her husband on these musical tours, though she barely glanced out of the windows and never followed the guides when there was a preferable café to wait in. Her only pleasure came from commenting on her husband's contributions. The nature of these comments could be judged from the amusement they caused with the other German speakers. Since she was not herself bilingual she could not offer the same satirical service to the English listeners, who had to endure unpunctuated Kirchelisms.

As the distinguished professor returned to his seat, stooping even further to protect the silver-teak arrangement of curls that he wore on his head, he received polite applause from the English and suppressed giggles from the German speakers, thanks to his wife.

Edward was grateful for the Viennese professor absorbing some of the derision that he had sensed earlier being directed at him. He was acutely self-conscious of their glances as though he was under surveillance for signs of madness, though so far the only sign of madness lay in his sense of being watched. This morning he had duly provided some evidence of loosened hinges, the worst part being that he had shouted at his children, who had done nothing to deserve it apart from being born. And he had shouted loud enough that even the offside passengers must have heard, giving them the enjoyable spectacle of an Englishman losing his cool.

The skies were darkening as they approached the outskirts of what Dr Dietrich cutely called the Bethlehem of Classical Music, that is to say Rohrau, described in the guidebooks as a neat and unremarkable town in lower Austria. They came to the old part of the village and the coach stopped alongside a single story building with a wide arch intended to allow for the entry of what in the eighteenth century were known as coaches. Their own coach driver put the Travego into park and opened the doors, which, since they operated by the compression of air, gave an apt sigh as they parted.

True to her habit, Professor Kirchel's wife remained on the coach, as did Carl, but the jolly Germans streamed off and scurried about like inquisitive rabbits released from an overcrowded hutch. The other passengers descended, Hamish and Sally refusing to hold their father's hand, but standing at his side in unimpressed silence. Their toys were weapons to be used against their parent. Sally made it clear by her caresses that Jemima was her only true friend and Hamish operated his game pad as a universal shun gun.

'What a *fetid* hovel,' was the frank assessment of the Duchess of Poundland, once she had been lowered from the coach – and she only expressed what several others were thinking.

Municipal touches, such as a white flagpole, a squat marble memorial plaque and rows of precision hedging showed that the place was meticulously cared for, if not loved. Having won the prize for Best Birthplace it persisted in a lifeless state.

Everyone gathered round Dr Dietrich at the entrance to the coach-yard. 'Haydn's father came of peasant stock,' she explained. 'Here he carried out the trade of a wheelwright and the hobby of a harpist, which is *most* interesting, when you think of it.'

Dutifully, Edward tried (as Dr Dietrich urged) to think of it: The Amalgamated Union of Wheelwrights and Harpists. Was that really interesting, or just unwieldy – turning spokes by day and tuning harp strings of an evening? Trying to accommodate both ideas in his mind comfortably at once squeezed out a mechanical instrument he and Pamela had once seen in Paris made out of an oil drum and an upturned bicycle, the spokes of which had been tightened to different notes, so that when the wheels were spun and strummed with a pair of spoons they played silly melodies. Part of a wheelwright's job is to balance the tensions within the crucial component: out-of-tune wheels loose battles, cost princes their realms, so wroughting wheels was an essential trade, whilst harpists were dispensable even in an orchestra, in fact they can only be heard if all the other musicians obligingly shut up. In any battle formation they would be a positive hindrance.

Haydn's father was wise to keep the day-job, Edward concluded.

Whilst Dr Dietrich was doing her spiel in German, Maximillian Kirchel watched with a meaningful smile. The distinguished professor and Friend of Music wasn't going to dignify the prattlings of a tour guide by contradicting them, but he spoke confidentially into Edward's ear. 'She is completely wrong about Bethlehem, of course.'

'Really?' said Edward with surprise. 'I don't think she meant it literally.'

'No, no,' said Kirchel, with relish. 'Haydn was the John the Baptist of classical music.'

The image of a severed head on its plate served up to a despot flashed through Edward's mind as Professor Kirchel set upon further explanation: 'Mozart was the marvellous child – the divine boy who could perform miracles. Don't you see, Edvard? And he died at the right age too.' Kirchel was laughing: 'You see, music is the national religion of Austria.' Then he added more cheerfully: 'Are you musical at all? I assume you are, since you have come on this excursion.'

Edward hesitated for a while before confessing; 'I used to play the viola.'

Musicians will already know how painful it must have been for Edward to make this admission. Professor Kirchel gave him a look of profound pity. Viola players are usually classed as people who hang around with musicians, and are the butt of innumerable jokes. Edward could not insist that he was no longer one of that contemptible species since it would entail revealing that he had descended to the only form of life beneath it, a banker. 'My wife got all the talent.'

'Did you play together?'

'When we were teenagers we had the same teacher, and we used to play quartets on Sundays.'

'That's marvellous,' said Professor Kirchel. 'You know Haydn played in quartets with Mozart?'

'Really?'

'Oh yes, and even when they were separated they shared their musical ideas by writing string quartets. They were very fortunate. It meant they could communicate when Providence kept them apart.

Edward was grateful that the professor was such a musical bore. It prevented the conversation becoming personal. Instead he unwisely chose to try Kirchel's sense of humour with the question 'What do you do with a dead viola player?'

'I am sorry, I don't understand,' said the professor.

'Move him back a desk,' said Edward.

These dank amusements failed to divert them from Dr Dietrich's summons and they joined the back of a long line shuffling into the building. One room had a period bed in it, nothing like a manger and almost entirely unlike the rustic cots the musical wheelwright's gifted little boys would have slept in. It also contained a copy of the parish register enshrined in a glass cabinet, at once testifying authenticity and destroying it. That object made this bedroom a notary's office, a place to register births and deaths, not a place to live.

Edward jiggled his children's shoulders. 'Look at this bedroom, kids, would you like to swap?' They looked up from their toys but gave no reaction.

Absolutely nothing was authentic, though all was admirably neat and clean. It had been scrubbed for two and a half hours this morning – eradicating all the evidence of a past epoch so recent as yesterday, and even on a cloudy day it shone with surfactant. There was no corner where the germ of memory could lurk.

As they finally trouped back out into the yard, Satma, in particular, seemed disappointed with the vacuous spiritual atmosphere: 'I'm not getting anything here,' she whined loudly to Anjali as she waved her arms in despair. 'I felt something pass through me earlier, but it was just wind.'

'Something you ate?'

'Oh come on Anji, this place is chicken-shit. Pure hillbilly.' Her unusual vocabulary was an acquisition from the American college where she graduated. It was not in her nature to neglect an opportunity to be interesting. She would have dearly liked to contribute some insights into this place, but, in spite of the urgings and encouragement of her psychic cheerleader, her powers remained unresponsive.

'Never mind, maybe we'll get something at the palace,' soothed Anjali.

'How do we know I ever went there?' questioned Satma, swishing her pleated coat-tails as though handling the hilt of a hidden sword.

How many people believe themselves to be the embodiment of Mozart's spirit at any one time I do not know, though I am sure that given the widespread belief in reincarnation and the attractiveness of Mozart I would guess that Satma was not a unique example. It was, however, a considerable inconvenience in finding her a match, as her parents had found. They had paraded, in a series of tea parties, young men with minimum grade-two piano before her. If the subject of samsara came up, Satma would not conceal her conviction from the timorous men and she argued so forcefully that none of them stayed for a second cup.

Her scholarship to an American college had given Satma the confidence to combat conventions and, having done so, to rescue Anjali from a future that she (with her degree from Pune and her lovely face) might have been unable to avoid. Anjali had no resistance to the schemes of mothers and potential mothers-in-law and there was no shortage of eager young suitors. She could have been married off ten thousand times, and knowing this devalued marriage in her estimation.

Anjali's parents blamed her reluctance to make the marital leap on her timid nature and her immaturity. After a string of refusals, they let her go to Europe to rectify these defects. A cultural tour in the company of a well-educated plain-faced friend (and American graduate) who would be sure to keep her out of trouble and show her a bit of the world could only enhance her long-term value in the marriage market. They never suspected that Satma was a more determined suitor than any of the sleek-haired Sanjays and Kishores with their excessively white trousers. With their parents' nervous blessings, the two friends went together to get a break from eligible young Maharashtrian men.

Satma and Anjali's European tour was a full blown psychic quest over an alien continent in search of previous selves. Satma, the self-attested second-coming of Mozart, had strict criteria for judging what they were shown: did it stir memories from her previous life? Experiences before birth and after death were the only forms of existence that should be recognised as reality, Satma argued with relish. She clearly enjoyed exploring the stamping ground of her previous incarnation. Then again, who would not be elated to be incarnated into the companionship of Anjali with her face of perfect symmetry?

Rohrau, however, was a spiritual vacuum and threatened to suck Mozart's spirit out of her. As Dr Dietrich told them, the building itself had been erased twice by flood and once by fire, so none of the original remained, which, she added, was a most interesting fact. Anjali had a further explanation for Satma's negative findings: 'There's no reason why you should have felt anything really, Sati,' soothed Anjali. 'I mean who says Haydn would ever have invited Mozart back to his childhood home? He was most likely ashamed of his homely origins.'

Satma was about to say 'Well, you should know', when they were interrupted.

'Never ashamed,' said Professor Kirchel with an introductory cough. 'The young lady's intuition has grasped at a commonly held falsity. If I may explain . . .' Undaunted by the heavy and intentionally audible sighs from Satma, the professor went on. 'The peasant stock from which Joseph Haydn sprang was a source of musical inspiration to him. As his genius took him into the greatest courts of Europe he brought with him his peasants, in sound at least, for the gilded halls of the aristocrats resounded to the Hungarian folk dances which he inserted into his music. It must have seemed that bucolic revelry had broken out.'

He was about to expand on several other ways in which Haydn's character had been shaped by his lowly origins, when Satma stopped him with these outstanding words: 'Drop dead, granddad.'

As Kirchel staggered away from this verbal blow, Anjali looked at Satma with a fixed expression of outraged delight. Too cowardly to take part in these acts of transcendental violence, she was in awe at the breathtaking audacity that could produce them. Her fixed expression was the result of having to restrain the urge to laugh, or cheer, or to kiss Satma.

Edward had left his children sitting on a bench kicking each other's heels and torpidly roaming their own private worlds. He had the same foolhardy intent as Kirchel, to strike up a conversation with the Indian ladies. However, he timed his approach so that he found himself in a space alone with Satma just as Anjali pursued the retreating Kirchel to offset her friend's acid tongue with her emollience. Edward had not heard Satma's brilliant bon mot and so began a conversation fearlessly. 'We haven't met – I'm Edward.'

'I think we may have – previously.'

Satma saw Edward's consternation and laughed. 'It's all right, you won't remember. It was in another lifetime.'

Edward felt he was being mocked again, which was easier to bear coming from this person who was somewhat clownish and squat. 'In that case it is nice to meet you again . . .'

'Satma.'

Now that he had discovered hers, Edward felt he was not far from learning the other one's name. He was making progress in his mission to rehabilitate himself in her unforgettable eyes after his terrible start. 'I am travelling with my children, Hamish and Sally.'

'I know.' With this response Satma gave the impression that she already knew the children's names, rather than simply being aware of their existence. She considered making a comment about Edward's wife hiding the passports and going shopping, but caution prevented her. She didn't want to freak this guy out.

Meanwhile, Edward had taken care to annunciate everything deliberately to establish the idea that this was a conversation in which many facts should be exchanged, particularly the name of her companion. 'You are travelling with . . .?'

'A heavy sense of déjà vu.'

'Oh really? Have you been here before, then?'

'You could say that – my interest in the place goes way back.'

'I should have guessed as much. You must feel quite at home here,' he said, making reference to the eighteenth-century cut of her coat.

Satma felt for a moment a fellow spirit. 'You too?'

'Yes, well – actually, yes . . . My wife . . .'

'. . . isn't with you.'

'As you can see . . .'

Edward was already collapsing under Satma's knowing looks. With silences and assumptions she made him feel he had a ball in his court the size of an asteroid. He found himself trying to tell her that his wife had been a violinist and that he had chosen this holiday as a way to compensate for her absence by introducing to his children the beauty of music. But he didn't manage to get it out like that.

'My wife, I mean my ex-wife – well anyway what I meant was, she's actually dead.'

'I know,' said Satma with the authority of aeons.

Edward sighed with relief that he would not have to go on trying to explain his predicament and did not even wonder how it had become known to this stranger. Satma's face had changed too – the wash of boredom flushed away and she beamed with shiny interest, like an old-master painting after the restorers have scraped off the candle smoke from it. 'This is so exciting!' she said. 'I can see that you are an old soul, Edward.'

'Am I?' He frowned. 'Not so terribly old, surely.'

Satma saw how he was trying to hold his stomach in and immediately slapped it, forcing a muscular relaxation. 'It's a *good* thing, you big baby! We will meet again, I am sure.'

'You mean in another lifetime?'

'No, later on today, probably.'

Laughing, Satma left Edward and joined her flawless friend, whom Edward still only knew as 'the other one', taking her arm and leading her to the coach, which had begun to throb eagerly under the gentle urging of Carl's foot.

Two universes had collided. Satma's psychically animated universe had just crashed into Edward's, which – so far anyway – had been rational. These two universes could pass through one another without explosive collisions; the changes would be undetectable at first, showing themselves in tiny alterations of the trajectory of his thoughts. By the end of this day's excursion his reason would be utterly adrift.

Before we judge him to be overly susceptible let us remember that despite having had his wife taken away, he has so far kept his family together and their lives on course for nine very difficult months. And let's admire Edward for this even more because his wife was well worth going to pieces over.

The first spots of rain were beginning to fall as Dr Dietrich curtly announced that it was time to resume the excursion. Edward found Hamish and Sally still sitting on a bench. Hamish was clicking away at his game pad and Sally was quacking to her duck. Neither of them looked up at his approach.

'Hamish, do you have to play with that thing here? I've brought you all this way.'

'I wish you hadn't,' Hamish moaned.

'You'll like the palace.'

'Why should I?'

Hamish continued taking his resentment out on pixellated helicopters.

'Did *you* like it Sally?' asked Edward.

'She didn't tell us about Haydn's mummy. She kept talking about his father, but I don't want to know about him, really,' Sally explained.

Edward grasped this opportunity to boost the popularity of fathers by setting off in search of Dr Dietrich. She was only a short leap away, standing by the coach smoking.

'Excuse me, Dr Dietrich,' he began, 'my daughter wanted to know about Haydn's mother.'

'There is nothing to say about her. She had children, she died.'

'Nothing else? Was she musical at all?'

'You had better ask Professor Kirchel that. He is on the coach.' She stepped out her cigarette butt to end the debate.

So Edward returned to fetch his children without anything to impart. Jemima was trying to jump onto Hamish's head and he was about to riposte physically when Edward grabbed his arm and tugged him to his feet.

'Upsies!' he said chummily. Sally took his other hand and the three of them (four counting the duck) stood in line to remount the Travego. Satma's coat-tails were disappearing into the coach and Edward smiled indulgently at her ridiculous clothing and her ridiculous beliefs. I suppose it's harmless nonsense, he thought.

As they waited to get onto the coach, Edward overheard the following conversation between the grand English lady with arthritis and Dr Dietrich. The agile Lakshman repeated the discourtesy of not waiting for the lady to go first, and had once again hopped on and disappeared to the back of the coach whilst she was still trying to persuade her hip to swivel sufficiently to get her foot onto the plate, though in his defence it must be said that in her preparations for the ascent she barely moved.

'Who is that *feculent* little man?' she said with considerable disgust.

'He's a Malaysian string theorist, I believe,' said Dr Dietrich.

'Really? Does he have a lot of *fundamental* theories about Malaysian string?'

This put a momentary smile on Edward's face and must have lifted his spirits, because he wasn't even offended when the woman turned her head and called down to him: 'For Christ's sake give us a hand getting into this *fuel-guzzling* charabanc.'

Eager to obey, he placed one spread palm on each of the woman's stalled buttocks, and once he had gained a purchase, thrust upwardly with all his might to hoist her into the vehicle.

You may lose your job at the bank, old chum, but you can be assured that there is a vacancy waiting for you, grabbing that lady's massive arse. You seem to have a vocation for it. At the bank Edward was used to being patronised by spivs, who treated him as a middle-aged dope. So he took no notice of the imaginary voice in his head as he handled his way down the narrow slalom of seats with dignity, and found his place across the aisle from his children who continued to hate him cordially.

The Germans, who were last on, scattered into different pairs, which came as no surprise to the Indian women. 'I told you they were wife-swappers, Anji.'

Carl took them away from Rohrau in the rain and Edward saw the departing town lit by a burst of sunlight through the clouds. With the Leitha Mountains in the distance, this was the sort of vision that rattled the spoons more effectively than thoughts of that bicycle wheel outside the Pompidou. Edward watched the landscape of the plain, with far spreading fields, its woods and promontories, spin backwards as they drove across it. Light was a good way to describe the classical style, music that did not have to be fast or slow, in the way dances are, nor either sad or happy, as romantics would see it. The classical style was composed of light and dark. It might help if he was able to see his life that way, too. When things looked black, like they did right now, he didn't have to degenerate into depression, and if he managed to muster a brighter mood, that was not necessarily a betrayal.

He looked at the profiles of his children as they watched the raindrops racing slantwise down their window. They were carrying their hurt feelings with them, rolled up in their laps. Edward knew that, whilst they were uppermost, these feelings had considerable mass and inertia, and the fact that on the appearance of an amusing distraction they would be dispelled like helium balloons did not help, since he had no amusing distractions to offer; only the birthplaces of dead composers. They were suffering pangs of loneliness, dislocation, nakedness – not literally, of course; in fact they were over-wrapped and almost smothered in intelligent fabrics.

Edward always felt it was necessary to explain to people he met (once they had passed the initial period of polite strangeness) that his wife was not separated from him by divorce or anything unpleasant like that – she was dead, which is a perfectly respectable position to find oneself in. There was always a bit of awkwardness as he was either offered sympathy or surveyed for signs of flakiness, but once he had satisfied them that he was not going to embarrass himself publicly, they could settle into a tranquil camaraderie that was almost as unruffled as their previous indifference.

This morning, however, he had shown plentiful signs of flakiness with this particular group of strangers, he had probably used up his stock of good will. Never mind, he could imagine that they would soon forget, and his stock would rise again. Then he thought of the mocking smile of the beautiful Indian woman whose name he had failed to learn. She had seen him behaving ridiculously, rummaging through the things in his suitcase; he had failed to replace that image in her mind with anything more acceptable. And it didn't help that they were such lovely dark eyes. He could only hope to restore his self-esteem by forcing those eyes to look at him with kindness or perhaps even admiration and forget that they had seen his children coming onto the coach tearful and unjustly scolded.

Edward looked over at his precious and vulnerable children across the aisle. They had started playing Squares, a game that offers a sound preparation for life; it begins with a blank grid of dots on a paper and slowly builds walls to entrap you into various dead ends.

We shall now relocate our inquiries to the Palace of Esterházy, which has already been described as a 'fairyland', by Dr Dietrich – not in search of fairies, but of human beings. Until fairies start reading and more importantly buying books, we will continue with human beings as our quarry. Another set of acquaintances will be made, with a new selection of personages who, in preparation for the arrival of the Mercedes Travego, are dressing themselves up in historical costume, though they themselves are solidly contemporary.

Some of these contemporary solids were bending over violin and bassoon cases on the floor of an unfurnished room, taking musical instruments out and wiping them down with dusters. Others were more advanced, applying rosin to bows, fixing mouthpieces and moistening reeds. They were forming themselves into Haydn's sixteen-piece orchestra. Despite the fact that most of them had not met, this being the first of these special gala performances for Euphony Escort Tours, they were able to play together as though they had spent a lifetime in a joint enterprise, which in a way they had. They did this as easily as birds flocking into formation.

They were of all ages, from students to retired teachers and all were male bar one. The lone female was Sophia, and for the sake of authenticity she was forced to wear the male clothing of Luigi Tomasino, the lead violinist in Haydn's Esterházy band. Still a student, Sophia was already a fine violinist, more than capable of playing the parts Haydn had written for Tomasino. Some of the musicians were surprised to find their leader was this slip of a girl, but by the end of the first rehearsal they had all fallen in love with her, except for Stephan the Strewelpeter-headed cellist, who was in her year at the conservatoire and had already been in love with her for some time.

Her role did mean that she had to entrap her breasts within a male jacket of the court uniform. She didn't mind sharing a single-sex changing room since the other musicians, though they were all male, were too preoccupied with their own struggles to get into costume to make lewd observations. For the sake of authenticity there was no conductor: the symphony they were about to perform came from a happy era when musicians were permitted to play unchaperoned.

In the grand Sala Terrena itself, chairs and ornate gilded music stands were being set out by a couple of stagehands with the deliberation of chess-players making their opening moves. All the preparations were being overseen by Teresa Martz, the *director*. Her job was to bring the past back to life and make it fit for modern travellers. Fit, that is, in a Darwinian sense. The past had to be made habitable by moderns, whether it was comprehensible did not concern her.

Though it was supplanted by the Empire style in European grand salons, the rococo never died. The colour scheme of white with aimless doodles in blue or pink or gold survived in wedding dresses and, of course, their associated cakes, and can still be found in some hair salons attracting the older clientele.

Teresa Martz never went to that sort of hair stylist, but tonight she was to play the part of the Prince's wife, Princess Maria, which demanded a spectacularly grand blue dress and wig. She was not going to do up the bodice for the rehearsal – it had to be uncommonly tight to squeeze a cleavage out of her modest endowment, and the wig could definitely wait. It lay on the seat of a chair, curled up like a sleeping lamb, and Teresa's bare head looked incongruously small sprouting out of that enormous dress. This show was her 'baby'. She had conceived it and spent months arranging every detail, and now she gathered the small cast for a run-through of the welcoming ceremony as Prince Nikolaus Esterházy and his court composer Franz Joseph Haydn.

'Where's the Prince?' she called out in German, then, in English. 'Kevin. Have you seen the Prince?'

A voice from the top of a ladder replied, 'Nahw Tess.' He was not up the ladder in order to look for errant princes; he was raising a suspended spot that would bathe the composer in a pool of enlightenment. It was almost fifteen years since young Kevin had decided to leave N.Z. and 'do' Europe, and he was still doing it, changing travelling companions and girlfriends as he went. With no destination or return date in mind he made his way across the continent from person to person, like a sub-clinical infection. He was very far from home, and climbing a ladder wasn't getting him any closer, but he was in no hurry to return, and he went on acquiring expertise as he went. He was now the best sound and lighting man in the business, though he said so himself.

A summer spent as a Smurf in a Belgian theme park was the colourful beginning (specifically blue) to a career in tourism technologies that took him from providing the lighting for an aquarium in

Brittany to installing the ominous audio at the Museum of Anne Frank. 'I did the Nazi footsteps coming up the stairs,' he would boast. He was now technical director at the Esterházy properties, where he was creating the ultimate sound and light installation.

When full of himself (a condition coincidental with being full of pilsner), he would proclaim: 'I've done *son et lumiere* all over Europe, mate and I'll let you into a secret. Next time you're sitting in your chair facing some historical edifice and waiting for us to throw a bucket of pre-digested history up against it, ask yourself – does this seem familiar at all? Because we use the same bloody sounds and lights every time. We had a film of some re-enactment guys walloping each other and shazam! It's the siege of Badajoz or the sack of bloody Lepanto.'

It was this sort of talk that had first aroused Teresa's interest. She had a thing for men like this, the attraction of their showmanship overriding the ridiculousness of their boasts. 'Wow, you almost make it come alive to me,' she gushed. 'How do you propose to do it?'

'I shall fill the palace with light. Make it literally *burn* with light.' As an ex-Smurf, Kevin didn't think too much, but even he saw that pleasing Teresa was an essential step to getting the job. 'As I see it my job is to make the place so blindingly brilliant you are unable to judge what you're seeing, that way you will really believe you have been taken back in time.'

Perhaps with his vigour he could take *her* back in time far enough to catch the last ovum before it left the station. He was eight years younger than her, he was tall, and looked virile enough. Yes, Teresa had allowed herself to build a nursery in the air.

Now, after nine months together, she had lost her faith in his powers. As a lover he was vigorous but neglectful. Whilst he continued lighting up the palace, he no longer did the same for her. The strain of getting the palace ready was prolonging their relationship and killing it. They had to keep it together for the sake of the Esterházys.

'If we could just get through today without a bust-up,' Teresa was thinking as she left him with his spotlights and went in search of the Prince alone. Pacing a corridor outside, she could see the veteran actor Bernhardt Croek, who was already getting into character as the wiry little peasant-genius, Haydn. He was mumbling his lines and visibly diminishing his gestures into small submissive hand movements that could have been arpeggios on a clavichord. The actor, whose renown once stretched maybe two-fifths of the circumference of the Ringstrasse and whose previous roles were far too numerous and at the same time not quite memorable enough to mention, was already in costume: the livery of an upper servant, for though master of the music he was a servant of the Prince. He occupied the middle rank of House Officer, an NCO in Nikolaus Esterházy's domestic army. He was acting young if this was really supposed to be a recreation of the year 1772, when Haydn wrote the Farewell Symphony at the age of forty. He was also not as authentic as he might have been, since the real Haydn would have played violin in the concert, but the resemblance was there – the long nose, the thin cheeks, the eyes that could express laughter or piety.

'Have you seen the Prince, Bernhardt?' asked Teresa.

Bernhardt's sigh was a soliloquy in itself. It was on account of the Prince that this evening's performance filled him with exasperation. Things would have been so different if his old pal Herman Fraenkl, who was cast as Prince Nikolaus, had not been struck down with his sciatica. The two performed together so often they were practically a double-act. In the initial read-through their interpretations of Haydn and Nikolaus exemplified a relationship comprised of mutual respect – love even – between the two great men. Herman would have given the audience a prince that exuded warmth and yet shone through with intelligence, and they could have shared the travelling expenses by coming together in Herman's little Skoda. Instead of which, he was obliged to fawn and scrape to a squat alcoholic peasant who hadn't learned his lines – and take taxis.

Teresa's search for the Prince took her into a side hall, where there were three trestle tables laid with white linen and ceramic dishes sealed with cling-film. She checked over the spread. There was some potato salad that could be mistaken for a bowl of calf vomit. There were prawn vol-au-vents topped with shrimps so tiny it looked as though they had been sprinkled with fishing-bait. There were some rustic hand-made mushroom flans, an entire local ham, a mountain of strawberries and some cakes and pastries. At another table there were glasses and bottles and a bowl of bright orange punch presumably made by fermenting glue and crayons.

'Is there proper wine?' she asked.

'Sort of,' replied the pinafored waitress.

'What do you mean sort of?'

'It's Hungarian. And there seem to be some bottles missing.'

'Oh really! By the way, have you seen the Prince?'

'He was here earlier, but he went.'

'How did I get lumbered with Tomek?' thought Teresa, but she knew perfectly well how.

For an out-of-town summer performance like this, no understudies were engaged, so when Herman Fraenkl pulled out, citing ill-health, a notice was posted in the area for anyone at all (of male gender) with theatrical experience. It is worth pausing for a while to relish the indignity done to the Prince, for whom lineage was so important. Correct gender and theatricality were precisely the requirements (in fact the *sole* requirements) of a European prince. Eventually the part was given to the only applicant: Tomek the village puppeteer.

Tomek's elevation to princedom was uncomfortable for him too. When Teresa finally found him he was sliding off a chaise-longue in a side chamber whilst trying to force his wide foot into a shoe fitted for Herman Fraenkl's narrow one.

'How much I hate Herman Fraenkl!' cried Tomek tearing the slipper open with his thumbs.

'Come on, Tomek, we have time for a *go-quickly* of the welcome speeches.' Teresa Martz's spoken Hungarian was acceptable but, like the wine, not proper.

Tomek tottered to an upright position and Teresa ran behind him to steady him and to make an adjustment to the straps that held his waistcoat tight, so that he might breathe. A few bulges were acceptable between buttons, as it was essentially a corset worn on the outside, but the gorgeously decorated waistcoat had also been made for Herman Fraenkl and it stretched unbearably around Tomek's ampler gut.

'Why did Herman Fraenkl have to be so thin?'

'You speak as though he's dead.'

'I wish he was.'

His shirt was still unbuttoned. His chubby fingers shook, fiddling the hooks into their tiny eyelets. Tomek had precious little help imprisoning himself like this. There were some servants but they were too busy putting on their own costumes. In this re-creation of the old regime they were all equally undignified.

'Shit on this collar, how could Herman Fraenkl breathe through such a scrawny neck? Won't you help me, Madama . . .'

Teresa Martz came round to the front and immediately the mystery of the missing wine bottles was solved. 'Have you got a mint? Tomek?'

He hummed, holding his breath.

'And no more until after the performance.'

'What performance?' he scoffed.

He had a point, as there wasn't much for him to do. He had his grand entrance in the legendary diamond jacket. After that he was required to sit and listen to some music. They weren't coming to see him anyway, even if it was (by an indirect last-minute inheritance) his palace.

The Communist Party had declared that the wealth of the Hungarian nobility should be shared by all Hungarians. This declaration proved almost as empty as the royal coffers. But he was at least Hungarian, a minority amongst all these Germans and Austrians and (for Christ's sake) a New Zealander, all of whom seemed to think they had the authority to order him around. Who gave them that authority? He was Tomek! No one got past him when he was a border guard! And he had outlived the tyranny that he so churlishly guarded. From now on he would concede to no more authority.

This was not strictly true since he habitually subjugated his mind (and, as the day wore on, his legs) to the higher power of alcohol.

'Look ahead, can't you, Tomek!' scolded Teresa. On the backs of her fingers she could sense him gulping as she tied his top-knot. She felt as nervous as a mother dressing her child for his first day of school. So much rested on the success of the day. After a few twists of starched cloth and loose fantasy, the Prince's collar was buttoned and cravatted.

They walked into the great hall together – the royal couple. 'Thank you, Teresa, I am now Prince Miklos!'

'No, Tomek, you are Prince Nikolaus, don't say Miklos.'

'Forgive me Frau Martz; I am only a simple Hungrarian boy from Fertod,' said Tomek.

'Our guests will know him by the German name,' insisted Teresa, speaking German pointedly.

Bernhardt was still pacing and muttering. He was rehearsing the lines he was expected to regurgitate when prompted by questions from the audience, in a reality-defying post-performance platform talk with the long dead composer.

Teresa did her best to beef up his part but there was not much to go on; all who left memoranda of meeting Haydn record his affability, but few found his utterances memorable enough to quote verbatim. So in devising a script for Bernhardt, Teresa had told him that his impersonation should be modest and wordlessly subservient. This did not enthuse Bernhardt to the role. He told her that it was not his business to do impersonations but to bring *Haydn the Man* back to life, although he wouldn't expect *her* to understand.

Teresa should have no worries about Bernhardt getting into his role, he had so much in common with Haydn, this was true: he was an artist trapped in a prison, a gilded one admittedly, and was underrated and menially exploited, his gaoler being the gruesome oaf Tomek.

So what kept him inside all this time?

When he had heard that Fraenkl's understudy to play the Prince was a communist puppet master, he imagined some aged apparatchik with dodgy connections. He hadn't realised that the word puppeteer was not an indication of political string-pulling. It was literally true that for many years Tomek had run his own puppet show using home-made folk and fairytale characters. The new intelligence did not cool Benhardt's hatred.

Bernhardt's disapproval of Tomek may have encompassed both puppetry and communism, but it was motivated mainly by snobbery. Tomek was a purveyor of low comedy and Bernhardt was a practitioner of high art. He watched Tomek slump down on a sofa and heard the waistcoat's audible rip as the silken panel at the back split along the seam.

'Take care with those clothes, they were meant for a greater man than you.'

'A greater man than me? Not Nikolaus Esterházy?'

'No, Herman Fraenkl.'

Tomek fumed visibly, his mighty fists clenched as he resolved that the next person to mention Herman Fraenkl would regret it.

The musicians trooped in to the Sala Terrena. Sophie (who had been transformed into Tomasino now) sat at the leader's desk and propped her violin on her quivering knee. She saw Bernhardt looking at her, his eyes expressed the pity of a fellow martyr. He did not see a young body squeezed into tight clothing – he saw a talented youngster starting out on a career and being put through the mortifications of Art – and once again he felt how unfair it was that great *interpreters* were always overlooked, whilst writers and composers monopolised the chances of immortality. The humble actor or musician who brought their works to life was forgotten as soon as the applause died. (Always proud of his humility, Bernhardt was unfortunately susceptible to musings of this kind.)

Sophie did not share his tragic viewpoint. She was still a student at the Vienna Conservatoire and had taken this job to pay for a holiday to Italy and she could write 'Leader of the Esterházy Orchestra' on her Professional Development module. Unlike Bernhardt she was young and optimistic, and unlike him she had succeeded in arranging a free lift, with Stephan the cellist.

Have we got time for more about Stephan? Probably not. He may have to wait. That seems to be his perpetual condition.

Whilst the ornate hall began to fill with some of the decorative musical ideas designed for it, the audience were unstoppably approaching in a coach that was being driven by a virtuoso of motoring, even in wet driving conditions. Once Carl had swung the coach into the stream of traffic heading south-west, Dr Dietrich stood and addressed the paired ranks of the English contingent as though they were an especially dim viola section. 'Good morning, once again. As we drive to the town of Eisenstadt, I will perhaps have time to tell you about the macabre adventures of Haydn's head before we visit his tomb.'

When he heard Sally asking 'What's a tomb, Daddy?' Edward tried to give her a pink-tinged explanation. 'It's a place where people are supposed to rest in peace.'

'You mean when they've been naughty?'

'He means when they are dead, that's where they are dumped,' explained Hamish, as part of his lifelong mission to crush the twee.

Dr Dietrich continued. 'Haydn's posthumous progress forms an unexpected subject. In relating it I am following the example of Haydn himself, who always liked to include something unexpected in his works. You may remember the Surprise Symphony. So I have warned you. The drive to Eisenstadt should not take us more than an hour, and so I have plenty of time to go from the birth of Haydn to his death.'

'That's because she is missing out all the stuff in between,' commented Anjali.

'Or the stuff on either side,' added Satma.

'Haydn's eventide, alas, was darkened by clouds of war. In 1809, when he lay dying, Vienna was under French bombardment and a canon-ball fell not far from his house.'

'Cool!' said Hamish.

'By the time he passed away, Napoleon's troops had occupied the city. Which is why, rather than receiving the state funeral that he deserved, he was given a simple burial in the churchyard in Gumpendorf, the suburb where he had lived.'

Gumpendorf was not part of the day's itinerary, but presumably the name conveyed the attractions of the place. Dr Dietrich did not have time to explain in detail how Napoleon's Army, promising liberation from old tyrants whilst delivering a new tyranny, went through Europe like hotel chambermaids, overturning everything without changing anything. She referred to it as an inconvenience for Viennese funeral directors.

'Following the ceremony, two men bought the sexton's complicity with some schnapps, and began with his help and his tools to dig up the corpse. With some effort and revulsion (for the body had already begun to rot) they opened the coffin, severed the head with a saw and the more recalcitrant tendons with some tree-loppers and finally made off with it in a bag.'

'That's disgus*ting!*' said Sally, the *ting!* rang out like a bell. Disgusting was one of her favourite words and she had her own special way of saying it. Most meals away from home received the 'ting' of disapproval.

'In 1820, a tomb was prepared and Haydn's remains were exhumed so they could be transferred to the family seat in Eisenstadt. When the corpse was uncovered, it was found to be *senza capo*,' Dr Dietrich went on, slipping a throat lozenge into her right cheek pouch. 'The coffin lid was lifted and revealed a headless body and an empty wig!'

The listeners gasped, and Sally squirmed in her seat.

'The Prince was absolutely furious.' Dr Dietrich seemed to share his outrage at this affront to his absolute right to dig up the corpse of a faithful servant. Such a corpse should be present and correct and serviceable for any further requirements the Prince might have of it.

'There was an outcry, followed by a police search. Prince Esterházy would stand no nonsense. The skull must be found; a reward was offered for its return.

'The mystery of Haydn's missing head was not so great a puzzle. It was the work of fanatical phrenologists who had already amassed a collection of skulls because they wanted to study the bumps. The new scientific cult of phrenology asserted that you could tell a lot about a person by feeling the bumps on their head. Cleaning the skull, washing away the remnants of brain-matter, which for them was simply a repulsive gloop, they declared that 'the bump of music' in Haydn's skull was indeed 'fully developed' according to the predictions of their theory.

'In order to retain possession of the relic, another skull was handed over to the Esterházys and so Haydn's bones were put together and the solemn ceremony of re-interment went ahead. Under a simple stone with a Latin inscription, the vault contained the body of Haydn accompanied by the stowaway head of an anonymous criminal.

'Over the years the wandering skull acquired the status of a relic. I don't know whether it was given to the Vienna Conservatoire or to the Anatomical Museum.'

Dr Deitrich administered to herself another well-earned throat lozenge and sat down, glancing at Carl, whose eyes were on the road and his mind on something else entirely.

As the macabre story of Haydn's skull progressed, Edward felt like clapping his hands over his children's ears, but it was the only part of Dr Dietrich's spiel they had so far paid attention to. They had personal reasons to be particularly afraid and fascinated by death. Afterwards Sally had asked 'Did Mummy have the bump of music, Daddy?' and Hamish said 'Shut up!'

'It's not fair, he told me to shut up . . .' whined Sally.

'Stop whining,' added Hamish.

'Daddy, why does he always say I'm whining?'

When Hamish reminded Sally to 'Shut up', Edward confiscated his son's game pad as a punishment for rudeness. Even as he did so, he secretly felt that Hamish was right to be annoyed; it was an excessively twee way to describe a brain tumour, calling it a musical bump. His sister had begun to manipulate their dead mummy like a doll.

It's not what she would have wanted, old chum, and you know it. Can't you hear her ghost pleading to be shown the kindness of being forgotten? Edward probably knew it, but would not have expressed it like that to an eight-year-old girl.

Dr Dietrich was obliged to go back over Haydn's posthumous career as a scientific guinea-pig, this time in German, but we need not concern ourselves with that unfortunate empty skull's journey when this story has a coach-load of skulls filled with more pertinent matter. They arrived at the Calvary Church in Eisenstadt, all but one of them in anticipation of something new to explore, the exception being Edward, who was asking himself why he had brought children on this sombre expedition.

At least the rain had stopped and the clouds were beginning to disperse on the fresh breeze. The pneumatic hiss of the Travego's parking brake accompanied by a sagging of the suspension expressed on behalf of one and all a collective sigh of relief. Another exhalation at the opening of the doors was followed by an inrush of air to refresh the endlessly recycled atmosphere maintained by the onboard climate control. Having existed in this synthetic environment they were highly sensitive to the aromas of pastry and coffee that lingered in the street.

Across the angled roadway was a beautiful white building with an octagonal tower built on the summit of a knoll, at the top of a flight of steps guarded by stone angels. All were equally charmed by the sight, bar the grandiose English woman who demanded to know how Dr Dietrich expected her to 'climb all those *forbidding* steps'.

Whatever their other drawbacks, churches present an occasion for milling about, bumping into somebody, whose name you may not even know, and casually beginning a conversation, the gloom preserving you from the awkwardness occasioned by her beauty. On this occasion Edward played his ace clumsily and far too early, as he deliberately pushed Sally forward at the bottom of the steps.

'Mind how you go Sally! Sorry, did she tread on your toe? This is Sally – say sorry, Sally.'

Anjali smiled 'It's all right dear' at the wide-faced girl, and Sally aimed her forehead back at the nice lady. 'Are you a Princess? My name is Sally.'

These awkward introductions were interrupted by the words 'Is there a toilet, Daddy?' uttered in a bored monotone by Hamish.

'I don't know Hamish, it's a church – can't you just do a wee somewhere behind a bush?'

'No. I need a toilet Dad. It's going to be more than a wee. I really need to do a poo.'

Hamish never spoke a word that was not both factual and actual. With the loss of his mother his mind had become earthbound – rooted to reality and suspicious of imaginary flight. Edward knew that his son would not be diverted by rococo architecture from his urgent needs. As the Indian beauty discretely receded, Edward dragged his children over the road and into a restaurant.

'I told you to go before we came.'

'No you didn't.'

'I shouldn't have to.'

Outside the restaurant they saw Kirchel's wife and the coach driver sitting at a table ordering coffees and pastries. The stately English woman whom the observant Indians had dubbed the Duchess of Poundland (and so, for the future, I shall call her) lowered herself onto a chair and called imperiously: 'Boy!' The waiter rushed to her side, by which time she had seen the prices in the menu card. 'I'm not paying that much for a cup of your god-awful tea!' she bellowed without first ascertaining whether her words would be understood. Her tone was unmistakable and irresistible. 'Bring me a cup of boiling water. Boiling, mind you, not tepid!'

Entering the restaurant itself, Edward Hamish and Sally pushed their way past another waiter unfurling tablecloths. By gestures he offered them a table, but Edward resisted, with wags of the finger and shakes of the head. Hamish shuffled into a small cubicle at the back, behind a bentwood hat stand and with profusions of apologetic hums and grunts, Edward tried not to take up too much space.

'When are we going to Mummy's palace, Daddy?'

'Soon, but it's not Mummy's palace.'

'But you did see her there?'

'It was only a dream, Sally.'

'Yes, but it was there, wasn't it? Otherwise why have we come all this way?'

In this particular dream, which had occurred to him the previous October, Edward had found himself wandering alone around an empty rococo palace. He entered an enormous white room caked with decorative plasterwork, when, from a side door, Pamela silently appeared. She was dressed for a concert in a long flowing black gown, tight to her body. Before it turned into a sensuous dream, his voice went: 'I am so glad I found you, we thought you were dead,'

'Edward you big idiot,' she laughed, showing her lickable teeth. 'I'm just on a European tour, remember?'

Hastily, the dreaming Edward said, 'Yup, well, I must get the kids; you don't know how much they have been missing you.'

He was about to lead her through to another room where Hamish and Sally were watching children's television in their pyjamas, but before he could reunite them he awoke.

The restaurant rang out with anticipatory clangs as the tables were laid. Edward waited and Sally tried to amuse herself playing with some toothpicks and napkins. Whilst his son's sluggish bowels were performing their functions Edward thought to himself, say what you like about Hamish, he doesn't skimp on ritual. It was as though he knew that to rush a ceremony like this would rob it of its pageantry.

All they had seen of the church so far was through windows, firstly of the coach and now of the restaurant, obscured by parts of the word *RESTAURANT* in reversed lettering. It was seemingly unobtainable. From time to time Sally's little castles of tableware collapsed. Edward had to work assiduously to replace the settings as they were intended, too inhibited by the silence to tick off Sally who delicately moved on to another table and began transforming the place settings into wigwams and giraffes.

At last Hamish emerged from the tiny *Herren*.

'I didn't hear a flush,' commented Edward.

'No point, Dad; nothing happened.'

'You mean the flush was broken?'

'No, I mean I couldn't do a poo, Dad.' This bulletin was delivered in a monotone.

Whilst Edward tried to remember the German for pharmacy, he knew that Hamish's intestines were immobilised by introverted tensions. The only laxative he required was one that loosened the pain from his head.

Conscious of having overstayed their welcome (one that had been grudging in the first place), Edward propelled his children out of the restaurant. It was a relief to be trespassers no longer.

'We didn't even leave a tip,' Edward regretted.

'No Dad,' Hamish explained. 'I told you I couldn't do anything.'

Outside the Duchess of Poundland was dipping a teabag into her cup of boiling water. This teabag had been part of the complementary facilities in her hotel room, and she emptied two spoonfuls of sugar into her cup, before putting the spoon into her Poundland bag.

They crossed the road and sprinted up the steps to rejoin the tour group just as Professor Kirchel was expounding: 'Here lay Papa Haydn, nestled within pine trees and shrouded by clouds.' The old professor was inclined to put it poetically.

The hill itself was actually prosaically artificial. It had been constructed not by the inspiring forces of nature but laboriously out of limestone brought from the nearby mountains to satisfy a princely caprice for contour. Repenting, perhaps, the decision to build upon the plains, the Prince decreed that a sacred mound should rise up in his hometown. Since he did not have the divine authority to command mountains to obey his will, the job had to be done by human brawn. It was a whim that had apparently been sated after just one mound, to the relief of the draymen contracted to manually relocate this geographical feature. I suppose the all-commanding Prince had made his point.

Edward's children seemed suddenly very perky. Hamish forgot the weighty burden he carried within him and ran around firing loud imaginary bullets. The child-sized hill was instantly recognisable as a playground and they could be heard exploring the labyrinth of steps and ramparts, their whoops of laughter, Hamish's bangs and Sally's screams going off like fireworks into the air.

Walking briskly to keep up with his children, Edward entered the church and enjoyably took his time adjusting to the cool and the diminished light. You could almost say he relaxed. He appeared to be scanning the place in search of Haydn's tomb, but we suspect he was actually straining to catch a glimpse of pale salwar. Unfortunately for him, whilst he was making his clandestine plan, his elbow was touched by the professor, who, while catching his breath from the short climb confessed: 'Dr Dietrich was quite wrong once again, I regret to say.'

'About what?' asked Edward, almost showing his irritation.

'About Haydn's head. It did not end up in the Conservatoire *or* the Anatomical Museum. It was finally bequeathed to the Society of the Friends of Music. I should know,' said Kirchel proudly. 'My grandfather was an elder of that fraternity, as was my father, and now myself.' Even when short of breath he was long-winded.

'Isn't that a rather appalling way to behave?'

'How do you mean?'

'Well – it makes you no better than head-hunters, doesn't it?'

Kirchel, unabashed at belonging to a tribe of head-hunters, recounted how his grandfather would on occasion proudly bring out the relic in its handsome wooden box and show it to visitors. 'I remember it well, the box had a carved lyre on the lid and glass sides, so you could look in without opening the lid. I saw it myself several times.'

'You haven't still got it?'

'Oh no, the time came to part with it. The bicentenary of his birth in 1932 seemed like an ideal opportunity, and the resplendent tomb you see before you was made. However, the advent of Hitler meant that the tomb remained unoccupied until 1954 when the burial process was finally completed. I was there myself so I can boast that I attended Haydn's final farewell – it was the most drawn out funeral in history.'

'The solemn ceremony took place when I was eighteen. It began with the head being carried in a hearse through the streets of Vienna, and then via Haydn's birthplace at Rohrau and on to this church. It is the very same route we have taken today.'

The sky had cleared and the pastel shaded English couple descended the church steps in brilliant sunshine. They were descending warily, the buttermilk man gripped his delicate young wife by the upper arm as though she was about to faint, or throw herself down the steps. When he saw Edward at one of the turns of the path, the husband beckoned him over urgently.

'Ah, I have a bone to pick with you. I think you should know that I have issues with your son.'

'You have what?'

'Issues. It seems to me that you are unable to control him, and he certainly can't control himself.'

Instantly a terrible notion entered Edward's head, there could be only one thing that could cause so much scandalised alarm. Hamish must have been overcome with a sudden and irresistible urge to void his bowels and had done so somewhere in the environs of the church. It was partly his fault for all his talk of bushes. He glanced down at the blazered man's shoes and saw with relief that they were unsoiled. Indeed they were immaculately clean, with a two-tone design reminiscent of spats.

'As I ascended the steps to the church he ran straight into me.' Edward was so relieved he laughed. 'It is no laughing matter. Imagine if it had been my wife he had crashed into . . . we are trying for a baby, the consequences could have been quite serious.'

'But he didn't run into your wife.' Edward smiled at the whey-faced woman. 'And he didn't hurt you seriously . . . I trust you will still be able to perform?'

The man in faux spats was not appeased. 'What is worse is that he sees fit to behave like an outlaw on consecrated ground, in the holy precinct of a church.'

'I shall speak to him,' promised Edward.

'So you should. If he was a son of mine I would have very stern words with him.'

Edward was already feeling sorry for the yet-to-be-conceived offspring who would be on the end of such parenting, but the outraged man wasn't finished with him. 'Now, can you grab this?'

In his confusion Edward thought his assistance was being sought in restraining the man's moon-complexioned wife, as though she was about to escape his custody, or float off like an un-tethered balloon, but instead he had a camera thrust into his hand.

'Not with the coach behind, with the church!' the little man instructed as he manhandled his wife into a suitable pose. They stood apart whilst Edward took the photo, and when he handed back the camera the man barked 'Pratt.'

'Sorry,' said Edward, feeling unjustly admonished.

'And you are?'

Edward's confusion gradually subsided and he said, 'Edward.'

They shook hands. Pratt's handshake was so insubstantial Edward felt he had passed his hand through ectoplasm.

Edward's untamed children returned to his side and the Pratts slipped back in the line, further down it than Edward, who wondered if this was to avoid being with him or out of excessive avoidance of pushing in. Queuing etiquette is a matter of national pride, if not quite a national religion. All of which meant Edward ended up entering the coach with Lakshman, the Malaysian physicist, who was at best a lapsed observant of the queuing creed and usually among the first on board. The arthritic English lady had been unwilling to attempt an assault on the holy mound without Edward's help, and was already on the coach, majestically consoling herself with a brioche bun.

'I hear you are a string theorist.'

'Actually I am a superstring theorist, which may sound a little boastful . . . Why don't you sit here beside me? Forgive the crumbs.'

Lakshman looked up at Edward with his eyes smiling, his skeleton was curled to suit the upholstered accommodation of the Travego, perhaps, Edward wrongly supposed, from years spent peering down a microscope, which in truth he had not done since his student days.

Edward felt that he had made a friend – or at least found another creature equally friendless, which amounted to the same thing.

As they were driven eastwards through the lower Austrian plains and Kirchel was bombinating in German, Edward and Lakshman had a very interesting conversation about Einstein. To Edward's relief this conversation never strayed into the general or special theories, but concerned the great man's brain, which ended up in 240 pieces packed into jars and carted around for years in the trunk of a Princeton pathologist's car.

'What did they find – any bumps?'

'It was smaller than average, but that was probably the effects of age. It was more spherical than usual, and more symmetrical.'

'Which means?'

'That his brain structure may have been unusual in some key areas that are important for spatial and reasoning skills.'

'Didn't we know that already from the fact that he came up with relativity?'

Lakshman laughed. 'Yes, but it is still good practice for neuroscientists. They are unwrapping the mysteries of the brain. With Haydn they had a look at the box it comes in, with Einstein they had a look at the hard drive – if we get just one more dead genius we might begin to understand the all-important software.'

'Don't we need live geniuses, rather?'

'Yes, I admit, that would be preferable.'

Lakshman was able to express his delight in paradox with his high chirpy voice, and the strange way his small body curled into a question-mark. Edward could well imagine him being admired and mocked by his university students in equal measure, probably at the same time. 'But do you really think we will ever understand how it works – the human brain, the mind, everything?'

'Oh yes, certainly,' chortled Lakshman. 'The mind remains a mystery to us because we haven't understood it yet, not because it is beyond understanding.'

'You think we are machines, then. What about the soul?'

At this, Lakshman guffawed so piercingly he interrupted Professor Kirchel's fluent German narrative as it went over the same ground for the second time, more thoroughly for his German audience who were clearly the smarter set. They were well informed and enthusiastic, whilst the Anglophones seemed to take a lackadaisical attitude, when they weren't being downright rude.

Lakshman scrunched himself into a ball and continued in a hoarse whisper: 'Anyone who accepts inexplicable things like the soul is copping out, and I for one salute that phrenologist fellow for setting off down the road to demystify the mind.'

'Even if he was on the wrong track?'

'Absolutely – that doesn't matter as much as you would think. The bumps in his skull had as much to say about the creative process as the shape of Haydn's hat, less, if you contend that you can tell a lot about a man by the type of hat he chooses, but it makes more sense than attributing his gifts to a supernatural source.'

Edward was surprised to find that a scientist would approve of such nonsense. 'Haven't you seen phrenological heads? They are sold in shops that also sell crystals and healing aromas and all that chakra crap! I mean! You know the sort of place: they have books on yoga and CDs offering panpipes for meditation. It's all balls.'

'Before you dismiss phrenology as balls because of the low company it hangs with, you should admit that the urge to measure the previously immeasurable is a fine ambition.'

'I suppose so,' Edward admitted.

'It is the same ambition that lies behind the MRI scanners that observe the activities of the brain, not as bumps but as brightly lit patches on a screen, but they have still not located the soul.'

Professor Kirchel had come to the end of his German lap and, looking directly at the pair of chatterboxes at the back, solicited questions in English. Edward felt obliged to supply one, and asked how the terrible crime done to Haydn's corpse would have affected the transit of his soul. He meant this in the context of Haydn's beliefs.

'The soul is like the music of a cello. It ceases to exist when the strings cease vibrating,' explained Professor Kirchel.

There came a loud cough from three or four rows ahead as Pratt asserted that: 'Some of us would have issues with that statement.'

'Ah, we have found another rationalist,' whispered Lakshman, 'and another for the other side.'

'You are keeping score?' Lakshman duly wrote a one in mid air with his finger. 'Anyhow, I am not sure that Professor Kirchel is a rationalist, he has substituted music for religion. You notice he didn't deny the existence of the soul, he just said it was music.'

'And music is irrational; Q.E.D. very good.'

By the time he died, Haydn was no longer a genius, he was a sentimental and kindly old man with old-fashioned courtly ways, whose eyes often filled with unprompted tears. He had outlived his tormentors, his detractors and anyone he had ever loved. He had even outlived himself, for there was nothing left of the energetic musical mind. It was exhausted at last, no longer capable of expressing human intelligence. To put it another way, he was a computer that was still warm but had no software running. But that too was nothing to worry about, because Haydn had already uploaded all the important files in a code of just twelve tones that could be run on a range of hardware interfaces, from pianos and violins to human voices.

Rehearsals of the Farewell Symphony were still in progress at the Esterházy Palace when Teresa Mertz received a call from Dr Dietrich, warning her of the proximity of the incoming audience.

'Sorry to interrupt, Sophie, but the coach has left Eisenstadt,' Teresa declared, with enthused tone. 'They will be here in approximately thirty minutes.'

'Okay,' said Sophie from her seat, addressing the band. 'Shall we take it from the coda and practice getting off stage quietly?'

The musicians turned to the last page of their parts and began to play the final adagio, and, as it progressed, the players one-by-one lowered their instruments from chin or lips and switched off the electric candle attached to their music stands. Taking care not to disturb the remaining musicians by scraping the furniture, they left the room with the soft tread of a parent leaving a sleeping child's bedroom.

It took infinite delicacy to perform this experiment. They were testing the idea, recently espoused by Professor Kirchel, that music was like the soul; that it ceased to exist when the strings ceased vibrating.

The last two players, the first and second fiddle, accomplished the fragile tailing off that Haydn gave to his symphony and tip-toed from the room. Their absence meant they were unable to observe whether the music continued on in silence. Tonight there would be an audience to correct that.

Having negotiated their noiseless withdrawal, the orchestra had twenty minutes in which to stretch legs, empty bladders and fill lungs with fresh air or nicotine, according to preference.

Her flat chest failed to justify the neckline's eighteenth-century plunge, so when Teresa Martz stuffed her mobile phone back into her bodice she offered a brief glimpse – to anyone who happened to be up a ladder – of a cigarette-butt sized nipple, a nipple that had never felt the drag of a baby's mouth. What suckling her nipples had to offer was currently monopolised by Kevin, who was no substitute. Not a patch.

Being a member of a social tribe, Teresa felt compelled to advertise her status as a non-reproductive female, which she had done by cutting her hair very short and not concealing its prematurely ashen hue with dye. The experience of early onset menopause had paradoxically given her youthful vigour; she was still as supple as a young woman unburdened with the moral and physical weight of maternity. For the purposes of historical verisimilitude tonight she would hide her boyish haircut in a pile of powdered bangs. Placing the perruquier's absurd creation on her head, she tried to glide over to keep an eye on the Prince. Kevin saw her talking to Tomek but concluded nothing.

Kevin's disembodied voice came over the PA system. His halting German intonated with Antipodean inflections sliced through the meticulously reassembled *ancien regime* ambience like a guillotine.

'Ready in ten! This is your ten minute call, folks.' For those able to unscramble his native dialect, he added: 'Remember, they want to visit another world, so if anyone asks you a question give them any rubbish that comes into your head, but remember to remove your wristwatches and switch your bloody cell-phones off! You can rest assured, no matter how little you know, there's people out there who know a hell of a lot less.'

'Kevin may be the exception to his own rule,' said Teresa to Tomek. As she attempted to neaten his appearance with various tucks and tweeks, Tomek shook with pleasure at her butterfly touch.

By the time the orchestral flock reassembled at their candlelit music stands and began tuning up, Kevin had completed his final sound and lighting check. He was extremely proud of the sensitive installation of lights and microphones that had transformed this bright and acoustically perfect salon into a dazzling modern concert hall in which your eyelashes stung with the reflections off the gilding and you could hear the oboist moistening his reeds as clearly as though he was sucking your earlobe. Which is why no one who was in the hall could avoid overhearing Kevin snarl at Teresa: 'I've heard of liking a bit of rough, Tess, but that what can you see in that old crock?'

'I was straightening his clothes, Kevin.'

'Trying to get into them, more like. Boy, I knew you were desperate, he must be fifty!'

'Oh Kevin, grow up.'

Stephan smiled across at Sophie over the top of his music stand. He was hopelessly in love. Meaning he was in love, and he was hopeless. He had made her lasagne and he had made her laugh, but he could not make her love him. Stephan was, you see, a romantic of the most idiotic kind.

To return to our dynamic main theme, the Mercedes Travego continued its merry trundle through the thoroughly uninteresting landscape of lower Austria, guided by the podgy fingers of Carl, who knew these roads so well his mind was almost entirely occupied with fantasies of a lewd nature.

Edward was occupied with persuading Hamish to use the onboard toilet at the rear of the coach. 'It will save an awful lot of time when we get there.'

'I don't want to, Dad. It's weird. Everyone will know I am in there.'

'Shall I create a distraction while you slip in, then? I'll come with you if you like, to stand outside. I can sing to cover the noises.'

'Dad no! You're so embarrassing.'

Sitting next to Edward, Lakshman was entirely failing to repress his giggles, and Edward abandoned his efforts of persuasion.

Despite her gingham charms and unswerving loyalty, Jemima was no longer holding Sally's attention. She was now twisted round in her seat resting her head sideways, gazing across at Anjali, transfixed by beauty.

For Anjali, the unrelenting stare of Sally's green eyes was extremely disconcerting. The pale lashes were unflinching and the skull beneath the blue-white skin seemed to show through. Sally's hair colour could be described as 'strawberry blonde'. She insisted on that ice-creamy phrase, as she did not so much like the sound of 'ginger'. It was pulled away from her face in the pincer grip of plastic butterflies to reveal her forehead in all its broad acreage. Edward had once made her cry piteously when he joked that she was growing horns.

What prodigious intellectual or personal powers would a phrenologist attribute to these cephalic protuberances? She now had this formidable forehead aimed directly at Anjali; convincing proof, Anjali felt, of psychic gifts.

By now Carl had taken the Mercedes Travego soaring across the border into Hungary. More sweat had seeped out of Edward at the approach, but his anxiety was ungrounded and they were not even stopped or asked for their passports, which at least gave him no further opportunity to loose them. Dr Dietrich confessed that the reputation for rigorousness had probably been earned by the border-guards protecting Hungary from incoming Serbians, to the south.

Henceforward, the landscape flattened out and became featureless. 'Eminently conquerable, but unlikely to inspire artists,' Edward observed to Lakshman. 'What do you suppose attracted Prince Nikolaus to this dreary spot?'

'A flat landscape provides a tabletop upon which to spread out grand delusions. The last thing your megalomaniac palace builder wants is a hillock upsetting the levels.'

'Unless he wants to plant a church on it.'

Soon they were motoring up the avenue through Esterházy Park. Dr Dietrich called it that, though it had been renamed, unhelpfully for promoters of tourism, Fertod.

'After Nikolaus the Magnificent spent something like eleven million gulden on it, the park was ornamented with groves, hermitages and temples, summerhouses and hot-houses.'

Hamish and Sally showed their disgruntlement with silence. Edward almost wished they were less well behaved. Since this tour was a quest to rekindle their lost mother, how could they be other than solemn? Forget the 'among other things', they felt overlooked by their mother's ghost at all times. They had brushed their teeth without being asked twice and hardly fought. And he had never seen them finish the plate before and, frankly, Austrian food stank.

This holiday-of-remembrance, with its beneficial effects on dental hygiene and sibling docility, was his doing: He had literally dreamed it up. Not being a practised hypnomancer, Edward did not know whether his dreams were steering him away from pitfalls or into them.

The dreams Edward sometimes had of Pamela were not always advisable from a banking point of view, since they made him sluggish the following morning. If his employers could have predicted the nocturnal appearances of his late wife they would probably have given him time off accordingly, but no one could foresee when these nights would come, least of all Edward.

One night last October Edward had that particularly lucid dream about Pamela in a rococo palace. It was so powerful and realistic he was condemned to waste his employers' time until three-thirty/fourish. The images in his brain had been ten times more intense than anything the fund markets had to put against them, and it wasn't until late afternoon that he realised he had lost the bank several millions.

The next evening at their bed time Edward made the mistake of telling his children about the dream and Sally immediately began a pestering campaign to be taken to the palace where he had found their mummy. He tried to explain that since it had been in a dream he didn't actually know which palace it was, so she told him to find out. Little girls can be very persistent and his research into palaces that Pamela might have been to on tour eventually brought him into contact with Euphony Escorted Tours, who had a brochure full of them. Edward warmed to the idea. This holiday might bring consolation. Meanwhile, it was the only way to get Sally to stop whining, and today was the climax of her unrealistic expectations.

She was buzzing with anticipation as the coach drove through the crested gateway. They were passing between curved stable blocks that joined the main building to form an enormous D. The wings were far off on either side and attached to the central block by quadrants, eliminating the need for corners and plasticizing the perspective, making the building as seemingly endless as the horizon. Now they were within this horizon they may have landed on another planet, so distant did the outside world seem.

Familiar exhalations from the Travego brought relief to the weary travellers. Firstly, the coach gave out a pneumatic flatus as the parking brake was applied, indicating that their journey was at an end. Shortly after that the doors opened with a gentle suspiration confirming that they were free to disembark. Once disgorged from the vehicle the passengers stood about on the newly laid turf like mariners who had reached a flat and apparently unpopulated island.

Unable to resist the opportunity to walk again, some of them staggered away on unreliable legs. These were not signs of sea-sickness, nor even coach-sickness, this was time-sickness. They had truly arrived at the eighteenth century, and it was cold and unwelcoming to outsiders. It was tempting to return to the coach, with its familiar bunks and bulkheads. But that was, for the next ten minutes or so, out of the question because the enormous Englishwoman was slowly descending backwards out of the hatchway, clutching her Poundland bag which was fluttering emptily in the breeze.

Rapidly, Carl closed the doors and drove the Travego away, carrying with him a single stowaway, Frau Kirchel. They headed for the more prosaic attractions of Fertod, leaving the time-travellers assembled on the vulnerable grass central area that (in a misunderstood attempt to avoid just this) was chained off with black parabolas, an authoritarian echo of the swags of stucco fruit on the façade. Large yew trees shaped into cones stood sentry, giving the palace court the air of an English churchyard. Before them there were two flights of stairs up to the pedimented entrance, lit by bronze lamps held by figures in flowing stone drapery unruffled by the gusts that blew across Lake Neusiedl.

Despite the fact that everything had been pre-booked months before, their arrival seemed to be completely unexpected. Dr Dietrich spoke to the interior of the building with her mobile phone. Then she told the party to keep waiting on the steps whilst she scuttled in through the service entrance below.

The English Dame had some words to say on this matter, covering the overall *farcical* incompetence and the implausibility of the assumption that she would be able to get herself up those *ferrule-less* stairs. She rhetorically asked who was to blame for this unbearable *fiasco-up*. Like courtiers in the days of Nikolaus, the stranded time-travellers were learning the importance of patience. The great man was keeping them waiting. Which one, in this case? Was it Haydn or the Prince?

Neither – it was Kevin. Just as she had been about to open the great doors, Teresa had noticed with alarm Kevin's buttocks half way up his ladder, half out of their denims. He was trying to maximise the candlelight by identifying and replacing a defective bulb in a sconce on the wall.

The fire prevention people had an enormous problem accepting the use of real candles. Artificial ones, which mimicked the flickering of a flame with liquid crystals, were outstandingly expensive and unreliable, but they couldn't risk burning down an irreplaceable building, even though (according to household accounts) a thousand candles a day had burned there in its pomp. Today, the lighting of just one would be a federal offence. Kevin was just screwing in one of the delicate glass replacement flames, when a voice came sharply behind him:

'What the hell are you doing here, Kevin? They mustn't see you.'

'For crying out loud, Tess, you made me jump,' protested Kevin as he fumbled with the tiny silica glow-worm.

'Really I don't think they would notice if one bulb was out.'

'I guess I'm a perfectionist, Tess.'

Teresa gave him a look expressing her doubts. The outward signs of perfection were not obvious.

Any attempt to put Kevin in a costume had been abandoned: he was far too tall for the eighteenth century, and a speaking part was out of the question since, like all his compatriots, he was unable to pronounce any vowels. So Kevin and his anachronistic buttocks were forced into semi-concealment.

Actually, Kevin preferred it that way. Having descended from his ladder, which he parked behind a fluted pillar, he disappeared through a door in the panelling to his control suite, formerly a valet's tiny bedroom, very content to be apart from those European snobs. From here he could vary the ambient lighting, the PA system, the microphones and all the other components of *son et lumiere* whilst monitoring it all on CCTV screens. In this way he could view the past as he had seen the so-called 'World' on New Zealand television news, in a way that only emphasised its remoteness and its irrelevance. Someone said the past is another country – for Kevin it was another hemisphere.

Meanwhile, the valued clients of Euphony Escorted Tours were having the flaw of a meticulously planned excursion driven into them with every blast of wind. They were prepared to endure considerable discomfort in order to learn about the past but their endurance was being tested now as they experienced the frustrations of the courtier together with those of a badly-served customer.

Alluring scenarios from holidays they might have booked instead of this one, such as lolling about by a pool, never fully sobering up for two weeks and never wearing more than three items of absurdly colourful clothing, ran through Edward's mind.

Old Professor Kirchel was stamping his feet to get the circulation going. 'This is a valuable insight,' he remarked to Edward, who felt he was being used as a screen to hide behind, or else a wind-break. 'As Haydn wrote to his brother Michael, this is a court. It is uncommonly hard to do what you like,' the professor went on. 'If you were married to my wife you would already know what that was like!'

It was vainly that Kirchel awaited a response, for none there came.

'Dad – I want to go inside, I'm cold.'

'We can't, Hamish, not yet.'

'Why not?'

'Because they haven't let us in yet.'

'Why not?'

Edward began to vent his frustration in a wordless growl but then he glimpsed the Indian beauty turning her head towards him and instantly he clamped his jaw to prevent further irritation leaking out. He furtively looked about to check if he was being observed and decided that being observed looking about furtively was probably more damning than being observed getting irritated with his son. 'It's going to be great, Hamish,' he said excessively brightly. 'This is what mummy used to do.'

'I bet they let her go inside.'

Edward felt that he had better do something with an even greater dosage of jollity to counteract his previous grumpiness. He took Sally by the hand and began spinning her round singing ring-a-rosie. Sally was not expecting this and began to scream.

Their rescue came at last when Dr Dietrich reappeared at the double doors and mustered them into a hall. There was a mass ascension of the steps with one weighty exception. Dr Dietrich retreated to offer whatever she could by way of encouragement or assistance. 'We do have a disabled lift, Madam – however, it is some distance away.'

'I am not disabled, I am in *physical* agony that's all. Do you know anything at all about rheumatoid arthritis?'

'No, Madam.'

'I thought not. You doctors are all a complete waste of time. I was meaning to ask – what are you a doctor *of*, exactly?'

'I am the holder of an upper second-class doctorate from the Higher Education Institute of Vienna.'

'What was your doctorate *in*?'

'Tourism,' hissed Dr Dietrich.

'Save us! Get that *fugitive* Englishman over here, he knows what to do!'

'Who?'

'The one with the two obnoxious *fidgeting* children.'

Dr Dietrich fetched Edward and he was once again put to work in harness. 'Would you like to take my arm?' Edward asked the Duchess, infected by some misdirected sense of etiquette.

'Of course not, you *folksy* idiot! Get behind me give me a bloody good shove.'

And so once again Edward took up his rearward post and began to elevate the pompous bulk of the Duchess up the long flight of stairs. Eventually he got his burden to the top and they joined the others who were waiting in what was an antechamber to the largest room of the palace, a room that was so important it merited its own introduction.

'Ladies and Gentlemen, this is the Great Chamber known as the Sala Terrena,' said Dr Dietrich. Once she was sure that the room's awesome size and grandeur had made its impact, she could afford to employ some false modesty. 'Here we shall be holding tonight's little entertainment.'

She humbly bowed her head as she went in through the doors that had comfortably enough clearance for a tall New Zealander with a long ladder. One wonders why a tiny Viennese woman without a ladder should have to constrict her stature, and also why the doorways were so abundantly capacious – had the architects anticipated Kevin's lofty requirements, or had they simply made an allowance for some shrinkage in palaces built in the damp environment of Lake Neustadl?

Dr Dietrich's obeissance was perhaps intended as a signal to her audience that they should prepare to genuflect. She clucked to get their attention and, preparing them for the disappointment they would surely feel when they saw the modest size of the band, spoke in a hoarse whisper: 'You will see the orchestra just as it was in Haydn's day. There were just sixteen musicians in the Esterházy Orchestra, but they were the very best.'

Young Pratt could not conceal his disappointment. He began to protest with his favourite opening words: 'My wife . . .'

The Duchess interrupted him. 'Don't tell us you need a full orchestra to impregnate your *fecund* wife.'

The poor husband began to blush, and said: 'My wife was expecting something bigger.'

This inadvisable remark caused a general titter, and ever more furious blushes on the little Englishman's cheek.

There were indeed just sixteen people seated at candlelit music stands of ornate wooden design. The candlelight everywhere was a masterpiece of expensive twenty-first-century technology. It looked exactly like cheap eighteenth-century technology.

'Let me introduce the celebrated Italian violinist, Luigi Tomasino,' said Dietrich.

The lead violinist, dressed in the militaristic uniform of the Esterházy musical corps, was a person of delicate features and small stature, who stood almost to attention with violin at present-arms as the audience filed past. Shaking hands, Edward noticed what elegant fingers this beardless youth had, and how soft. *Watch it, chum, you don't want to start falling in love with boys at your age,* chided his mockney mucker.

Tomasino bowed but didn't speak.

'Tomasino, though a brilliant virtuoso, was just a servant in the economy of the day,' explained Dietrich, filling the silence. 'He wore a uniform, to remind him that he was expected to behave at all times with the utmost decorum and humility.'

Pride filled Sophia's chest at leading the historic orchestra, though she took care to hold it in. Bernhardt sour commentary was unheard, decorum prevailing: 'This is progress; we are now nothing but synthetic servants in an ersatz Esterházy,' he muttered inwardly.

The baffled tourists were passed down the line of musicians like visiting royalty, the more eager ones crushing the poor fiddler's knuckles in their grip. They came at last to the slumped and grumbling Tomek and his twitchy consort Teresa, who were seated on two throne-like chairs and both failing to carry off the sublime poise of inborn superiority.

'May I present you to His Excellency, Prince Nikolaus Esterházy.'

Tomek remained seated to receive their tribute of awkward bows, his arms remained stiffly at his sides. He swallowed his mint but wisely chose not to speak.

'And the Princess Maria Elisabeth,' continued Dr Dietrich. Teresa smiled – not too widely – and welcomed the guests in German. 'And finally here is the man we have all come to see, Papa Haydn!'

As our sham Haydn came forward to greet the admiring throng he had an aged but kingly aspect that Bernhardt had perfected on the stage in various roles, including Shakespearian ones. There was nothing Teresa could say to rid him of this manner, which was very impressive but so inappropriate for this role of a forty-year-old servant. As he swanned forward he just couldn't prevent himself receiving imaginary tributes. He seemed to be simpering 'thank-yous' under his breath, but actually he was addressing Tomek with the words 'you are certainly no Herman Fraenkl, you tongue-tied clod'.

Behind him there was the scraping sound of a heavy chair being moved aside. Tomek had got to his feet. Rude, disturbing, fat and overdressed, he was as incongruous as a trombonist in a string quartet. Immediately, Teresa tried to interpose herself, putting her back between her prince and his audience, a breach of protocol that would have been inconceivable in their day. Since this was all a huge conspiracy to pretend that they were in 1772, and that this colossal oaf was supposed to be a prince, it made perfect sense for her to make her announcement still in character as Nikolaus's wife: 'His Imperial Highness is unaware of this, but tonight Papa Haydn has a surprise for us . . .' She spoke in English, a tongue unknown to Maria Therese, but you probably understand by now that pedantry is futile in the realm of re-enactment. '. . . A new symphony!'

You know you are approaching the final bars of the first movement of a symphony because you feel the satisfying reassurance of having heard everything twice. The listener is sated with thematic completeness and no further novelties are required – only an emphatic end, some kind of bombastic punctuation mark. The red-faced Tomek, who began to topple forwards in his unfamiliar indoor shoes, provided the punch line of this history's foremost portion. Bernhardt turned to him just in time to receive a heavy agricultural fist in his face. He fell to the parquet and to make it clear this was no random attack, the Prince gobbed a large bolus of bronchial fluid on the unconscious maestro.

II

SENSES

Adagio

When this story is adapted for the cinema, the screen at this point in the narrative might be expected to wash, or perhaps to *fade* out, resolving either to black or to white; fade out, like a light; black out, like Bernhardt; or washout – which is what we seem to be left with. Why not fill the screen, or even this page, with a curtain of blood red, in the style of a horror film? That would be highly expressive, if we were pursuing this history through what film-makers call the POV of Bernhardt.

The screen had certainly gone blank in one way or another for him when his brain was shaken within its skull by (as he saw the instant before it came) a blow from Tomek's crusty fist. What colour his closed eyes were seeing I cannot say; what colours his brain was imagining, I cannot guess.

It wasn't that hard a punch. Bernhardt had lamented the blow with a single tear of blood that swelled from his nostril. He lay on the floor as though he imagined he was in the last act of Hamlet. The musicians looked down at him awaiting their cue.

From the point of view of Bernhardt, the story has an intermission, but for everyone else it had just taken a busy and unexpected turn.

'Daddy, why did that man hit him?'

'I don't know Sally; perhaps he didn't like him very much.'

'But why not, Daddy?'

'I still don't know, Sally. Why don't you ask me again? Maybe after the fiftieth time of asking I'll have an answer. Oh Sally don't cry!'

He could see she was close to tears, which meant she was not so far off lacerating him with the words 'I want my Mummy'. Edward handled her like an emotional hand grenade, grabbed the duck that she was letting drop from her fingers and began to quack 'Jemima loves you'.

The blow had not been uniformly distressing; the range of responses went from laughter to derision. Other alternatives that were available included: 'Did you see that Satma? He knocked him clean out with one punch.'

'I know.'

'Do you think that was the disaster you foresaw?'

'Except he's not dead is he? I had a premonition of death, not a smack in the face.'

'Yes, but your premonitions are not always a hundred percent accurate, are they, Sati?'

Satma snorted. 'That little girl doesn't look very happy – see she's going to cry.'

'Her name is Sally,' Anjali informed her impressively.

'I know,' said Satma.

There were, of course, various further commentaries in German, but to avoid confusion and indeed tedium, they have been left unrecorded.

The Duchess of Poundland turned to Rosie and expressed her opinion of the organisers of this *futile* excursion, the pale English woman didn't give any reply, so she raised her voice even further and addressed the following remark to the husband: 'Does your wife ever say anything or is she always too wrapped up in her *fallopian* tubes?'

After a day that had been fast-paced and cinematic, with the onrushing momentum exemplified by rapid cuts of dialogue and sweeping pans across the landscape, the tourists were now becalmed in a pool of idleness. What did they have left to entertain themselves, this audience waiting to be amused? As if searching for an answer they looked at themselves in the mirrors that lined the walls. They waited in the Sala Terrena reflecting and being reflected. They were turning themselves from an audience into courtiers.

They were left hanging like an unresolved chord.

Teresa Martz, whilst straining to keep in character as the Princess Maria, furtively beckoned Dr Dietrich over to her, which is something the Princess Maria would never have done. 'You had better make an announcement. I have got to get this hooligan out of here.'

'I don't know what to announce.'

'Since when did that matter? Tell them anything you like. Explain that there will be a short delay. Talk about the history of the palace to keep them interested.'

Dr Dietrich had already given them a complete history of the palace (and they hadn't been all that interested). 'Can't the concert just go ahead without him?' she asked.

Tesrea gave her an aristocratic look of disdain, and she wasn't acting. 'They have come to see Haydn,' she said, and, leaving Dr Dietrich to stitch up the torn soirée, she took the arm of her historic consort and with all seeming decorum dragged him into another room by the ear. Whether she intended to instil discipline or display wrath once she got there, she hadn't quite decided yet.

The room into which they had just come had glass doors leading out onto a terrace and was filled with superb orange sunlight. The sun was descending into Lake Nieusdl and shining directly into Tessa's face as Tomek stood defensively with his back to the windows.

'That wasn't a very aristocratic thing to do, Tomek.'

'Wasn't it? I thought it was, from what I learned at school.'

Tomek had a jocular defiance backed by generations of history and a bellyful of alcohol.

'What you learned at your communist school doesn't apply anymore, and you know it. What the hell was it *really* about then?'

'I did it for Hungary,' Tomek declared. Then seeing this wasn't going to work, he added, 'but mainly it was because he kept going on about Herman Fraenkl.'

Teresa appeared to be entirely satisfied with the explanation. This was probably what made her unusually good at her job. 'How drunk are you, Tomek?'

'I am as sober as I will ever be.'

Teresa was unsure whether this was an assertion that he was currently sober, or an admission that he had no intention of ever becoming sober at any time in the foreseeable future. He was giving her a challenging stare and standing very upright, benefiting from the backlit nimbus that surrounded him. But he was swaying in his eyeballs and he smelt like a distillery, so Teresa felt she could have knocked him out herself.

'Tomek, for all I care, you can hit Bernhardt as hard and as often as you like, but after the performance if you don't mind. I've got an audience. They've paid good money to see eighteenth-century aristocrats at play; what you have given them is a grand display of low-class thuggery.'

This moment of weakness was brief. She looked at his face, with its saddlebag eyes and jawbone inherited from generations of tripe-eating peasantry. It was a chin that you could shave five times and still leave a blue shadow. He was never going to be mistaken for an aristocrat. When this palace was run on principles of hierarchy he wouldn't have got past the stable block.

'Honestly, Tomek, why did I ever think that *you* could play the Prince?'

'I don't know, to be sure,' frowned Tomek. 'I came here to work the puppet show, remember? All this was your idea. You said it was your baby.' He began undoing the buttons on his waistcoat. Suddenly Teresa knew she was staring at the solution as well as the cause of her problem.

'You are going to save the day, Tomek.'

'How? I was hoping that I had spoilt it.'

'That smack in the face was just the opening number, you're going to knock 'em all dead!'

She was inspired by the spirit of showbiz. Teresa gave Tomek a slap on the back, and instead of the stern and lengthy admonishment he was expecting, administered a motivational talk. She was tireless in her praise of his abilities as a puppeteer, but was met with stubbornness: She coaxed him with a little team spirit, which he countered with surly non-cooperation. When all else had failed, they stood apart in undefeated frozen silence. The tension mounted between the two protagonists as they faced each other, pausing over another unresolved chord.

Meanwhile, the orchestral players were tending to their fallen maestro and the Euphony Escorted Tour party shuffled around awkwardly exchanging bemused expressions. Reluctant to recapitulate themes that had already been rehearsed, Dr Dietrich sought out Professor Kirchel and propelled him towards the stage.

'What are you doing with me?' he demanded, even as his feet obeyed the thrust in the kidneys that was impelled by the handbag, and behind it, the ferocious willpower of Dr Dietrich. 'Get up there and tell them something!'

'I am not sure they want to know any more. They have reached saturation point.'

'Yes, well, we've got to do *something*. You're the musicologist – what would the court of Esterházy do when they had time on their hands, Professor Kirchel? Or did that case never arise?'

'Oh no, they had almost limitless time on their hands. Their hands were dripping with it,' he added angrily.

'Good – then talk about that.'

So Professor Kirchel stood in front of the audience wringing his time-drenched hands. 'Ladies and Gentlemen, this is an opportunity for us to experience the condition of perpetual deferment that was courtly life. No wonder they were called ladies in waiting, or gentlemen of the antechamber! This is a lesson in how stricken they would have been without Haydn, since mostly they made time pass by listening to his music. You could almost say that Haydn was indispensable to the sanity of the place. Without his soothing music, who knows what savagery might have arisen in their breasts?

'Under his influence the Esterházy courtiers were cultivated into one of the most sophisticated audiences that has ever existed. Even those guests who attended the nightly concerts merely in order to conduct romantic liaisons, or to catch the Prince's eye, were as sensitive to the changes in his music as they were to the shaded utterances of their Prince.

'And for those that were, despite their craven position, still human beings, the music pulled strings that went straight to their hypocritical hearts. Whilst his music was playing, they were transformed. No longer the *courtiers* of Nikolas Esterházy, they became instead the *audience* of Joseph Haydn. Haydn was providing a brief glimpse of freedom from the continuous demands of service. If only we could retain the thoughts that filled this room, but thoughts die away as quickly as musical notes.'

Kirchel heard his own voice stop. Then he said: 'There is nothing more for me to say. Quite literally the only information we have about those musical evenings is preserved in the scores that Haydn left. Tonight we are all ghosts of the audience that sat in this room and heard this beautiful music for the first time, so perhaps we can try to imagine that we have heard no Beethoven, no Bruckner or Mahler. We are witnessing the unveiling of a new art form, and we are very demanding clients. Yes Haydn was required to fill many aristocratic evenings over the years in Esterházy, but he couldn't get away with muzak.'

The audience chortled sleepily.

Kirchel continued: 'Now I shall just speak to my German friends, whilst you may think of any questions you may wish to ask me.' He had kept going in English for too long, and had lost half of his audience. He hurriedly began again in German, but he could not actually recall what he had been saying. The English speakers hadn't had time to come up with any questions when Kirchel surveyed their blank faces with an exaggeratedly raised eyebrow.

Finally, it was Hamish who bravely raised a hand and asked the professor: 'Why is it called the Farewell Symphony?'

'That is easy. The symphony was a way of hinting to Prince Nikolaus that it was time for the summer holiday to end, because, you see, the musicians wanted to leave Esterházy and go home.'

This answer received a murmur of empathy. Professor Kirchel had expressed a sentiment that was shared by all.

At that moment not a single person was moving. The palace was stopped in time.

From the sunlit side room there came a rip of Velcro as Teresa tore the wig off her head and threw it aside in frustration, then charged at Tomek's belly. Before he could recover his wind she had succeeded in launching him out of the double doors and down the steps of the building. Far from being angry, Tomek enjoyed this treatment enormously; he even tried prolonging the fun by running ludicrously over the lawn. At last he allowed her to catch him and pull him in the direction of the cave. She had her man.

'This is your chance to show Berhardt up for what he is, Tomek! You can be the star of the evening – knock him off his underserved pedestal – permanently.'

Tomek was about to agree when his bloodshot eyes scanned the figure of Teresa. She may have had no tits to speak of but she had great legs, especially when she stood aggressively with hips thrust out. Even in that skirt, which fell to the floor but showed the angle of her pelvis and the length of her upper legs, she was an invitation to an eighteenth-century ruffle. If he had ever been subtle this was not the moment. 'I want more.'

'What?'

'This!' he said, making a grab between her legs.

'Oh I see,' said Teresa, wriggling away. 'What do I get in return?'

'First I'll give them a show they will never forget,' said Tomek, 'and then you.'

'It's not just Bernhardt you want to knock off his pedestal then? You want to topple my boyfriend too,' she replied, although she knew this was ridiculous. Kevin was unlikely to ever occupy the summit of anyone's pedestal – he would first have to come down off his own step ladder.

'Have you ever heard a slow movement that was so still, so perfect, so sublime, that time seemed to stop altogether?' asked Professor Kirchel, who had resorted to asking the questions, since they had none for him.

'To be honest, I find my mind is apt to wander a little in slow movements,' replied Rosie Pratt, nervously picking a lavender bobble off her lamb's wool sleeve.

A chortle floated around the group that may have contained a sneer of superiority in certain quarters, but it was overwhelmed by a wave of recognition. In fact, in Edward's opinion, Rosie's confession was an understatement; *his* mind was not just apt to wander, it was apt to get up and leave the concert hall altogether. When he came to think of it, had he *ever* in his entire life sat through a slow movement and not gone over some financial work-issues in his head?

Professor Kirchel was patiently addressing Rosie's admission. 'Yes, I understand – it is certainly the most perilous time for the composer too; he might transfigure his audience – or lose them altogether; he might show them a glimpse of infinity – or have them making eyes at the light above the door that glows with the seductive little word: Ausgang.

'The slow movement – when it really works – doesn't hasten the passage of time,' he concluded, 'it quells it altogether. It may be as delicate as a bubble and just as briefly existent but it contains eternity within it.'

This was exactly the sort of pretentiousness that would invite derision from Kirchel's wife, and yet he did not hear one of her sharp comments popping this particular bubble. This was because she was enjoying a peaceful snooze along the back seats of the Travego, which was now parked in the town square of Fertod. Carl was keeping himself awake with coffee in the nearby café. The intimacies the two absentees had shared were those of escape, a little conversation, and now silence. Despite the perfect innocence of the affair, Frau Kirchel slept the delicious sleep of the adulteress.

I shall leave her and all the rest of the cast in these doldrums for a while to allow you to forget what you have read. The distractions of action: the Mercedes rolling along the open roads; the landscapes of Austro-Hungary sliding past the panavisual windows; the nipple-slip when the flat-chested woman put her phone away; or the New Zealander's demi-denimed buttocks as he climbed a ladder; the mocking smile of the beautiful Indian woman and the sullen face of the constipated boy; the stricken weight of the colossal-jointed duchess; not to mention the moonlit face of the English wife and her pastel-blazered hubby. All these phantoms can be taken away in an instant, those attachments to character and plot dissolved as easily.

Which may be just as well, since my intention is to introduce you to a boisterous new cast. These baffling characters will shortly invade our undefended history, armed with giant syringes, excessively bright clothing and a complete disregard for decorum. This story, which so far has been populated by personages who, between them seem to be indecisive as to which era they were supposed to be occupying are going to be knocked dead (that was Teresa's phrase, I think) by this advancing army of anarchists.

The Prince's original troupe of marionettes had long since passed into dust – after all, they were only pliable mechanisms clothed in pretty rags. In recent months a new generation had been constructed and costumed, to coincide with the appearance of the musicians at Esterházy who had been assembled in readiness for the tourists who themselves were summoned up by Euphony Escorted Tours.

It turned out that the contractors engaged in building the grotto in which the puppets were to dance had not been coordinated into this grand plan.

In the back-stage area behind the artificial cave, the crate containing the marionettes had been levered open and, as Tomek went to work, Teresa lowered her bodice to retrieve her phone and dial Dr Dietrich to explain the new arrangements.

'We're going to have a puppet show in the grotto.'

'But it's not finished.'

'I know. I'm handling Tomek this end,' Tess replied. 'Bring the audience. Kevin will show you the way.'

Snappily putting her phone away in her bag, Dr Dietrich rose to address the assembly. Having got their attention with one of her penetrating coughs, she announced the good news in German and English that they would be offered an alternative entertainment elsewhere. At this the Germans whooped with good cheer and the English continued to grumble. Then Dr Dietrich went over to the side wall of the Sala Terrena and tapped on the panelling.

'What's she doing Dad? Why is she knocking on the walls?'

'I don't know, Hamish. Perhaps she's lost a mouse.'

'She might be looking for fairies,' suggested Sally.

The panelling broke open along an invisible join and a head appeared.

'Yes?' snapped Kevin.

'Teresa Marz just called.'

'What does she want now?'

Kevin opened the secret door a little wider and the tourists craned their necks to see into his hi-tech lair. Their natural curiosity was particularly aroused when they saw that, amidst the chaotic scribble of state-of-the-art electronics, Tomek's killer punch was replaying on a colour screen.

'Ah yes, I was checking through that for security reasons,' said

Kevin, pressing pause. The motion froze as Bernhardt's head took on an unnatural angle. Kevin hurriedly slapped another button and the screen went blank.

'This is the lighting and sound control room,' he explained. 'It's not safe for the public.' He emerged without opening the door any wider and stood in full view. His unhistorical denims that had been banished from sight could no longer disturb the ambience; the precious spell had already been broken.

'You are to take us to the grotto,' said Dr Dietrich.

'But it's not finished.'

'I know.'

'I'm the technical director not her personal dogsbody. Why can't she take them herself?'

'Because she's already there, with Tomek.'

'Oh really?'

It was a resentful dogsbody that led the paying customers out through the side room where Teresa's empty wig lay on the floor, and onto the lawns lit by the late afternoon sunlight, to begin the long march through the grounds. It looked as though they were going to be put back onto the coach, and sent back to Vienna without having heard a note. Dreading this, they huddled into a collective shudder like sheep when the slaughterhouse truck arrives. Every shudder was amplified by the cold pike-scented wind that swept continuously off Neiusdl Lake, and there was widespread regret amongst those that had left their coats behind.

Did they rise up and protest? No. As if infected by the spirit of courtly behaviour the group processed in a very stately fashion along paths of newly laid pink gravel. Edward found himself walking behind the beautiful Indian woman, and saw an opportunity for emergency repairs to his reputation. He had Hamish and Sally flanking him in either hand, and he told them in a distinct and cheery voice they were going on a magical mystery tour. Sally cheered and Edward felt like cheering too. At last here was some light relief from deathbeds and empty cots. He briefly attempted to initiate some skipping and over-did the loving father act to such an extent he probably only made himself appear even odder to the Indian beauty. He certainly succeeded in confusing his kids.

Along the way, Dr Dietrich said she regretted that the original puppet theatre had been demolished once it was no longer required (had it ever actually *been* a requirement? Edward wondered), and the new one, a faithful reproduction, would be finished in time for the next season. With this statement the guide not only disappointed her paying customers, she also made them feel like uncouth visitors who had arrived prematurely.

'The puppet theatre was of a most unusual design,' she went on. 'It was brilliantly ornamented in the manner of a cave. The puppet shows were in the *commedia dell'arte* tradition, with characters you may already know, such as Columbine and Harlequin and Scaramouche. So, you see, the Prince was not always for the serious and the tragic.'

'At last,' said Hamish, sounding unconvinced.

The party were led onward through the twilight until they reached some stone steps cordoned off with orange plastic mesh. Kevin had to squat to pull back the temporary barrier so that Dr Dietrich could lead them down.

'This is a strange journey,' said Anjali. 'Where are we going?'

Flashing safety lights and some high-visibility tape marked the way.

'You will see, ladies and gentlemen, as Kevin obliges us, the beautiful curves and sculpted form behind the covering.' But when Kevin drew aside the blue weather-sheet the volutes and scrolls of a rococo façade were not there as promised. Misshapen stumps of cement sprouted electrical wires in anticipation of sconces bearing synthetic torchlight, as the second fixing had not been completed. Instead of a fantastic grotto, they were facing a mound, with, admittedly, a hole in it.

'This is like waiting to be born,' jested Satma. 'You see what that looks like, Anji?' The entrance of the grotto formed an unmistakably vulvic form, fringed with moss and ferns.

'Except that we are on the outside waiting to go in,' answered Anjali, giggling quietly.

The resemblance of the cave's mouth to that by which we make our first entrance into life was inevitable and therefore cannot be seen as symbolically significant, whatever ideas may flourish in Satma's psychically fertile mind. The cave that does not possess this characteristic is as rare as a sports car that isn't phallic or a potato with no resemblance to a politician. There was no mistaking the similarity in this case; numerous giggles and mutterings betrayed the fact.

'We're not going in there,' said the Englishman, Pratt. 'My wife!'

'We can get her a wheelchair, sir,' said Dr Dietrich hurriedly.

'A chair – what do we want a chair for? – we're trying for a baby.'

'A bed then?'

'I'm talking about the dust. Do you want my unborn child to get emphysema?'

Dr Dietrich attempted to make the best of it. 'Doesn't anyone here want to see a puppet show?' Her enthusiasm was reflected back in the form of a wave of indifference, except that in normal circumstances waves carry energy. She tried again to rouse their spirits: 'Come on everyone, show some enthusiasm!'

Dr Dietrich overheard the following snippet of dialogue in German: 'The English are wary of puppets because they might come to life.'

'Who, the puppets?'

'No, the English.'

When this was greeted with a hearty roar, Dr Dietrich said: 'I am so glad some of you are keen; Prince Nikolaus, too, really loved puppets.'

The Duchess of Poundland muttered: 'Control-freak!' and laughter rippled across the pool of heads.

'Yes he was a bit of a control freak, I suppose,'

'I meant you.'

With professionalism and a complete lack of a sense of the ridiculous, Dr Dietrich ushered her group towards the entrance with undaunted rectitude: 'It may seem to some of you a little bit exotic to have a puppet theatre in such a place – I mean in the garden – but it is really not so strange. Think how many rich persons today have home cinemas.'

'That's true,' corroborated Hamish. 'There was someone's house on the telly that had a bowling alley.'

'So you must imagine we are going to a rich man's private cinema.'

Edward was glad to see how widely Hamish grinned at this idea. Both Hamish and Sally loved the movies. There had been a cineplex near the hospital where Pamela had been admitted for her final stay, so when visiting time ended they would go and treat themselves to a film. When they came out of the cinema they could pretend they had left their mum watching the rest of the double bill rather than undergoing treatment in a cancer ward.

Hamish put up his hand with a question. 'So why is it in a cave, Miss?'

An audible smirk passed round the whole group that the kid had outsmarted the all-knowing guide, but to everyone's disappointment Dr Dietrich welcomed the incoming question because it gave her the chance to unleash her ready riposte.

'I suppose you know, young man, when cinema was invented?'

It was one of those questions that you don't like to be pressed into being specific about – even if everyone has a rough idea – so Hamish shook his head with the sagacity of a twelve-year-old.

'Perhaps you should ask your Daddy.'

At once Edward was in a panic. 'Before your time, Hamie,' he said with anxious levity.

'Yes,' corroborated Dr Dietrich, 'even before yours, I think. The earliest ever description of a cinema is – I am quite certain – a lot earlier than you think, young man.'

Edward was busy backdating his unspoken guess. Being put on the spot like this was discomforting – especially by Dr Dietrich. She was hired to be the know-it-all, why did she have to ask the questions too? And while we're at it, why had she just called him a young man – how old did that make *her*?

Edward had still failed to come up with an answer, wrong or right, when Dr Dietrich seemed to confirm his estimate of her extreme antiquity with the following utterance: 'I am confident you will be surprised when I tell you that the first cinema predated modern filmhouses by twenty-five centuries.'

Other emotions elicited by this statement included incredulity, confusion and disappointment, none of which retarded Dr Dietrich in her onward gush.

'In a work that some of you may know as *The Republic*, the Ancient Greek teacher Plato described a cinema audience as captives in a cave, unable to turn their heads away from the wall across which moving lights and shadows passed, making it a sort of primitive screen. The shadows they were watching were cast by people outside the cave, out of sight, passing in front of Plato's projector, a great fire.'

'I don't see any fire,' objected Hamish.

'No, neither would the captive audience, they were born in the cave and believed that they were seeing all that there *was* to see.'

There was one among Dr Dietrich's listeners who responded with engorged interest. 'You have shown us a strange image,' said Satma, 'and they are strange prisoners.'

'Like ourselves,' Dr Dietrich replied.

Satma nodded and gave a look to Anjali. This cave, whatever it was, must be extremely significant. This was like finding the Mouth of Hell, except she didn't believe in Hell. This was the orifice of rebirth; a place to explore past incarnations.

They entered the cavern's dark interior, which had been decorated with gargoyles and monsters, entwined in foliage and encrusted with shells. It was too dark to perceive how well these were carved, or for that matter how badly. They were, in fact, moulded out of preformed plastic.

It is customary to leave a pause before a theatrical performance begins, allowing the audience time to lose its memories of the outside world and prepare themselves to enter a new reality. Our audience lingered in the cave of rebirth like souls gathered together before their mass-reincarnation in another realm. Their chances of an afterlife rested on the violently unpredictable Tomek doing his work.

There they loitered, longing for chairs, staring at the curtains, willing them to twitch. The Duchess of Poundland, in particular, had numerous things to say about standing around in a *fibreglass* cave.

Around the back, Teresa watched Tomek prepare for his performance with rising admiration. He surrounded himself with the marionettes, propped up in sitting postures with their strings carefully stretched out to prevent them tangling, emanating from their wooden heads and wrists like screaming lines of panic. Tomek addressed the cast in Hungarian: 'Scaramouche, you bastard, it is always a joy to see you – all in black, ready for the skirmish, but oh dear they have given you a terrible haircut. And Arlechino! What is this ginger hair made of, bailer-twine? Still you have a fine suite of patches . . . And who is this? I'll call you Scapino. Let's see if together we can't make some mischief.'

Tomek addressed his cast with the air of a commander giving his squadron a pep-talk before a daring raid. 'And Il Dottore, here is your doctor's bag and it's well equipped – have you got your clysters? Giangurgolo you crazy poltroon – can't you keep your big mouth shut?' Testing the mechanism of the jaw, he adjusted the v-spring that made it snap shut on his finger and then, when he pulled a cord, gape implausibly wide. '. . . And Columbine,' he sang, 'my *inamorata*, you are so beautiful I see – no one can resist you . . .' and he gave the painted face of the puppet a lingering kiss.

Finally, Tomek took off both his shoes and removed one brown sock. As he did so he muttered to himself, mentally running through the ribbons of comedy.

The audience collectively shushed themselves as the velvet curtains parted, and Arlechino was discovered on stage, alone.

'I can't see, Daddy, lift me up!' squealed Sally.

'I still don't get it, Dad, why is the puppet show in a cave?'

Although Edward knew he should admit he had no idea, instead he said: 'It's all to do with Plato, Hamish. It's a little complicated.'

Though his father's answer was thoroughly unhelpful, Hamish did not pursue the matter, and as his sister was hoisted to shoulder height he pushed his way to the front to get a better view. The inadequacy of Edward's explanation was entirely understandable since he was utterly perplexed himself. Everything would become clear later, he thought, as the puppet show began.

Arlechino resembled a pile of piebald rags until he twitched into life and groaned. His body lifted slowly as he dragged his head off the floor. Tomek may have been unprepared, but he was a very dextrous puppeteer, and he was transcendentally drunk, his mind pulled along by its own invisible strings of inspiration. Poor Arlechino cried out in agonised fury, using extremely foul language. Most of this crudity was perfectly clear, even to the English speakers, despite his use of Hungarian, but it was, perhaps, more warmly appreciated by the Germans present. There were guffaws of laughter as Arlechino shrank back from the painful reverberations of his own voice, racked by a fit of coughing, followed by an equally unstoppable bout of flatus before he floated back to the floor on a cushion of his own wind, in defiance of both gravity and good taste.

Edward had no doubt that this would be going down well with Hamish.

Tomek, who was also playing the tambourine between his knees to provide sound effects, continued to have enormous fun with his hungover puppet, bringing him to delicate motion and then slapping his head against the wings, causing him to stagger in mid-air, a feat both impossible and instantly recognisable, for the sufferings of this puppet are common. Edward could feel Sally's giggles transmit themselves down his spine.

In the next scene the Doctor arrived and tried to determine what was wrong with the twitching Arlechino. After a couple of false remedies, il Dottore seemed to give up, and Arlechino, apparently dead, was raucously mourned by some sections of the audience. Il Dottore went off stage and shortly returned dragging a syringe that was as big as the puppet itself. With this he gave Arlechino a shot in his backside, and after a suitable pause the patient revived. Arlechino celebrated his recovery with a little dance, then suddenly clutched his stomach again and lay on his back with his knees in the air. Some of the audience seemed to be ahead of the rest, but all was made clear when a baby emerged from the puppet's body. Tomek was able to express the pain and joy of childbirth with twitches on his strings. A second baby immediately followed since they were strung together like sausages, their birth pangs drenched with the laughter and encouragement of the audience.

Edward thought that perhaps he had been too quick to assume the puppet show was suitable for children, but he disliked the idea of censoring harmless fun. Even Sally knew where babies came from. What harm was there in it?

The Doctor picked up the first baby, joyously at first, then with concern. He listened to it, turned it upside down and finally slapped it violently. Then he shook it, before throwing it over his shoulder and picking up the second one by the foot. Holding this one upside down he gave it a shake and a sniff before it too was rejected and tossed away. These outrages were greeted joyously by the crowd. Whistling a merry air, il Dottore left his two infant patients strewn lifelessly across the stage. The thrill of such un-Hippocratic behaviour could be said to have overpowered the audience's ability to repress their laughter. In other words, the show was going well. Not so much with Edward, perhaps – he was becoming a concerned parent. And yet there was no squeak of alarm from the eight-year-old atop his head.

Arlechino, alone now, seemed exhausted, until he was struck with a new spasm. He adopted the knees-up position. Evidently a third baby was due. At this unassisted delivery Edward involuntarily gripped Sally's leg. Foremost among the things he wished Sally had never known about was her mother's third pregnancy. This unsought blessing was the last occasion of perfect joy that he could remember. Pamela was delighted with what she called her 'third mistake' and could not conceal the news from Sally, who so wanted a baby sister and never for a moment considered the terrible possibility that it would be a boy.

No one for a moment considered the possibility of any of the terrible things that happened next. It was at one of the routine health checks for expectant mothers that the cancer was discovered. They were presented with a choice – see the pregnancy through and put up a belated fight with the cancer or terminate the pregnancy so that Pamela could undergo chemotherapy right away.

Sally had to be dealt with very sensitively. No further mention was ever made of the little sister that had been growing inside her mother. They hoped Sally would forget the whole thing, were optimistic that the disease would be beaten, and foresaw a future filled with baby sisters. As it turned out, the abortion was merely the first of a series of defeats.

Edward may be forgiven for squeezing his daughter's chubby calves a little too tight. All these traumas were about to be grotesquely lampooned.

The surviving baby was a simple two-string puppet, but Tomek played upon those two strings like a virtuoso. It wriggled and cried out. Awoken by the cries, Arlechino revived himself and, apparently a much more self-possessed individual than Edward, tenderly picked the baby up. Soon the newborn child was pacified and belched contentedly whilst Edward was horrified at himself, for the guilt and panic that he was feeling as he watched.

Arlechino went off; the baby was left on the stage but the show was not over. The beautiful Columbine entered, in a dress of Andalusian orange. She did a little dance with many curtsies to present herself; she saw the baby, was instantly charmed, and picked it up. Arlechino returned with a book bearing a pink heart on the cover and began to read to Columbine. It was clearly love poetry; Tomek mimicked the yearning strains and ridiculous whines of the genre. Meanwhile, he extruded a brown sock from within the baby puppet by pulling a string.

This happened to be Tomek's own sock, and was a refinement (if one can call it that) on the equipment he had found in the crate. Very effective it was too. By pulling it out of the baby puppet to the accompaniment of infantile groans, it appeared that the child was relieving itself of a piece of excrement that was at least as big as the excretor. Tomek was an absolute master at expressing through puppetry the pleasures of expulsion; his marionette skills made the puppet purge itself with such realism you could even sense the moment when (at the tug of a certain string) the baby was tying off the arabesque with a final twist, and the woollen matter fell into the book on Arlechino's lap while Tomek supplied the cutest possible expressions of voided babyjoy.

His recital rudely disrupted, Arlechino slapped the book shut and Columbine fled. The audience were delighted both by the crapping and the critique of poesy; they uproared with splendour. Even Edward felt his shoulders bouncing under Sally's giggling weight.

This was *Commedia del' Arte* of the most astonishing crudity. It was a show that consisted mostly of violence, obstetrics and now scatology, but he could congratulate himself that his children were well-adjusted enough to see the show as a huge joke about a laughable species that was supposed to comfort rather than offend us, because we are all equally ignoble.

Then he heard a high-toned 'ting!' It was Sally's cute way of saying 'disgus-ting'. She was tugging on her father's finger and the final syllable rang out like a bell, causing several people to look in their direction. She kept repeating the word, of which all that could be heard over the hilarity was a cantabile *'ting!'*

Edward looked back at the stage to see what, after all that had gone before, had finally gone too far for Sally's eight-year-old head to take in.

Arlechino, alone again, with the book lying beside him, was breast-feeding. A good single parent, he nursed the baby's head as it began to suckle noisily at his teat. So it seemed that Sally had no objection to cruelty and excrement, but a male parent suckling a baby was too much for her. She pulled her father's hair and said loudly into his ear, 'Take me away, Daddy.'

Leaving Hamish at the front they headed for the exit. Kicking her heels into his flank to urge her father onward, Sally led the way with her 'ting, ting, ting.' She had to dismount to get through the entrance, and even before they got outside they felt a gush of air cold enough to restore the sanity to a sufferer of daemonics. Edward shuddered and held Sally close to warm her. It was only a partial relief for Edward to get out of the cave – now he would have to withstand Sally's naive but penetrating inquisition.

At the top of the steps was the beautiful Indian woman. The breeze and the early evening sunlight were having a splendid effect on her draperies. She smiled when she saw the father and daughter huddled together; the smile was probably meant for Sally, though Edward gratefully took a share in its warmth.

'Not your kind of thing?' he asked. *Of course not*, he corrected himself. *A refined and exquisite girl like that isn't going to enjoy such vulgarity.*

Sally tore herself away from him and danced over to the beautiful lady. She was not at all shy, since she constantly watched films or read books that included impossibly beautiful princesses and would not have been surprised if this one was accompanied by a tame unicorn or carried a potted genie.

Meanwhile, Edward was also smiling inanely, alert as he was to the possibility that this was finally a chance to discover her name and repair the low opinion she must have of him. He had had only one experience of another woman since Pamela's death and it would be fair to say that it didn't go particularly well. It was the condoms that did for him. Trying to commence love with another woman, with condoms that Pamela had bought for him to use with her, proved to be the trigger of farcical disappointment. Even the word trigger was an unhappy reminder. He should have thrown them out with her cosmetics. He had learned his lesson and had a fresh supply now, unopened.

However, he was unable to think of a conversation starter and only smiled and kept on smiling. Brightly, the beautiful lady suggested to Sally that they explore the gardens, which she enthusiastically accepted. Edward, immobilised as well as dumb, watched them depart together.

A blue plume of smoke advertised the fact that Dr Dietrich was also standing outside the cave. Assuming Edward had come outside for the same reason as her, she offered him a cigarette. Then, upon receiving a non-verbal refusal, tempted him with some chewing gum, which Edward also declined.

'Are you not feeling well?'

'No, I mean yes, perfectly fine, thank you.'

'But you came out of the puppet show.'

'Yes.'

Their dialogue was not exactly Socratic so far.

'This puppet theatre; my son still doesn't understand why it has to be a cave, and I know he's bound to go on about it until I give him an answer. He hasn't got the connection with Plato.'

'Has he not?' queried Dr Dietrich, 'are *you* perhaps familiar with Plato's *Republic*?'

'I suppose we did it at school, but I never got beyond the first few pages. I'm like that with books.'

The *Republic* is a struggle, particularly if, like Edward, you don't want to get caught up in someone else's argument. He was ill-equipped for its relentless question and answer refrain. Edward had to get drunk in order to pluck up the courage to contradict anyone, which meant he had never won an argument in his life. He was such an able member of negotiating teams at the bank because all arguments seemed futile the moment he planted his broad seat at the table. As a force he was never irresistible, but as an object he was usually immovable. Tonight he was in a sober yet belligerent mood, and Dr Dietrich annoyed him sufficiently to get a response when she declared: 'You will probably not remember the beginning of book seven, when Plato shows how dim our understanding is. He does this in a very clever way . . .'

'So he is the one exception, then, to the general dimness of humanity – good of him to put his brilliance to work pointing it out, and leaving it to book seven, where most of us are bound to miss it.' Edward obviously wasn't really peeved with Plato, he was simply taking his frustrations out on him.

'This was his reason for inventing the cinema, to illuminate how easily deluded we are.'

'Really? I always thought people go to the cinema to enjoy fresh delusions,' Edward mumbled.

'Plato is not so interested in the cinema-goer,' said Dr Dietrich. 'He is interested in the cinema-comer.'

'Oh, I see! Why is that?'

'Because people going into the cinema never give anyone any trouble; he was concerned with people coming out.'

'You mean people re-enacting shootout scenes, dancing in the gutter, driving recklessly – generally causing a public nuisance in their excitement?'

'No, not really.'

Dr Dietrich asked Edward to imagine what would happen if one of the captive cave-audience was somehow released from his bonds. He would make his way out of the cave and into the light, stumbling, groping. 'At first blinded by the glare,' Dr Dietrich suggested, 'he would fancy that the shadows he had once understood are truer than the objects now shown to him, no?'

Edward assured her of his complete agreement.

'Like you, now, coming out of the cave, and talking to me – you understand better now, yes?'

'No, not really.'

Dr Dietrich fell silent, wondering whether it was worth pursuing this explanation. An awkward pause was broken by Sally's voice calling. She was standing a little way off, hand in hand with the beauty of the world.

'Excuse me, I have to go and see what she wants.'

'Of course you do,' remarked Dr Dietrich, watching him hurry off.

'You two seem to have made friends,' said Edward, and then to the beautiful young woman, whose name, agonisingly, he still did not know, he added: 'Thank you for looking after her for a while.'

'That's quite all right. She's been quite a chatterbox!'

Naturally, Edward dreaded this. He bent to Sally and gave her an exaggerated smile. 'What do you think of the gardens, darling?'

'They are a bit flat, Daddy.'

'Didn't you find any fairies, Sal? Remember, Dr Dietrich said this was Fairyland!'

Sally looked very serious for a moment as though deciding whether or not in her mind fairies still existed. If they did it probably wasn't for that much longer.

'There weren't any here because they don't like bulldozers, Daddy.'

'Bulldozers?'

'Yes, Daddy. We saw one, but it didn't see us. It was sleeping.'

The lower terrace would soon be an overflow car park. In the modern world large gardens were doomed, along with their fairies.

Now Sally was excited about something else that was suddenly urgent. She was jumping up and pulling on her Daddy's corduroy sleeve. 'Daddy, do you know who Anjali's friend is?

Edward was too busy relishing that precious name to heed the question.

'Daddy! You know Anjali's friend . . .'

There it was again, a beautiful name – Anjali. How like an angel. Why would anyone want to discuss her plain-faced friend?

'What about her?'

'Do you know who she is?'

'Yes, we met earlier. I think it was Satma, wasn't it?'

'But really she is Mozart! Yes, well it's true. You can see that it must be true from her funny coat. It's straight out of the olden days.'

'Mozart is dead, Sally.'

'That's what I said. But Anjali says it doesn't matter because he can come back. And he has!'

Now that it had been divulged he would be able to call her by name, speak to her face to face, and oh, that face! Putting a name to it would be really something...

'Are you listening, Daddy?'

Anjali began to explain to the disorientated Englishman; she had been through it so many times before, her explanation ran along familiar lines, reincarnation being part of Hinduism and encompassing every living being. That was an accepted fact, as far as she was concerned, and yet this Englishman had apparently not heard of it.

'Daddy, don't you see?' squealed Sally. 'Anjali says that absolutely everyone comes back – that means Mummy will too. You did say that didn't you Anjali?'

Anjali lowered her eyes and said: 'Yes, that is what I believe.'

Edward's weak smile faded as he heard Sally coming to a terrible conclusion. 'Oh Daddy, I was right, she's coming back tonight isn't she!'

Edward could not bear to look at the sincerity in his daughter's eyes, but knew he had to kill this idea at once. Was he too much of a coward to strike? Taking cover in the growing darkness, and with his gaze held downward, he spoke to the Indian woman: 'Do you know what you have done?' Then he added brightly, ostensibly to Sally, but for the other's benefit: 'I think that people who are so sure of the afterlife should go there.'

Edward realised that this was not a light-hearted comment and that his anger had just leaked out.

'You don't mean it!'

'Of course I do. I could even lend a hand if need be.'

Edward hurriedly tried to cover himself, saying it was only a joke, but he saw at once that he had failed to convince. She gave him a look that confirmed he had frightened her.

And Sally? He saw that she hadn't understood the words but recognised his false laugh as a sign he was covering something grown-up and dark.

Edward also saw that it was futile getting worked up when the damage was already done. He would have to spend the rest of the night dismantling that airborne castle, turret by fairytale turret.

'I think I need a walk,' said Edward hurriedly. 'Sally, come with me.'

'No, Daddy, I don't want to. You're a grumpysaurus. I want to stay here with Anjali. I've been round and round the garden already.'

Not trusting himself to stay, and reluctant to compound matters by dragging Sally away, Edward had no choice but to leave them alone. He strode off into a part of the garden that was cast in shadow by the palace. He walked in rapid circles, as though his mind was rewinding back to the previous night in his room at the Imperial, when he had dreamed he was walking barefoot with his wife on their back lawn in Putney. They walked around the small back garden together to get away from the smell of paint. Edward wanted to tell her that he was stuck – that he felt he was wasting his life – then, suddenly remembering that she had lost hers entirely, he realised what a self-centred clumsy fool he was being. She drifted off the way people do in dreams, and he felt that if only he had kept up a light and inconsequential conversation instead of moaning about his sorrows, she might have stayed around a little longer.

For a while that morning, as he padded barefoot on the deep pile carpet of his hotel room, he felt as though the soles of his feet were still wet with dew. Rationality rejected these phantasms and yet part of his brain had to keep asking the questions: Can I get her back? What if Pamela (wherever she exists) is dreaming of me? If she is somewhere – anywhere – please let her dreams come true!

He ruthlessly repressed such thoughts. Of course dreams don't come true. He knew that, but did Sally? She was bombarded with assertions that they do if you believe in them enough. Admittedly, these assertions occurred in animated feature films, which were waking dreams themselves, never mistakable for reality. Besides, what sort of parent would proscribe believing in dreams?

Without dreams, life would be a lobotomised existence. Longing for the impossible return of his wife encouraged nocturnal phantoms to appear, but he would never choose painless, dreamless nights.

He had calmed down now and his swirling thoughts had slowed into a story he thought he could spin to Sally, preserving dreams and memories but discouraging delusions. However, when he returned, Edward saw that Sally and Anjali had gone. The indomitable Dr

Dietrich was still there, puffing like a demon on the bottom quarter of her cigarette. In some sort of shock at his own vulnerability, Edward hurried up to the cave.

'You are in quite a rush to find her – I saw you together – she is very pretty'

'Well to me, she's beautiful,' said Edward.

'I can tell you love her.'

'I absolutely adore her, thank you – have you seen her?'

'She's just gone for a walk with your daughter.'

Edward could not respond to untangle this misunderstanding because it was simultaneously entangled in his own mind.

Dr Dietrich was chortling privately. 'Plato warned that this would happen,' she said. 'Walking around outside the cave the watcher slowly grows aware of what he saw only dimly before. For the first time he will understand, as you have.'

'What have I understood?' begged Edward, genuinely exasperated.

'You have seen what is real and what is not.'

Edward was about to demand 'Which?', when Dr Dietrich recommenced quoting chunks of *The Republic* verbatim: 'And when he remembers his old habitation, he will surely pity the ones still imprisoned inside.'

At once Edward thought of Hamish, who was of course still inside the cave, and was possibly deserving of pity. He told Dr Dietrich that he was going back in.

Dr Dietrich put out her arm to warn him of what Plato said would happen to people who decided to re-enter the cave.

'What will happen?'

'You will find your eyes blinded with the gloom of the place, yes?'

'Certainly, I expect I would,' Edward concurred.

'Now when you go back in you will stumble, and most probably to all those inside you will appear ridiculous – mad or drunk.'

'They may already think that.'

'Besides, they are watching the show. While you try to get your son out, they will angrily resist; they will try to silence you with shushes and when that fails, by pushing you away so you don't block their view.'

'Now, honestly, I can't believe they would behave like that.'

Dr Dietrich gave him a cold stare: 'You would do the same if someone started tugging you out of your seat in the middle of a film. You would tell him quite bluntly to find his own seat.'

'I suppose so.'

'And if you didn't know that what you were watching was a film, and thought it was real life, how would you feel if someone slipped into an empty seat beside you and whispered into your ear, 'This is unbelievable nonsense! How can you believe in this nonsense?', and getting quite carried away with his own message, ends up waving his arms and blocking as much of your view as he can . . . screaming, 'This isn't real!'

'I wasn't planning on doing anything so ostentatious as that. I only wanted to fetch my son.'

Dr Dietrich took a long draw on her cigarette and said: 'Take it from me, if you go in there and break into their reality, they will pull you down into the darkness at their feet where they will kill you, almost absentmindedly, because to them you are the one who is unreal. They will stamp you to death without missing any of the *real* action on the stage.'

Dr Dietrich threw down her stub and laughed a coarse throat-clearance. 'It is alarming how far people will go to keep what they think is reality from being challenged.'

Had Dr Dietrich overheard his embarrassing outburst a few moments ago? She must have; and clearly she believed in the supernatural, too. When Anjali tried to reveal things that were beyond his comprehension his reflex had been to kill her. Of course he would never act on such an instinct, but Dr Dietrich knew it was there even if he didn't.

Edward was still absorbing the oracular utterance when two members of the audience came out. On closer inspection they were the tender-hearted Pratts. Both of them were flushed, their eyes wide, the whites of them shining; but Rosie was just perceptibly still shivering with the aftershocks of laughter, in contrast to her husband who approached Dr Dietrich aggressively. 'I am quite disgusted!' he began. 'I have never experienced such horror before. My wife has been subjected to scenes of indescribable depravity, and, I'll have you know, she is a very sensitive person.'

'I am sorry you and your wife did not enjoy the puppet show.'

'Do you call that X-rated disgrace a puppet show?'

Dr Dietrich looked blank and lit another cigarette. 'It had puppets and it was a show, so yes, that is what I would call it.'

'Is this what Euphony Escorted Tours calls a Feast of Festivals? A Feast of Filth, more like! My wife had to stand there and watch such scenes involving babies and human waste.'

'No harm was meant by it,' said Dr Dietrich, forgetting that other defence that no babies or faeces were involved – it was only a matter of some socks and pieces of string.

Pratt had to pull himself together to be strong (and righteous). He was surprised to find his little wife standing beside him looking flushed and elated, her moon-face warmed in the sunset.

'My wife is very sensitive! She is – I mean we are – trying for a baby – how do you think that makes us feel?'

'Very angry, apparently.'

'Never mind, James, I thought it was funny,' said Rosie, as she pulled him away from Dr Dietrich.

'I think we are entitled to some compensation.'

'Yes, well, if you feel that strongly about it . . .'

Rosie was pulling at his arm: 'James, it was only a joke.'

'People should not make jokes about some things. Some things are sacred!'

'Maybe, but not puppets, surely.'

Dr Dietrich showed the outraged Englishman and his tender wife the way back to the palace. As they set off along the gravelled path she promised to do something straight away. What she would do, she did not know yet. She opened her phone and rang Teresa. 'Is our fallen hero back to life yet?'

'Still out to lunch,' said Teresa.

'That gives me an idea. Can we go straight to the interval buffet? I'm getting some discontents here.'

'Oh dear, was the puppet show no good?'

'Not to everyone's taste, but it's still going. I can hear the laughter from out here. I've just had to deal with a couple of walk-outs.'

'Okay, we can do that. You bring your discontents straight back and I'll send Kevin out to bring the rest back round the long way. That should give us time to sort the problem out.'

Whilst Dr Dietrich was making her call, the Malaysian physicist, Lakshman, waddled out of the cave. Edward greeted him with immense relief. Here was a scientific man, a cheerful example of rationality and robust mental health: 'Was it too much for your taste, too, Lakshman?' he asked.

'To tell the truth, I don't actually know. I could not see anything at all from the back.'

Edward was so relieved to find backing for the rational cause, he decided to recruit Lakshman to his side of the argument. 'Dr Dietrich here tells me that if I go back inside they will probably murder me for interrupting the show.'

'I don't doubt it,' said Lakshman, laughing. 'But you look shaken, my friend.'

'It's not that – I am afraid I may have made a blunder. I seem to have threatened to murder someone myself. It was a misunderstanding, but it must have caused offence. You'd assume so, wouldn't you?'

To Edward's relief, Lakshman continued to laugh. 'I am constantly making such threats to my students, and the lab technicians, and to my Dean of Faculty, and to the car park attendants at the campus, and to anyone who serves me weak coffee. I hope all these lapses will not all be held against me.'

'No one could imagine for a second that you were capable of it,' Edward assured him warmly. He related to Lakshman the incident with Anjali that could be interpreted as a murder threat.

'No one could imagine for a second that you were capable of it,' was Lakshman's generous-spirited echo, which may have been an endorsement of Edward's gentleness or a reflection of his cowardice.

He cut through Edward's groan with the counter-proposal that, since they were still there discussing this now, it was safe to assume that they all (Anjali included) possessed at least some doubt about whatever is beyond. 'If he had had access to telescopes and microscopes, Plato might have realised that there is plenty of science to be done inside the cave, and that *speculating* about what is outside, like he did, is mystical nonsense.'

'It's a good thing Dr Dietrich's not here, she would be horrified to hear you dismiss the work of our greatest philosopher.'

'Yes, well, she has a little too much respect for authority.' Lakshman had a habit of chewing his words. It was more probably a result of poorly fitted dentures than what it seemed, the nutritious cud of a ruminative mind. 'Disrespect is our most precious commodity. Our future depends on it. Perhaps Plato's story is just a way of disparaging people who doubted his fantastic stories,' he began. 'Obviously most people would rather not be stuck in a cave. It makes them seem like bats.'

'But not you, you don't mind seeming like a bat?'

'Oh no, I am very happy to be a bat – we can see in the dark!'

Edward felt restored to sanity by Lakshman's cheerful rationality. Then he remembered Hamish. 'Perhaps I should go back in and get my little boy.'

'Aren't you scared that they will tear you to shreds?'

Edward was stunned by this apparent contradiction. 'That was Deitrich's argument, or Plato's . . . not yours.'

'On the matter of human psychology they may be right, I'm no expert.'

If Edward had been bold enough to ignore expert advice and enter the cave, Hamish would most certainly have greeted his parent with a punch in the lower abdomen as an indication that he had no wish to be distracted from the show. But Edward procrastinated, leaving Hamish as incapable of tearing his eyes from the action at the front of the cave as if he had been fitted with Plato's manacles.

Kevin strode back across the darkened lawns to the grotto, shirt-sleeved and immune from chill, although physicians, if they could monitor him fully, would observe that the muscles of his jaw were clamped. He was muttering bitterly, not from cold but about not being the bloody Pied Piper of bloody Anywhere. When he got to the mouth of the cave Lakshman barred his way with a gesture of his arm and said: 'Take care, young man, if you go in there they will tear you to pieces and stamp your broken limbs into the dirt.'

'Are you pulling my tooleywag?'

Edward was irresistibly infected by Lakshman's schoolboy

mischief and added: 'They have become a mob in there. If you go in you're a dead man.'

'We'll see about that,' said Kevin, and in he went.

The lights came on suddenly and brutally in the grotto, silencing any predicted fury with illumination. Kevin had not yet fitted the concealed halogens with dimmer switches that would, by next summer, allow the rocks to glow in a soft luminescence. Instead, he plugged some 1,200 watt work lights to the mains and when he flipped the rocker the cave was instantaneously exposed in harsh white light. The stepladders and tools of the plasterers who had sculpted the rock formations were left incriminatingly displayed.

Kevin was an unexpected bringer of enlightenment, and the audience duly cowered, as Plato had foretold. Some of them clearly blamed him (Kevin, that is, not Plato) for ending the fun, and made comments as they passed him on their way out; amongst the German disapproval he caught snippets translated for his own benefit such as 'typical English', which hurt his kiwi pride.

Satma, who had enjoyed being outraged as much as she enjoyed outraging others, was not surprised that Anjali had walked out of the puppet show. But she didn't expect to find her friend close to tears when they met up afterwards. Sally was gone and Anjali had a mild tremor, like a frightened whippet.

'Oh come on, Anji, it wasn't that bad!' said Satma, slapping her friend on the back.

'It's not that, I was just feeling sorry for that poor little girl.'

Satma wasn't paying attention. The puppet show had given Satma something to chew on. It was jumbled, but what can you expect from a message from beyond existence? It would take a while to disentangle the meaning of the string of babies and the brown sock.

Plato, the advocate of enlightened despots, would surely have approved of Nikolaus Esterházy's construction of an artificial cave in which he and his courtly guests could laugh at baser versions of themselves. When they emerged they could congratulate each other on how noble in reason, how infinite in faculties they were, and how their royal host was the perfect ideal of a prince. Neither of them would have liked Kevin.

When standing on ceremony Kevin never had a secure footing. He broke up the marionette gala with inelegant cheer.

'Hi guys! Come with me and there's a bonza treat for you all . . . grub's up!'

Meanwhile, in a quiet room of the palace, Bernhard's body was as inexpressive as that of someone who was feigning death, or if you prefer, someone who has fallen into a dreamless sleep in his seat in the cinema. When he wakes up the flickering dreams will resume. The trouble is he might have missed a few vital flicks. He will find the actors' dialogue discontinuous.

Bernhardt was not dead; his mimicry of the revered composer was not so perfect as that, he was a marionette that had been dropped. Meanwhile, his skull was a darkened cave wherein no puppets danced. Outside it, though, the puppets were as animated as ever. We shall rejoin the show after this short intermission, when, to everyone's relief no doubt, the pace briskens. In the next movement we shall be livened up with a dance, to get the circulation going.

III

MANNERS

Menuetto

'The minuet and trio portrays only too well the tedious intricacies of courtly life,' said Professor Kirchel. The oboist chuckled, and the others sighed in agreement. They were lounging around in their dressing room, where the distinguished professor had paid the musicians a visit while awaiting the call to perform.

'But the minuet and trio is the most inoffensive thing in music.'

'And yet it is the most hated!'

Like all orchestral players, they measured their work by the line and had been tricked by repeat marks.

'As far as I can see, the minuet and trio has only two virtues – it passes the time and saves paper,' said the oboist. 'More than half of the material is repeats and the original two-fifths is calculated to be as unchallenging as possible.'

'Wish we could skip it.'

'The minuet is rather leaden, I admit,' concluded the professor, 'but it was an expected part of the symphonic form. It would not be good manners to disrupt the stately progress of the symphony.'

The musicians yawned.

Teresa Martz popped her head round the door; the domesticity of the act was inconsistent with the grandeur of the door and the fact that she had her Pompadour-style wig back on.

'Sorry to interrupt . . . ah, there you are professor.'

'Miss Teresa. How's the fallen maestro?'

'No change – he grumbles a lot. He says he doesn't know where he is.'

'He is milking the scene,' said one musician.

'He is a terrible old ham,' added another.

Rather than waste time choosing between metaphorical offerings of dairy and pork, Teresa began issuing instructions: 'Professor Kirchel, I have a favour to ask of you. Have you met Kevin?'

'G'day,' said Kevin, reaching an arm round the doorjamb.

Kirchel sycophantically held out a hand.

'He's the technical director,' explained Teresa, and the hand withdrew.

Teresa was certain that Kevin was about to make one of his over-familiar remarks, so she forestalled him with excessively bright instructions to 'take the professor with you to the grotto and bring the audience back, if you don't mind, Kevin.' Sexual relations with subordinate male colleagues turned them into uncooperative teenagers. Or maybe that was just Kevin.

While Kevin led the professor down the west wing, the musicians perked up from their previous lugubrious talk of minuets and discussed football instead.

Teresa went back into the Sala, bustling with urgency. 'Keep everyone sweet!' she trilled. Her command swept across the busy catering staff. 'Do whatever you have to do – smile, flirt, supply them with plenty of drinks.' She had decided that it was essential that the audience were either too happy or too drunk to complain.

'What did she say?' asked one Hungarian waitress.

'Let them eat cake.'

Teresa continued: 'I have sent Kevin and the professor over to the puppet theatre and they will be returning shortly.'

'How shortly?'

'I told them to take the long way round.'

Teresa twitched her hands, unaware yet whether the audience would arrive in the form of stroppy customers, sycophantic courtiers or an angry mob. Unusually for her, she was achieving nothing. At some point these twenty-first-century tourists would wake up and remember that they were the ultimate stockholders of this dream, and they hadn't invested good money to have it turn into a nightmare. At least

– she reasoned – some tolerance could be put into the mechanism with alcohol. 'More peach schnapps in the punch and keep refilling, okay?'

This decision was risky since the uprisings delayed by wine are more violent for the same reason. A reign of terror might ensue. The delays to the performance of Haydn's 45th symphony had strained everyone's good manners, and Teresa was not certain that more good manners could be presumed from people who were already under some strain. They had been transported back in time to the courtly atmosphere of Esterházy in which no one was ever allowed to relax. Admittedly the Prince himself had done his best to shatter the courtly ambience with that brutal punch in the face of his Kapellmeister, but this had only added threat of further random violence to the already elevated level of tension.

Meanwhile, let me assert that the real Prince Nikolaus would never have punched Haydn; that was not his style. If he had wanted Haydn punched he would have sent one of the under-gardeners to do it.

'I thought the cave was somewhere in the park,' said Professor Kirchel, panting.

'It is.' Kevin was striding with no concession to the elder man's slower pace.

'So why are we going down this endless corridor?'

'You can go outside if you want; this is a short cut, under cover.'

They came to a long gallery that Kevin called the Display Room. This gallery's refurbishment was almost complete and Kevin was particularly pleased with his part in it. He put the ambient ceiling lights on and whistled for Kirchel to enter. They stood among the display cases, which were of various sizes, from tall wardrobes to tea chests. They were all constructed from glare-free glass with invisible joints. They resembled cubist crystals, bricks of solid air or, if you prefer, precisely defined portions of space, and they seemed to float, since the boxes on which they rested were matt black. One or two of them enhanced the illusion of weightlessness by also being vacant; the others contained the musical instrument collection.

Kevin left the professor admiring the collection and set to work with a small electrician's screwdriver, disabling the alarm so that he could open the emergency exit without setting it off. When the doors opened a gust of cold air blew in.

'Are you coming?'

'I think I'll stay, if you don't mind,' said Professor Kirchel, affecting an interest in the objects displayed.

We have already been told of the brusque manner in which Kevin declared that the farce was over, not by bringing down the curtain but by turning up the lights. He now allowed the disorientated exiles from the cave of delusion to return to the palace across the lawn – no actually *encouraged* them – to take a short cut across the grass, wilfully ignoring both Teresa's instruction that he should take them back by the longest possible route and the little black signpost that indicated such herbal transgressions were verboten. For this reason they re-entered the palace through the Display Room, avoiding a long walk that would have brought them round to the front where they could have been welcomed once again by Teresa with due decorum.

'Put some zip in it, folks, it's perishing!' Kevin chivvied, as he allowed them to enter – traipsing mud into the Display Room where Professor Kirchel was peering deeply into a case. Dr Dietrich preferred to remain outside to enjoy a cigarette. Kevin had also disabled the smoke alarm, but she preferred to stay outside anyway.

'As you approach the displays an infra-red motion sensor detects your presence and brings up the illumination on the nearby object. Bonza, isn'it!'

He showed off his bonza lighting scheme by sweeping into range of a detector until a cross-beam of light brought up a cabinet containing a headless mannequin in a peach-coloured gown, which appeared to be perpetually accepting an offer to dance.

'Beaut!' said Kevin.

Such a description was too brief.

'Is this supposed to be Princess Maria?' asked Pratt.

'Nahh, it's just some Sheila. They wanted her to rotate, but I insisted she should oscillate. It took a bit of doing with the reciprocating motors, but in the end I got her waltzing.'

'Why hasn't she got a head?'

'Since when did a Sheila need a head?'

This remark provoked a retort from Rosie.

'Why do you talk like a two-dimensional Australian?'

'Actually, I'm from New Zealand.'

Having corrected that misunderstanding, Kevin guided Hamish and Sally towards the case that contained a gilded birdcage, which, in turn, contained bejewelled songbirds on an ornate perch. 'Now, take a squizz at this, boys and girls.'

When Hamish got close it not only illuminated itself but also broke into a blast of cuckoo sounds and other bird noises. Kevin gesticulated flamboyantly, as though conjuring magical light and sound at once. 'Pretty spiffy, don't you think?'

Professor Kirchel took this as a cue to speak: 'It is true that when you hear the Toy Symphony with its perky melodies accompanied by a cuckoo and a torrent of other unrealistic birdcalls made by various whistles and rattles, you would be justified in holding the opinion of Haydn that he was a composer of Silly Symphonies and Looney Tunes.'

Kirchel's note of derision struck damply. There was a murmur of amusement, mostly from Kirchel himself. 'And so, what does that tell you about the Palace of Esterházy? This was nothing but a toy palace, populated by clever mechanical toys, automata that were so life-like they made the humans seem rudely mechanical. And for them, Haydn wrote another symphony, his Clock Symphony.'

'Cool,' said Hamish.

'The palace ran on clockwork. Clockwork was state-of-the-art technology in those days. It became an obsession for Louis XV of France, who, by constant tinkering, kept all the clocks of Versailles going. When urged to attend to business he would answer "Bah! The crazy old machine will last my time, and my successors must look after themselves." In his Clock Symphony, Haydn satirised the ancien regime by depicting the crazy old machine running down, reminding them that precious time was slipping away.' Professor Kirchel's phrases always ended on a dying fall.

Edward wandered towards a cabinet inside which a mysterious boat-shape lurked. As soon as he got close, Kevin's *fiat lux* revealed a musical instrument of russet wood inlaid with decorative purfling and topped with an oversized scroll studded with numerous black pegs. More numerous than were the visible strings, this plantation of ebony gave the thing the look of an aristocratic guitar that still had its curlers in.

'What's that?'

'No idea mate, it looks like some sort of violin or something,' replied Kevin without concern.

Professor Kirchel spoke up. 'I can tell you exactly what it is. This is the Penny-farthing of the Viol family.'

'What did you say it was?' asked Rosie Pratt.

'It is a baryton.'

'Never heard of it.'

'I'm not surprised – even when it first appeared it was a superfluous variant of an obsolete model. Whilst new musical species are constantly evolving, there are offshoots that get stranded up a musical creek. Starved of an audience or anyone to play them, such instruments fall silent and are ignored until eventually they turn up fossilised in a museum. This is a particularly sad example of the type.'

Those who stood at close quarters could see that the object was receiving glares of hatred from Professor Kirchel, not sympathetic looks.

'Only a sentimentalist would mourn the demise of such a thing. True musicians talk of the baryton's passing without regret; like the extinction of an ugly reptile. Look at this loveless thing! It had seven bowed strings and a second set strung behind them for the player to pluck with his thumb.'

'Can we get it out of its case and hear it played – bring it back to life – perhaps the Prince can oblige us.'

'Tomek? He wouldn't know which end to blow down,' said Kevin.

'That,' added Kirchel, 'is an undisguised blessing. It was said to be fiendishly difficult to play, but its true defect was that it was impossible to play well. The sound it made was like a patient with tuberculosis coughing out an aria.'

As the party drifted away from the shunned instrument, Edward, feeling perhaps a kinship with the friendless survivor, asked Kirchel why he was so reluctant to hear the baryton being played.

'Because it was responsible for wasting so much of Haydn's time. Prince Nikolaus fancied himself as a barytonist and demanded a hundred sonatas for it.' (Edward hmmned.) 'Imagine being the most innovative musician in the world.' (Edward nodded.) 'Every day you have to dress in a servant's uniform and create easy pieces for your employer to play on this unworkable contraption.'

Professor Kirchel made a dismissive gesture at the object with one hand, knocking the glass case with his knuckle.

'Watch it mate, the cases are alarmed. Touch them and all hell breaks loose.'

'I thought you had disabled the alarm,' observed Edward.

'The security is on a different circuit,' said Kevin, raising a suspicious eyebrow at the Englishman's interest in the alarm system. It wouldn't surprise him if this guy was casing the joint. Kevin wafted the Euphony tour group in the direction of the doors. 'There are dunnies over here, if anyone wants one,' Kevin added as an aside. 'Guys, Sheilas and Crips.'

Though politically incorrect, this was the most gratefully received piece of information that the travellers had been given for a long while. They formed an eager queue in an adjacent lobby of recent construction that terminated in three doors to the facilities. The facilities advertised their sanitary credentials by being as unsympathetic to the surrounding décor as possible.

Edward suggested to Hamish that he might like to take the opportunity to go, but apparently his urge to purge had passed.

Kevin nipped back into the Display Room and was about to reactivate the alarm system when he saw Dr Dietrich banging on the glass door to gain admittance.

'You were going to let me freeze to death?' she accused, once he had allowed her in. She had an almost supernatural imperviousness to cold, so she was only complaining to put Kevin in his place. 'Whilst I was out there Teresa Mertz rang and told me to send you back to the Sala Terrena at once.'

'For crying out loud, what for now?'

'I don't know, she just said it was urgent.'

Kevin began muttering formless expressions of discontent, and by the time he reached the Sala Terrena, having kept up his muttering all the way down the corridor, he had worked them up into the single interrogative 'yes?' that expressed his pent-up rage and frustration without violating what was left of their professional relationship.

'Nothing,' said Teresa. 'I just didn't want you saying anything stupid to the guests.'

Kevin did well not to explode. He would go back to his control room and explode there. As he went, his muttering gained an angrier tone, like a car being driven in the wrong gear.

With Kevin safely out of the way, it was left to Dr Dietrich to usher the guests through the sequence of rooms, accompanied as always by a torrent of facts and enthusiasm.

'Ladies and gentlemen, your feast awaits you at the end of this corridor.' This was repeated hurriedly in German to compensate for her recent neglect.

She opened her factual spray-gun, drenching them with information in two languages. 'This is the west corridor – the east wing matches it in length, but those rooms have not been renovated yet.'

The Duchess of Poundland interrupted her in mid-spurt. 'Tell me, Dr Whatever, is this a very long corridor?'

'Oh yes, it is the longest in this part of Europe, second only to the one at Versailles. Esterhaz was second only to Versailles for many things, not just the length of its corridors.'

'Do you intend talking to us all the way down it?'

'Well . . .' stuttered Dr Dietrich, 'there is no need . . .'

And she fell silent, cowed by an expansive gesture made by one of the Duchess's eyebrows.

The procession passed through a series of rooms that progressively swelled into ever-grander pomp, forcing them to cower beneath the ornamental mass until they grumbled like children who have been brought down from their nursery to be displayed in front of a formal dinner party. They were on best behaviour and yet seething in a cloud of disparate mutterings.

Back in the silent Display Room the automatic timer extinguished the lights, returning the baryton to its well-deserved obscurity. No one could spoil it now; it was preserved from being damaged, scratched or – worse – played. Haydn had been more generous to his patron than Kirchel; his baryton sonatas are very pretty pastoral sketches, they sound like the music of shepherds in Arcadia. Though forced to write these pieces by a humiliating obligation, he performed the tedious chore with good grace. Prince Nikolaus was very pleased with them, and never noticed their Parnassian mediocrity. They enabled him to prolong his delusion of being a musician, for even bad music is preferable to reality.

As the Euphony tourists were escorted past, their fractured and fractious voices disturbed the consciousness of that great actor and aesthete Bernhardt Croek. He was sitting up on the sofa where he had been laid in what had been a quiet room. Slowly, he was recovering from the blow. More accurately, he thought that it was time he recovered. Being an actor, he wanted to pace the scene. He was unaware that thanks to the frailty of the arteries in his brain, he would never recover from Tomek's punch: The blow had triggered an extra-dural haemorrhage. Bernhardt's life was a theatrical event that had over-extended its run; he had just over two hours to live.

His remote voice lugubriously intoned these words in English: '– all those fine musical evenings – which can only be remembered, not described.'

The memory of an actor is a wonderful instrument; in return for services rendered it demands control of the entire mind, which is why none of them is capable of uttering an original statement.

Any discontent within the cultural explorers was dispelled when they saw what was ahead of them as they reached the Sala Terrena. They were wide-eyed with ocular greed. At the back of the room were three trestle tables laid out with white linen, upon which splurged a buffet intended for the interval, but now moved forward to cover the hiatus in Bernhardt's consciousness. To the side was a makeshift bar with a few non-alcoholic drinks as well as a wide selection of beers, wines, and a fruity punch of high alcohol by volume and more than usually revolting syrupiness. The audience were urged towards these temptations by Teresa Mertz, *wig on*, resuming her role as Princess Maria but still breathless from her exertions as event organiser. She had to strike a balance between largesse and her concerns that the pre-show buffet would last until their replica Haydn, whose continued obliviousness was beginning to become more than a little irritating, could somehow be restored to working order. Before she went to check on him she told Kirchel to get the party swinging.

'How am I to be expected to do that?'

'Mingle.'

'Mingle?'

'Use your charm. Get them in good spirits.'

'Have you actually had any experience of these people? They are terrifyingly ignorant, and some of them are very blunt.'

'I am sure they don't mean to be ignorant, Professor, they're not doing it on purpose.'

'I really have no idea why they are doing it.'

Professor Kirchel glowered at the ravenous mob – instinct was bound to conquer manners. After a collective hesitation, the group found their appetites arise rampant. Edward saw his children heading for the pyramid of profiteroles and implored them to try something savoury first. They were about to ignore him as usual when the Indian couple, Anjali and Satma, came to the rescue with apparently genuine enthusiasm for mini quiche, or dolly tarts as they called them. Satma and Anjali took both Hamish and Sally off to the food board in victorious spirits and loaded their plates with food.

'Ting!' chimed Sally when a small tartlet caught her censorious eye.

'What's wrong with it?'

'It's got mushrooms in it! Ting ting!'

'I'll have that one then,' said Satma, taking the pastry tart from her plate.

'Actually, I don't like mushrooms either,' Hamish informed Satma flatly.

Whilst Satma relieved Hamish of his tart, Anjali found a dish of flans uncontaminated by mushrooms for the picky English children.

Rosie Pratt appeared with an empty plate and declared cheerfully: 'Have you had one of these mushroom tarts, children? They're absolutely amazing; out of this world!' She was elated and her face for once matched her name. 'I hope they're not all gone,' she said, scanning the array on the serving table, with a sideways glance at Satma's plate, which was overly supplied with the articles in question.

'Here, you can have the last one,' said Anjali, serving Rosie from her plate.

'Oooh yummie!' sang Rosie, and skipped off.

'She's come out of herself,' commented Satma dryly.

The Germans were tucking in with equal gusto and filled the room with appreciative remarks, none uttered by vacant mouths.

With superfluous zeal, Teresa had also encouraged Dr Dietrich to unleash her charm. Consequently, the concise Viennese compendium approached Satma and Anjali and offered them some chewing gum, which Satma declined, having a plateful of food to get through first. 'Thank you, Dr Dietrich,' said Anjali sweetly, taking a stick of gum and slipping it into a hidden pocket. She went on to extract the first name of the tour guide, something which no one had ever managed to do before, and went on to tell her that according to her friend, who was never wrong about these things, the palace was drenched with the presence of death.

'Really?' said Dr Dietrich, turning to Satma with interest.

'Don't tell me you haven't sensed the deathly aura in here,' asserted Satma, her mouth full of flan. 'It's literally choking my heart.'

Dr Dietrich (her first name was an intimacy that she would not want to have more widely shared) seemed to welcome this insight and empathised with her new friends. 'Yes, unfortunately even princes and princesses cannot live happily ever after. The royal fairytale ended with the death of the Princess Maria in 1790. The Prince was devastated, and he died later that same year of a broken heart.'

'I knew that,' confirmed Satma.

'Ahh!' sighed Anjali. 'Perhaps that is what you have been picking up, Satma.'

'Of course it is,' Satma assured them.

'Ah, here is the professor; he will be able to settle the matter . . .'

On hearing his name, the professor's long face, on which the furrows tended to a downward inclination, appeared to experience negative gravity. This rare and exotic phenomenon was a Kirchelian smile.

'Professor, we have been discussing the tragic mood of death that seems to pervade the palace.'

'Does it? I hadn't noticed.'

'This lady says she can certainly feel it.'

'Bloodstains on the fabric of reality,' said Satma impressively.

'She is very sensitive,' said Dr Dietrich, invoking the proverbial righteousness of customers.

'Dr Dietrich was telling us that the Prince died of a broken heart after the death of his beloved wife, the Princes Maria,' said Anjali.

'The Prince's broken heart, as you call it, was mended in less than a week.'

'You don't know that; you can't see into someone's heart.'

'No one who had Haydn's music played for him every day could possibly die from a broken heart,' the professor asserted.

'But he did die, in the same year as his wife,' Dr Dietrich reminded them. 'Perhaps that is the fatal blow that gives the palace its overwhelming air of doom.'

'The Prince's death was, I imagine, an inconvenience for him, but for the world of music it was a great blessing, since it marked the end of Haydn's incarceration in this out-of-the-way place. It enabled him to compose his last and boldest works, orchestrated with vivid colours unimaginable in Esterhazy with a sixteen-piece ensemble. I can't see why it could possibly leave any psychic residue in your 'fabric of reality', other than relief.'

Satma, having an empty plate, excused herself and headed for the buffet table, followed by Anjali. Dr Dietrich had no intention of trading strained bonhomie with Professor Kirchel and claimed to see his wife coming towards them with an extra glass of punch in her hand.

'Oh goodness me,' said the hunted professor, 'I had better check up on how the musicians are getting on,' and the sprightly septuagenarian was gone. Dr Dietrich chuckled with satisfaction, which might lead you to suppose she was well aware that Frau Kirchel was not nearby, since she had seen her drive away in the coach with Carl.

Meanwhile, Edward found himself gravitating towards the physicist, who was standing somewhat apart from the others. After opening remarks about the food, Edward asked him why he had come to Esterházy. 'What brings you here?' was his actual question, so the answer could have been 'the same as you, I came on the coach', or 'millions of years of evolution'. Realising the question was too vague, Edward waved his glass around to indicate the immediate surroundings as the 'here' to which he referred.

'I am interested in Universal Intelligence. Perhaps you have heard of it.'

'No, but it sounds like something one ought to be in favour of.'

'It's the subject of a paper I'm giving at a conference in Vienna,' said Lakshman, straightening his spine. 'It's about how intelligence shapes the universe, and vice versa.'

'Really? And tonight is your night off, then . . .'

'Oh no, I'm researching. It is very rare to be able to recreate a distant moment in time, for example when a room full of people first heard the Farewell Symphony. I want to know if that moment has really passed.'

'Surely it has.'

Lakshman raised a crooked finger. 'Maybe not! Music is one of the only ways of expressing thought without using words. The other is mathematics.'

'But surely when something's gone, then it's gone,' said Edward.

'You wouldn't say that of an idea, though, would you? You see, if my theory is correct and there *are* countless parallel universes, then the ones that contain a Haydn are exceptional. They will stand out against the run-of-the-mill universes. If you were able to sweep through all the possible universes looking for intelligence you would inevitably find Haydn. Why? Because intelligence organises stuff better than stupidity does. To be honest, stupidity leaves it in a mess. And the more intelligence in any given universe the better its chances of survival.'

'Have you told the orchestra that the fate of the universe depends on their performance? It might give them stage-fright.'

Lakshman sniggered and took another bite of food. After nibbling rapidly he went on: 'I flew here from Kuala Lumpa; where did you travel from, Edward?'

'Putney.'

'Oh, very nice.'

'Do you know it?' asked Edward eagerly.

'No. I just wanted to be polite. But you seem to think this 45th symphony of Haydn's is worth coming all the way from Putney to hear, and I travelled further still to hear it. Would you say it was worth crossing the galaxy to hear?'

'Well, I don't really know.'

'When you consider how great the distances, perhaps not – particularly if they were to be disappointed, as we have been by unintended delays. But just as you could have stayed at home and listened to a CD or the radio, other intelligences in alternate worlds don't need to come all this way. They could be listening in on us from far away, if my theory is correct. They can do it by quantum entanglement. . . . Excuse me, I shall go and get another chicken leg.'

Entanglement – that's a good word for you, isn't it, old chum? Of course you have absolutely no idea what it means. To think that you arrogantly rejected reincarnation earlier because it was too crazy and now you're sucking up to a scientist with theories that take the biscuit and wipe the bloody floor with it.

The voice in his head was getting more truculent. Edward blamed the punch.

Also growing beerily truculent was Kevin. Teresa Mertz was shocked to find him sitting at the back of the hall, drinking from the neck of a bottle with his feet up on an empty chair. 'What are you doing?'

'I'm just having a pilsner, Tess.'

'But they will see you – it's not very authentic is it?'

'They've already seen me, Tess,' said Kevin, and he loped off into his control room to get away from her, muttering 'my authentic arse' as he went.

When he was satisfied that his sarcastic spouse was physically remote, Professor Kirchel came out of hiding and selected Edward as the next individual to benefit from his charm. The renowned musicologist was showing a tendency to gravitate towards the English speakers. Although they were far more ignorant and blunt than the Germans, conversing in English was preferable to being understood and mocked by his wife, whom he assumed was somewhere in a knot of German speakers. He had been avoiding her so assiduously he had not noticed her absence. In fact, she was enjoying a pleasant but inexpensive meal with Carl in a small restaurant in the town.

Edward could not avert the slow, dreadful approach of the learned professor, whose face showed the strain of maintaining an uplifted expression.

'We are certainly getting a first-hand experience of *Sturm und Drang* this evening, are we not?' said the professor.

'What? Yes. I mean, no, it's no use, I have absolutely no idea what *Sturm und Drang* is – you mentioned it earlier, I was going to ask.' Despite their numerous encounters, Edward still felt the uneasy queasiness of a schoolboy meeting a master in town.

'It means storm and stress. It was a mini Romantic movement that broke out in the midst of the eighteenth century, largely inspired by *The Sorrow of Young Werther*.'

'I haven't read it.'

'There's not the least need to. It was a book that young men carried about with them to indicate to young women that they were intelligent and sensitive.'

'Oh yes, I know the sort of thing – in my student days it was *The Unbearable Lightness of Being*.'

'Yes, I think that would do it. But this one is a more chaste story about a young man who can't have the woman he loves.'

'Oh?' said Edward, more interested than he expected to be. 'What does he do?'

'He kills himself.'

Edward was so shocked by this comment that before he could stop himself he had popped a prawn canapé into his gaping mouth.

'I see you have a liking for the vol au vents!' said the professor, nodding at the little plate in Edward's hand, where three more pastries sat, rejected by his children owing to the presence in them of prawns.

'Not really, they're disgusting.'

'What do you call them in English?'

'Vol au vents,' confirmed Edward. 'Would you like one?'

Picking one up from Edward's plate and waving it about, the professor mused: Yes, but what is the English word you use for them?'

'We don't have one, we just call them vol au vents.'

'That is a pity, I was hoping to extend my vocabulary. Do you know what it means, however?'

Edward shook his head, not sure what meaning was being conjured here.

'In French. I speak French as well, you know.'

Edward hummed and nodded.

'It means thrown on the wind, it's the pastry – and do you know maybe what we call it in German? No? We say blatterteig!' said Kirchel with triumph.

At these percussive consonants, a fleck of blatterteig flew out of Kirchel's mouth and landed on Edward's lapel where it clung wetly to the corduroy. Edward could not prevent a reflex glance at it, but quickly forced himself to look straight at Kirchel, whose face expressed agony at the embarrassing situation. What should the professor do? He was supposed to be spreading good cheer not spraying pellets of food. In Prince Esterházy's day he would have flourished a white handkerchief, or else left the court in shame, never to return. Now he was paralysed, unable to avoid staring at the tiny beige fragment of ballistic pastry.

Edward was, if anything, more mortified than the Viennese academic.

'Now I must circulate,' said Kirchel. 'I have been instructed to mingle, whatever that means. I only hope I don't bump into my wife. Edward, you are wise to come on vacation without your spouse. Unfortunately mine follows me everywhere.'

Edward's children returned with empty plates. They had clearly revised their opinion of the local cuisine. Hamish now wore an agonised expression that betrayed recent overindulgence. 'Dad, I need the lavatory,' he advised. 'Now.' Adding for further emphasis: 'It can't wait.'

Overhearing this, Professor Kirchel overcame his fear of Frau Kirchel and sauntered off.

'What did *he* want?' asked Hamish.

'Nothing – he just came over to spit at me,' said Edward, wiping his flecked jacket with a napkin. He put his plate down with a sigh. 'Why didn't you go earlier, when everyone else did?'

'I didn't want to.'

'Okay, but must we go all the way up that corridor again? Let's look for a lavatory closer-by. Dr Dietrich will know where to go.'

They found Dr Dietrich waving her arms in the air evidently explaining the iconography of the fresco on the ceiling. She was speaking to three people who were holding plates under their upturned chins. 'These angels are carrying the letter E for Esterházy, so Prince Nikolaus could be assured that he would be recognised when he got to paradise. His idea of heaven was quite exclusive, and like your luggage, it was monogrammed.'

Edward pulled Hamish over to the guide and said: 'Can you help us, please?'

Dr Dietrich came down off the ceiling with its personalised angels. 'Of course,' she said, changing into English effortlessly.

'Toilets,' said Hamish.

Dr Dietrich, remembering her instructions to turn on the charm, squeezed out a smile. 'Certainly, you young people are so fascinated with this subject. The necessity of always being within calling range of the Prince meant that courtiers preferred to urinate down the back staircases than risk offending their Prince with their absence. This was the practice at Versailles and here too. All palaces are designed for the convenience of one person, no matter how inconvenient that makes them for everyone else. They must have reasoned that their liquid waste would find its own way out of the palace on its own, though it can't have been pleasant for those unfortunate enough to be coming up the stairs, and may have given rise to the phrase *après moi le deluge.*'

Hamish appeared to be splitting his sides, but not with mirth. He pulled his father's hand so forcefully that Edward realised that they didn't have time for a digression on light sewage in eighteenth-century palaces. He allowed Hamish to tug him away from Dr Dietrich.

'Where are you dragging me to, Hamish?'

'The toilets next to that room with the exhibition.'

'What? All the way back up that corridor?'

'I don't want to go back there,' said Sally, pulling in the other direction on his other arm. 'By the time we get back, all the strawberries will be gone.' She seemed ready to wrench off an opposite finger in her stubbornness, so Edward, knowing that Hamish had issued his third and final warning, told Sally to go and find Anjali to look after her.

'Are you really going to kill her, Daddy?'

'No, sweetie, you can tell her she's quite safe.'

'You do like her really, don't you Daddy?'

'Yes, she's lovely.'

Having carelessly scattered these seeds of gossip to any eavesdropper within range, Edward and Hamish set off manfully, hand in hand, down the second longest corridor in Europe (according to Dr Dietrich) in search of plumbing. Hamish strode with the determination of a pocket chancellor until he attained the lobby, welcomingly bathed in orange light, with its three doors labelled with hieroglyphs depicting archetypes of a man, a woman and small chariot.

Once Hamish was securely enthroned, Edward paced the empty room with its displays of costumes and artefacts that each required atmospherically controlled imprisonment to preserve them. He struggled to resist falling into that thoughtless state usually called pensive, but the soporific weight of his surroundings dragged him into their idle gravity and he lost track of how much time passed.

Satma, too, was becoming truculent, without the help of wine. She wanted to have the last word with the sceptical Professor Kirchel. She was confident that the evening, which had already been disastrous, had not exhausted its potential for further disasters.

'You don't get it, do you, Prof?'

'What do I not get?'

'The overpowering sense of death. You consider yourself too sophisticated, I suppose, too *rational*.'

This was a slander; sophisticated he may be, but the professor was not a rationalist. 'I certainly hope not,' he said. 'There are more things in Heaven and Earth than ever dreamed of in philosophy.'

'That's so true. You are quite insightful after all.'

'That was Shakespeare.'

'Yes, well I knew it couldn't be you because it was so short and to the point.'

Kirchel made a weighty suggestion: 'Perhaps the death that you have foretold is your own.' He said this without apparent malice, but it was nonetheless a powerful statement. It sounded almost like an omen, and had the effect of silencing Satma.

'I was speaking about the premonition of your death when you were incarnated as Mozart,' Kirchel hurriedly explained. 'You believe that you were once Mozart, do you not?'

'Without question,' asserted Satma.

'Perhaps you would like to hear how the news of your death was received by your mentor? Don't worry, it is very flattering to yourself – and it may be the source of your morbid anxiety.'

In what was, for her, an unusual state of earnest humility, Satma bade him speak.

'Haydn last saw his beloved Mozart in the days before he departed for London in December 1790. All of Haydn's friends were concerned at his bold expedition; they reminded him of his age, of the discomforts of a long journey, and of many other things to shake his resolve, but in vain. Mozart especially took pains to say, *"Papa!"* as he usually called him, *"you have had no training for the great world, and you speak too few languages"*. *"Oh,"* replied Haydn, *"my language is understood all over the world!"* Kirchel said these worlds in a heartfelt tone and his eyes moistened.

'As soon as Haydn had settled his household affairs, he fixed the day of his departure. On this day Mozart never left his friend's side. He dined with him, accompanied him everywhere, and said at the moment of parting, *"We are probably saying our last farewell in this life"*.

'Tears welled from the eyes of both of the friends. Haydn was deeply moved, for he applied Mozart's words to himself, since he was the older by some twenty-three years. The possibility never occurred to him that Mozart's life would be ended within the following year.

'That is a death that might have sufficient significance to cause ripples – or vibrations – or whatever you call them, through history. Whilst he was in London, Haydn heard news of the death of his great friend Mozart. *"The world will not have such a talent again in a hundred years"*, he said. We have waited more than two hundred years for your return, Madam.'

By now, Satma was pitching like a rowboat in choppy seas. Kirchel helped her to steady herself, wondering how she had managed to get drunk so quickly. But Satma wasn't drunk. The Sala Terrena was *not* rocking about either, though this is perfectly feasible with pneumatic pistons and a convincing interior, the sort of thing you might find in a haunted house. Ask Kevin, he had operated one such attraction in a theme park outside Krakov. The rocking sensation Satma was experiencing was caused by lysergic chemicals found in certain funghi, some of which had found their way into the mushroom flans, and these complex acids were now busily turning her brain into purple sprouting broccoli.

'I think I'm going to be very, very . . .'

Before she could either say the word or suit action to it, she sprinted out of the side door, throwing her paper plate aside, and Professor Kirchel was once more left in that solitude that one can sometimes experience even at a cocktail party.

Anjali had not seen her friend's sudden departure, being occupied with helping Sally reach some of the more distant delicacies on the Tapeziertische using the plastic tongs provided. Sally had latched onto Anjali, and from the first encouragement had tirelessly poured out a stream of inanities whilst eating iced fancies. As a rule, Anjali encouraged the child with a sustained smile, but now, noticing Satma's absence, she frowned, a sudden look that gave Sally a fright.

'Are you getting over-tired? You look grouchy.'

'No, darling, just run along and find your Daddy.'

This was brusque, but Anjali didn't see why she should baby-sit for someone who wanted to murder her anyway.

'Daddy has gone to the lavatory,' said Sally.

'Oh, well then run along and find Dr Dietrich, she has lots of good stories about ghosts.'

Sally tottered away, stabilising her plate of iced fancies against her chest. Anjali was unable to prevent the approach of Professor Kirchel, who, seeing her unprotected, determinedly advanced like a club-footed dancing partner who sees his chance with the young heiress.

'Miss Anjali, are you enjoying your visit to Esterházy?'

'Most of it, yes,' she replied enigmatically.

'But this part is not so good. I know. It reminds me of the minuet and trio, which is a rather leaden-footed convention that always leaves the listener with a sense of incompleteness. Would you like some punch? It's a local speciality.'

'I'll stick to the wine.'

But the wine had all gone. The last six bottles could now be located in the back of a certain cave, nestled among the skirts of a cast of puppets. Anjali sighed, her eyes searching for Satma.

'Are you looking for your friend?' asked Kirchel, without pause.

'Good manners require a quality of patience. Your friend has not this quality, I find. She suddenly ran out of the room whilst we were speaking.'

Anjali handed him her empty glass. 'Excuse me, I have to go and find her.' And she too fled, but out of a different door.

'Hamish – has the nose-cone descended from the clouds?'

From beyond the locked door of the lavatory came a weak voice. 'Not yet, do we have to talk about this, Dad?'

Edward paused and then carried on with this apparent non sequitur: 'Have you been given permission to land?' This evasive style of language was the by-product of a chronically constipated child who didn't want his condition referred to in plain terms.

There was no reply.

'Hurry up Hamish, lets finish off the paperwork and go through to departures.'

'Go away!'

'I'll wait out here.'

He wandered into the Display Room, which was lit only by the orange light from the lobby, and made his way past the glass display cabinets that resembled cuboid ghosts, one containing the dark human shape of a headless mannequin. One, he knew, held in its humidity-controlled interior the mechanical heart of a baryton.

There was nowhere to sit and he was feeling tired and depressed. He didn't have time to feel the loss of his wife; he was too busy losing his children. Sally to the fairies and Hamish to intestinal introversion. He doubted whether Hamish had made the connection that his bowels were blocked with the emotions that resulted from losing his mother, but that was how Edward saw it. You have to do your grieving somewhere, he supposed. All the pain Hamish felt came out – or rather didn't come out – behind the locked door of a cubicle. While Sally, who had constructed dreams of a reunion with her dead mummy, was at this moment probably preparing for the reunion in her dreaming mind. Powerless to comfort either of his children, Edward felt helpless with love for them.

Carefully avoiding the obscure obstacles, he turned back towards the orange light of the lobby, with its three mysterious doors, and cleared his throat. He knew how sensitive Hamish was, and the slightest impatience in his tone could be disastrous. He had to tell Hamish that he loved him, so he practically sang his son's name to eradicate any harshness of his tone: 'Hamie? Are you going to be much longer?'

Hamish's reply was strained and entirely lacked the quality of mercy.

'Dad, I'm twelve, I'm old enough to go to the lavatory by myself. Leave me alone!'

Edward sank to his knees and began to beg in the fervent whisper, almost like a prayer: 'Please shit! I'm begging you, just shit for mummy's sake.'

From his control suite, formerly a valet's tiny bedroom, Kevin was engrossed in some patterns of light flickering on his screen. It was the latest equipment; the closed-circuitry picked up the sharp images from the ballroom and displayed them in high definition on a flat monitor. Here, as in the cave, there were drip sheets spread over the floor and decorators' ladders left in various parts of the room.

Kevin watched the monitor with rising interest. Lead violinist Tomasino's outer clothing was being draped over a chaise whose embroidery and gilt were protected by white dustclothes. A splendid female creature was stepping out of the masculine attire. Dressed now in white trainer socks, some plain but very satisfactory white knickers, and something that wasn't a bra but was something like a curtailed vest (Kevin had no idea what this garment was but he heartily approved of its semi-transparency and tight fit), the feminine violinist picked up her instrument and strummed the open strings with the fingertips of her left hand to check it was still in tune.

The female that was observed emerging from the male cocoon was Sophie. Being in her final year at the Conservatoire, she intended to take this delay in the show as an opportunity to prepare for her finals recital. Unable to play properly in the restrictive and ill-fitting costume of Tomasino, it made perfect sense to do it in her vest and knickers, since no one was watching. Except for Kevin, who was savouring the transformation from eighteenth-century male to a present-day woman – Jeeez there were compensations for being stuck in a valet's cubby-hole.

Then she started to play, and it just got better. Kevin hadn't been aware of this particular work before, but he was a big fan now, and growing bigger. The girl was struggling to control the violin like someone flying a kite on a blustery day, on tiptoe, arching her back, her abdominals at full stretch.

Another gust of music tore across the instrument, and her bowing arm was pulling it back. Kevin's bowing arm was too. Still, he was probably only using this valet's cubby-hole for the same thing the valet had used it for.

Teresa was content with the way things were progressing except for the absence of His Rustic Majesty. She was going to tell Kevin to go and fetch him, and strode over to the door concealed in the panelling when something made her hesitate. Kevin was growing more irritable as the evening went on, so, rather than risk annoying him further, she opened the door a crack and peered in, and then decided, on second thoughts to give up on Kevin and get the prince for herself.

Tomek was backstage at the Platonic cave, seated amidst his cast, enjoying a post-performance glug from a stolen bottle of wine.

'Tomek? You're supposed to be a prince.'

'Ah, won't you join me, Madama?'

'Very kind of you, but the Prince is needed in the palace. You have to come back with me.'

Tomek grunted. 'The whole thing makes me sick – why should I prance about with those revolting snobs in honour of a tyrant? I am a peasant. I hate snobs and I hate princes.'

'Tomek, you are mistaken. The reason we are all dressed up like this is to honour Haydn, not the Prince. And Haydn was a peasant like you.'

'He was born a peasant but he became a flunky – we would call them running dogs, in the old days.'

'And you, Tomek, you were a good communist – didn't that entail some flunkeyism at times?'

'There is a difference, Teresa. Sit with me.'

Teresa thought the difference was that Haydn had been refined and polished by aristocratic patronage whereas years of obedience to the Hungarian Communist Party had entirely failed to buff Tomek up to a shine.

'The difference was I never meant a word of it. And by the way, Teresa, I was never a communist.'

'Fine, apart from your membership of the Party and the fact that you were a border-guard . . .'

She knew this from Tomek's work record, and was sure this would be a decisive blow. Tomek's bellyful of alcohol was shaken with laughter as his memory was stirred. 'Twenty years ago! And do you remember what we did in the terrible communist border police? We had a picnic.'

For a moment Teresa couldn't think what he was talking about.

'1989!'

'What about it?'

'The pan-European Picnic! But you were probably still at school.'

Indeed, Teresa had been a student then, and now he mentioned the date she understood what he was referring to.

'That was when the fortified border between our countries came down, don't you remember? Thousands of people left – East Europeans fleeing West. Do you know why it came down? I took it down with my own hands. So don't call me a communist,' he roared, thrusting out his chest, 'I am the destroyer of communism!'

Tomek took a huge swig of wine and sighed. 'Do you know what is the funny part? We began cutting down the wire in April, in strictest secrecy. By the time the announcement came in May that the border was to be opened, we had already dismantled most of it. By the time the politicians were finally ready to announce the end of the iron curtain, in June, there was nothing left of it.'

'But I remember it on the news.'

'Okay, well what you saw on TV was fake, little girl. They arrived in their city suits and ties, so clumsy with the wire cutters, with no strength in their puny arms, and they tried desperately not to get too muddy, because they were all wearing the wrong sort of shoes. What did they expect in a field full of shit?

'So they tip-toed up to the fence and somehow managed to mangle their way through the little wires and the news cameras took their shots of these pinstriped clowns smashing down the iron curtain like big heroes.

'We were laughing because we had put that fence up ourselves a week before. You call that history? It was a farce.'

He placed a big iron-curtain-destroying hand on her leg. Teresa was the first Austrian Tomek had liked, and he liked her a lot. Yes, she was here to boss him around, just like all the other Austrians he had ever met, but at least she did it with some gypsy swagger.

They drank to Revolution, then to Hungary, then to Women, and with each toast, Tomek got closer to Teresa, until at the end he was on top of her.

'I can't do it here – not with them all watching.'

'Yes you can – it makes it much better.'

They debauched with vigour in front of an audience of marionettes, whose lopsided heads and slack jaws maintained the blasé indifference of true courtiers. Tomek overcame Teresa's objections by persistence, and at the end of it they fell as limp as their audience – except that unlike their strung-up fellows they were gently giving off steam.

'I can't believe I let you do that to me, you're a dirty old man,' said Teresa with no regret in her tone. 'Do you rape all the women who come backstage?'

'The ladies tell me I can still look quite handsome on occasion.'

'Oh yes, Tomek, when might that occasion be?'

'After about a bottle and a half of this fine wine,' said her squat lover, pulling another bottle out from Columbina's motley skirt.

'Tomek, that was for the guests; they'll be running short.'

'Ha! Let them drink punch!'

Teresa laughed and then swigged from the bottle to enhance her lover's appearance.

In his continued search for someone who might serve as a recipient of his charms, whilst carefully avoiding his wife, whose malign presence he wrongly felt was always at hand, Professor Kirchel now made an advance on the lone figure of Rosie Pratt, who had somehow eluded her clinging husband and was swaying about near the glass doors. Rosie greeted the professor with a shriek. 'Have you had a mushroom flan? They are wonderful.'

'No, there were none left,' said the professor.

'That Indian had two, the greedy bitch, no wonder she's so fat.'

Leaving Kirchel absolutely stunned, Rosie performed a pirouette out of the open doors onto the terrace.

Trio

For those who are afraid of attending a concert for fear they will clap at the wrong moment (the same people who would be sure to scratch their nose in an auction-house just as the Renoir reaches its selling price), the third movement is a minefield. It starts, stops, starts again with a different tune, then stops and (after a pause to catch unwary clappers) restarts at the beginning.

Having offered that explanation, if it was one, we may now proceed.

I wanted to say that mushrooms were tiny protrusions into our world of an alien species that mostly occupies another dimension entirely, but I never got a chance to put that phrase in the first section, so I have saved it, along with other material, for this one. Neither plant nor animal, mushrooms are related to those other intimate friends and foes the gut-borne pathogens and parasites with which we interact unconsciously, with whom we share our inner space.

Consider the piles of warmed-up objects that we inconsiderately throw into ourselves: it is amazing that we don't end every day either vomiting or dead. Once in a while the stuff being eaten bites back, as was currently happening to Satma whose accidental ingestion of magic mushrooms was cause for alarm.

Satma was, a few minutes ago, in a state of emergency as she felt a need to rid herself of the alien insurgents in her gut. Not content with storming that stronghold, they seemed set on staging a coup de tête and taking over the government of her brain. Soon they would be organising reality along completely different lines.

She crashed into a sequence of rooms, all magnificently proportioned, parts of which were cordoned off with red velvet rope, leaving her a straight run from one pair of double doors to the next. The rooms flashed past – she was barely conscious of their décor, except that they were all extraordinarily ornate and beautiful and all of them were quite unsuitable places to be sick in. She was looking for a bucket, but you are as likely to find a bucket in the staterooms of Esterházy Palace as to find a Ming vase in a potting shed. As she went on, the realisation grew that she would be forced to vomit into a Ming vase.

In desperation, she looked about her and leapt towards a black box that was on a console table beneath a painting of a classical hunting scene. It was made from ebony, and the lid had a bronze lyre on the top – rather like the flames of enlightenment depicted on the top of the Buddha's head. The sides of the box had bevelled glass panels set into them, which was how she knew that it was empty even before she pulled off the lid. It was not empty for long.

Leaving Satma hunched over the malodorous box, we must trail Anjali's pursuit. Noticing the absence of her friend, she had torn herself from the adoring and jammy fingers of little Sally and the gimlet eye and clinging bones of Professor Kirchel, and was now stepping hesitantly into an endless series of rooms. Unfortunately, this set of rooms led off in the opposite direction to that taken by Satma. The palace was curved, the east and west wings bent round until both women were heading north, although the two wings were not sufficiently folded to allow them to actually meet. Anjali and Satma were now travelling along parallel suites separated by the wide court. After calling out Satma's name, Anjali began to wander through the answering silence whilst Satma (much less cautiously) travelled along her plane.

As Satma closed the lid, now almost sure her final paroxysms were over, Anjali was opening the doors into a large white chamber that was decorated with gold piping – a process of decoration that had apparently been resumed, since the restorers had left their ladders and dustsheets and, ironically, buckets. Had Satma selected this wing to vomit in, she would have had an embarrassment of receptacles. The ballroom was probably in the proportion of a double cube, but there were no straight lines, as if the whole thing was padded. Anjali was reminded of expensive pillowcases embroidered with gold piping. But what struck her most was that this room was filled with the sound of a violin being played with astonishing virtuosity somewhere beyond. Sonic arabesques blew around the ballroom out-swirling the rococo decor. Drawn towards it, Anjali opened a door into a further apartment and saw a young violinist, her straw hair shaking as she played from memory with her eyes closed. It was Sophie, still in her pants and vest and still practising for her concerto performance – and still being monitored remotely by Kevin.

The solo, or cadenza, Anjali was not sure which, was surely not the work of Haydn. It had notes in it that Haydn wouldn't have dared to write. His music only ever toyed with the irrational without ever breaking the form to let it free, whilst this woman was dragging irrationality out of her self and throwing it around the room. Sophie's violin was unhitched, tossing in a storm of accidentals. To Anjali, she appeared to be a lunatic, standing there in her underclothes and in her bare feet, which were planted wide apart, her knees bent to give her the stability she needed to sway about so expressively.

Anjali particularly admired how her thighs tensed like a bareback horse rider. As though her violin was a wild pony and she was breaking it in. But why was she playing this terrifying whirlwind of music alone, and why do it in her vest and pants? Anjali could only stare from the doorway, as her body vibrated to the sound like the sympathetic strings of a baryton. She didn't dare interrupt.

Movements on another screen, showing views from another part of the palace, disturbed Kevin's furtive enjoyment of Sophie's performance by coming into his peripheral view. Lights were coming on in the Display Room. Regretfully he switched his attention to the monitor and saw that Pom, the one in the brown jacket with an unhealthy interest in burglar alarms. He couldn't think of a good reason why the Pom should be there, so presumably he was there for a bad one.

He was talking to the barrytron (or whatever it was called). Kevin surmised that if he didn't have some criminal intent, it was just as likely that he was simply out of his wits, which, when he thought about it, only increased the likelihood that the Pom would try to release the flightless barrytron from its glass case and reintroduce it into the wild. He clearly thought it was trapped because was talking to it.

Checking he had zipped himself, Kevin sprinted up the west wing, past the room where Bernhardt was moaning and the room where Satma was moaning. When Kevin reached the Display Room and peeked round the door his suspicions were confirmed. The Englishman was alone and behaving very strangely. He was talking loudly so that Kevin could hear every word.

'How long are you going to spend stuck in there?'

There came no reply.

'You're missing the buffet, and you're making me miss it.'

This mad Pommy was really giving that musical contraption a tongue-lashing, observed Kevin.

'I mean you can't spend the rest of eternity locked up. Have you actually done anything since I last saw you?' Edward was looking into the glass case and speaking very clearly, so that his voice would carry through a solid barrier. 'Have you made any progress at all?' he demanded of the ancient instrument.

There was no sound for a long while. Edward wandered over to another case, which was instantly illuminated by Kevin's wizardry. The headless Sheila began to swivel, accepting an infinitely deferred invitation to the dance, and Edward briefly made an answering pose. This is the sort of thing you might do in such a room if you were bored shitless waiting for a kid that wouldn't shit. Unfortunately, Kevin didn't see it that way. As he peered around the door jamb, what Kevin saw was confirmation of his insanity theory: the bonkers Pom was talking to the woman in the glass case like she was real. What's more he was chatting her up with zero finesse.

'Come out, won't you?'

There was no response from Hamish, who was preoccupied, and even less surprisingly the lady mannequin gave no reply.

'Do you want me to come in a get you out?'

Kevin expected to hear the sound of breaking glass and then the deafening screech that alerted the local police that one of the cases had been tampered with.

'If you don't come with me I'm going back to the party without you.'

The angry and disturbed man began walking about in frustration and waving his arms emphatically. Still no alarm sounded. Instead, he triggered off the irritating Toy Symphony with its mocking birdcalls and gold-filigree treetops.

'I've had enough of waiting. You really are impossible. You say you want to be left alone, see how you like it,' said Edward, stumbling out of the room. He came through the doors and Kevin ducked out of the way so that he wouldn't be seen, which made him look foolish when Edward nearly fell over his crouching form.

'What are you doing down there? Are you desperate too?'

'No, I was just checking the wiring,' said Kevin, remaining asquat. 'Not that it's faulty.'

'Good. Shouldn't be too long now. Formalities . . . Customs . . . Nothing to Declare . . .'

Edward strode purposefully back to the buffet to check on Sally.

Bernhardt heard Edward's defiant footsteps outside the room where he lay and groaned out for help, in vain. A short while later some more footsteps shambled past and he called out once more, but Kevin did not stop either. He was beginning to despair of attracting the attention of a good Samaritan when he heard some different, slower steps approaching and hesitating outside the door. He summoned up enough energy to cry out and the door opened.

Someone in eighteenth-century garb tip-toed into the room carrying a box – perhaps it was a musical instrument, he supposed. Bernhardt tried to express some suitable greeting, or remember his next line. He wasn't sure which cast member this was and he was pressed to fall back on some emergency rhubarb: 'Now – here I sit in my wilderness – deserted – like a poor orphan – almost without human company – sad – full of the memory of precious days gone by.'

Satma listened to his mumblings with unusual interest, feeling sorrowful that her great friend Papa Haydn was so distressed. She allowed him to continue. 'And who knows when those pleasant days will return? That charming company? Wherein a whole circle shares One heart, One soul – where is all that enthusiasm? Gone – and gone for a long time.'

Satma knew these words were specifically directed at her, though as yet they didn't make much sense. Which precious days were these? And when he said 'gone for a long time' did he mean a long time since they left, or a long time to wait for their return? In either case it must mean that Haydn had been waiting for her to come back.

Dialogue between a man who has had a recent head injury and a woman who is woozy with food poisoning is never easy to follow. Add to this the further confusion occasioned by the fact that the one had memorised the words of a composer long dead, and the other believed herself to be the living spirit of another long dead composer and it was impossible to disentangle who was speaking to whom. There was evidently still some entanglement of Bernhard and Haydn, of reality and fiction, of past and present. Satma's mind was further destabilised by the lysergic fungus. It was so difficult to keep track of what was happening on that night. They were, between them, proof of the non-existence of identity.

'Where have you come from, Wolfgang?' asked Bernhardt, beginning at a loose thread. 'Call Luigi – perhaps we can make up a quartet, if we can find that sentimental cellist. He'll be mooning about here somewhere. I am quite accustomed to taking the part of second fiddle, and someone will lend you a viola. You know that we understand one another best when we play music together, and I have something very interesting to play you . . .'

Fittingly, Satma responded as Mozart would have to the real Haydn. 'I have just come from your birthplace – you always wanted to show it to me. You are held in great honour there. Tonight I am returning to Vienna.'

Bernhardt groaned at that word, a groan that expressed all his squandered potential. He moaned and swayed, rocking his sore head.

'You seem to miss the city very much. Don't you like it here?'

'Here, I don't know whether I am Kapell-master or Kapell-slave,' he said with some of the emotive power that he had displayed in leading roles in the city theatres in precious days gone by. 'It is melancholy to be always a slave, but Providence wills it so.'

Satma had no idea what Providence was supposed to be; she would have to discover more about this occult power and start believing in it.

'I am an unfortunate creature!' Haydn went on. 'Always plagued with much work, very few hours of repose . . .'

He ran dry once more, but was prompted when he saw the box she was carrying. It was *his* box – an important prop that he recognised instantly by the lyre on its lid. 'I see you have decided to return my old skull to me – about time too, this new one is hurting me dreadfully.' He held his head and groaned loudly to make the confusion stop. Satma was delighted to have found at last the purpose of her visit.

'The box was just a way of bringing me to you,' she explained.

'What's in it?'

'That is not important.' She put the box under the seat and sat herself down beside Bernhardt. I don't know if part of Bernhardt's wobbly mind thought it was engaging with his absent friend Herman Fraenkl, or if he was so deeply in character he truly believed he was Haydn speaking with Mozart, but it doesn't matter; a plant growing on different soil is the same plant. An unforced tear filled Bernhardt's eye, and Satma gently wiped it with a white handkerchief produced from her sleeve with a very eighteenth-century flourish. Soon they were holding hands like long-parted friends, which is precisely what they each believed they were.

'I thought that Providence had taken you away forever . . .' muttered Haydn.

'I'm back now,' soothed Wolfgang, 'I have come to pay a visit.'

'That is so kind. You don't know how much I have missed having you; a soul to be fellow to my soul.'

'Come back with me and join the others,' said Satma, taking his hand. 'There are strawberries.'

'You must not leave me again, I couldn't bear it,' groaned Bernhardt as though in sleep. His arms moved as a sleeping person's arms move, groping blindly, softly.

The large heavy tears returned. When Satma had finished dabbing, the patient insisted he was not well enough to join the party, even for strawberries.

'You are not well?'

'No. I think I may be dying.'

Satma promised she would get help *and* a plate of strawberries.

The Sala Terrena was already notable for its absences when Rosie was declared a missing person by her keeper/husband James.

'It's nothing to worry about,' he said needlessly, 'but have you seen my wife anywhere?'

The Duchess of Poundland was filling her plastic bag with whatever edible goods seemed capable of surviving a journey back to Vienna. 'So far from being worried, I hadn't even *faintly* noticed.'

'I have to take great care of her because, you see, we are trying for a baby.'

'Yes, I believe we are all aware of that fact. Tell me, is your wife barren or are you firing off blanks?'

'It's really a mystery – there's nothing medically the matter with either of us.'

'Well, I have no medical qualifications but might I suggest you try having a good old-fashioned fuck? I'm told it can be tremendously effective.'

James looked shocked. The Duchess went on with frowning pugnacity. 'Still, I expect you are not in the mood to hear my advice since you have so recently lost your wife. But you mustn't worry for her sake. She must be quite euphoric without you hanging around her depressing her spirits – that is when you are not disappointing her uterus.'

Admonished by these reassurances, James set off in quest of his wife. The Duchess went back to grazing at the tables. Meanwhile, Edward returned to the Sala Terrena and found his daughter sitting alone on a chair with only Jemima for company.

'Sally! I thought you were with Anjali.'

'She went,' said the little girl gloomily. 'Then the Lady Doctor had to go outside, but you can wait with me if you like. She will be coming back, won't she, Daddy?'

'Anjali? – I have no idea.'

'Not Anjali.'

Before Edward could ask why they should be waiting for Dr Dietrich, Professor Kirchel limped over and made a joke of how unpopular he must be because everyone kept running away. It wasn't a very humorous observation, but it was at least true. Edward sympathised and told him that he had not been a popular boy at school, he had no real friends at work, and here on this trip he was actively shunned. He meant all this to be a comfort and consolation to Kirchel.

'I can see why,' said Kirchel.

'What?'

'I see you as an artist who has lost his muse,' Kirchel sang.

'Right. Except I never wanted to be an artist.'

'Popularity is just another art, Edward.'

'I'm tired, Daddy,' whined Sally, pulling a parental finger. 'I wish Mummy would come soon.'

In order to explain why a man who lacked the gift of popularity could be the hero of this day's events, it would be necessary to infill with back-story, which I have resisted up to now, though there is much to tell. Edward's winning of Pamela is a story that would require a further regression to their teens, when Edward, a mediocre viola player, was in a string quartet with the brilliant fourteen-year-old violinist. Non-musicians can only imagine the gulf between a brilliant violinist and an adequate viola player. However, Pamela was such a high-spirited girl she bounced across any social gap and continued bouncing until Edward forgot his shyness and became an energetic and instinctively happy boy.

So, when they chanced to meet again in their twenties, in the interval of a concert at the Royal Festival Hall, their shared experiences as teenage musicians bridged the gap between their adult worlds. She was through music college and he was starting work at a banking firm in the city. Although he hadn't seen her for seven or eight years, Edward was very disturbed by her unaffected friendliness. He would have expected a friendship restarted after a long gap to be awkward, but Pamela was so natural it terrified him. By now, he had got used to his inability to make friends and bore it like a birthmark. He wasn't bad looking, he hadn't filled out so much then, but he attracted no one. Quite casually, in the midst of catching up on their shared youth, Pamela had said that she had liked seeing him again and he was about to say that seeing her again was the best thing that had ever happened to him, when the interval buzzer rang.

Once out of her magical orbit he reverted to his usual lethargy and went back to socialising with bankers. One night he was wandering past the South Bank and ran into another musician friend from the past, and among the usual whelps of reunion, Pamela's name came up.

'You should ring her up, I'll give you her number,' urged the friend.

'But I'm not her type – she's so glamorous.'

'What?' shrieked the mutual friend, 'You haven't seen her on tour! She's a pig!'

If she was a pig, she was also a pig in a relationship. The story of how Edward won her from a better looking rival would fill a book, but cannot be allowed to clog up this one. Edward might prefer to re-read that earlier narrative in his mind, but we must press on with the current gruesome tome.

His banking colleagues certainly didn't think Pamela was a pig when she was introduced to them. Edward had somehow bagged this beautiful outsider, Meanwhile, her musician friends continued to treat him with the mockery reserved for viola players and he was never more comfortable than when in their company. They never attempted to mix the two groups. Now he had lost her, but was she, as Professor Kirchel seemed to suggest, his muse? Although he was most unlikely to use the word, Edward supposed that if Pamela had been, she was one he had taken for granted. She did the artistic stuff so he didn't have to, which made her seem more like a labour-saving appliance for people with pretensions.

Though these biographical reminiscences took up much of Edward's time, they needn't take up ours. Perhaps it is enough of a character reference to say that Pamela loved him.

At the Palace of Esterházy, despite the fact that the tourists were not supposed to be wandering around unsupervised, the corridors were flowing in a manner that would be instructive to the bowels of poor Hamish, which had not moved for some time. Among the humans being impelled down the corridors as if by peristalsis, was the beautiful Anjali, who dragged herself away from the vision of the nearly naked violinist and resumed her search for Satma. Satma, too, out of concern for the convalescent patient, had come in search of the palace physician. Their paths met not far from the Sala Terrena.

'Sati, Sati! I've been looking for you. You'll never guess; I've just seen a ghost!'

Whilst Satma was too astonished to resist, Anjali took her by the arm and led her back through the sequence of east wing interiors to where the apparition had occurred. When they got to the ballroom they passed Tomasino coming out – Sophie was fully dressed and outwardly masculine once more, carrying a violin under her arm – now the crook of an apparently male fiddler's elbow. Anjali ran back to check out the empty room.

'She's gone!'

'Who?'

'The girl playing the violin.'

'There is no one in there playing a violin,' said Tomasino. Sophie was playing a trick on these tourists, but in her defence I should assert that she had no idea of the overexcited spiritual plane they inhabited, their cerebella inflamed by psychic phenomena. 'There was a girl,' insisted Anjali, 'a woman playing wonderful music.'

Sophie smiled at the compliment and added truthfully: 'There were no women in the Esterházy Orchestra.'

'But I saw her!' protested Anjali. 'She looked real to me!'

The exercise had cleared her mind somewhat and Satma had returned to her normal self. She slapped Anjali on the arm. 'What are you talking about you silly thing?'

'Oh Sati! – I *must* have seen a ghost. Oh I'm so sorry Sati, I know you always wanted to see one, and now *I* have and not you. I didn't mean to, honestly – she just appeared right in front of me. Don't be angry, Sati.'

'Who do you suppose it was, exactly, that paid you a visit, Anjali dear?'

'How would I know? It could have been Haydn's wife or someone. Did *she* die?'

'Obviously she died, but why would she manifest herself to you? You really are too proud. You will tell me it was that Englishman's wife next.'

Anjali gripped Satma's arm. 'Sally's mother? You could be right.'

Satma liked being right and smirked, despite herself.

'Why didn't I think of it?' Anjali went on. 'The little girl told me that they came here in search of her. She was a violinist.' Before Satma could claim to know this already, Anjali said, 'Or did you know that too?'

Satma laughed brutally. 'As a matter of fact I did. But that still doesn't solve the big mystery. What did she want with you? Was she simply begging for you to take her place?'

'I don't think so.'

'I've seen the way he looks at you, or the way he tries to avoid looking at you, which is worse. You've done pretty well getting his attention. And now, it seems, you have the blessing of his first wife.'

'Sati, how can you say that?'

'Easily! You have no idea how easily. He probably killed her. You said he goes around threatening people.'

It was a long-established foundation of their relationship that it was she, Satma, who had the insights and visitations, and it was Anjali's role to look on in beauteous wonderment. Satma was not prepared to have these arrangements altered suddenly. And, if further proof were needed, she had just been having a tête-a-tête with Haydn. They began the return journey to the Sala Terrena separated by an empty space as though the ghostly figure had *literally* come between them. They were both determined not to speak to the other, and sustained a resentful silence until Satma suddenly exclaimed 'Oh! My box!'

'Sati, are you okay?' Anjali asked. 'What box?'

'I had an out of body experience,' Satma explained. 'I guess something didn't agree with me.'

'That was very brave of it.'

Satma was startled by the approach of Teresa Martz. 'Your majesty, I think you had better look after your maestro.'

'Bernhardt? How is the old ham? Still milking it?'

'Who's Bernhardt? I'm taking about Haydn.'

Slowly, Teresa realised that this was not one of the orchestral musicians but one of her paying customers, with no reason to be here at all. What reason there was for the historic costume she couldn't guess, nor why she went on saying, in an agitated way: 'You must do something to save him.'

'There is no need to get upset, Madam, we have a trained first-aider in the orchestra.'

'I think he requires more than first aid. He said he was dying.'

'Well, he always was more for the *tragic*.'

'He kept talking about slavery. It is very cruel. The Prince must be a tyrant.'

Teresa had not come upon a problem like this before. She decided that it was better to throw cold water onto this writhing mass of blind misunderstandings, so she explained: 'You were talking to Bernhardt Croek, the actor. He was speaking Haydn's words, Madame.'

'Is he a clairvoyant, too, then?'

'No, Madame, he is speaking words that Haydn wrote in some letters. I thought you would have seen through the deception.'

'It is you who are deceived. When I left him he was too unwell to speak.'

'He must have run out of script.'

Bernhardt was indeed running out of script. The blood vessels in his brain-box were leaking quite freely now and within twenty minutes or so he would be dead. Unaware of the seriousness of the situation, Teresa sent Kevin to check on him.

'Why should I?' asked Kevin, reasonably enough, he thought.

'Because I say so.'

It was clear that they had abandoned any pretence of professionalism and descended to bickering. But Kevin went, after making a passing comment that he was not her personal slave. Teresa remarked that his behaviour was juvenile, and reminded him that he was employed as a technical designer under her directorship, so she had the authority to tell him to carry out any reasonable tasks as circumstances demanded. Plus he was her boyfriend, which covered any unreasonable demands.

When he got to the sickroom Kevin found that the situation required the use of his full range of empathetic skills to coax Bernhardt out of his moribund condition. 'Yeah mate, I wish I wasn't doing this either, it's so bogus! I could have got a job at Disneyland, but I decided to stick it out here, Christ knows why!'

'What are you saying?' mumbled Bernhardt.

'I'm just saying I know how you feel, mate.'

Cheerily slapping Bernhardt on the shoulder blade was not a good idea; it goaded the old man into one last display of his favourite emotion – peevishness.

'You think you know how I feel? I am a true artist and this is how I am treated – and for what? Or perhaps I should ask – for whom?'

'Calm down, old feller; not for my sakes, anyways!'

'For you,' said Bernhardt, adding with more contempt than was absolutely required, '. . . and people like you.'

Kevin was somewhat hurt that his well-intentioned sympathies had been rejected, and his irritation showed in his voice. 'I was only trying to say that I feel your pain, Bernhardt.'

'Do you? Well I don't.'

'Don't you?'

'No, right now I am trying to feel Haydn's pain, and it's not being made any easier with all your interruptions.'

Kevin was duly silent, and his lack of interruptions proved just as irritating to the great actor. 'Do you know how I feel his pain? When I think of him stuck out here when he could be playing to packed houses in Vienna. That's when I feel his pain.'

'It sounds to me like you're feeling your own pain there, mate. We all know you have played to much bigger and better dressed audiences before . . .'

'I have played before the most sophisticated audiences in Europe,' asserted Bernhardt furiously.

'Styles change, old mate,' Kevin went on. 'There's no shame in it, mate.'

Bernhardt clutched his head in what Kevin took to be exasperation but was, in fact, a portion of his brain flooding with blood. Kevin made another attempt at consoling him with sincere empathy, which is a terribly hard trick to pull off when you don't give a shit. 'Bernhardt – you won't let us down, will you, mate?'

Bernhardt slapped the proffered hand away and announced, so that it could be heard at the back of the gods (if there were any), 'Noli me tangere!' and crumpled to the floor.

At that moment Teresa appeared in full princess regalia, including the wig that added forty centimetres to her height. She saw at once that all of Kevin's efforts to handle the situation were having a counter-productive effect on the prone actor. She fell to her knees and turned his chin to face her. Then she took his pulse and announced: 'He's dead, Kevin. Did you say something to upset him?'

Gathering herself quickly, Teresa pulled out her phone. 'I'll get an ambulance. Tidy up in here.' She spotted the casket. She carefully picked it up and handed it to Kevin.

'Dispose of this somewhere, Kevin,' she snapped. 'And do be quick!'

'What is it?'

'It's Haydn's brain. It's gone off.' And as he disappeared, she shouted after him: 'And come straight back!' Fuming with resentment, Kevin carried the reliquary down the corridor to a rear entrance of the palace. On the way, he made the mistake of inspecting it. From the side it looked like an aquarium into which someone had dipped a blender.

When Kevin reached for the handle of the lavatory door it twisted but wouldn't give. This was because Hamish was still in there.

'Are you going to be long, mate?'

'Can you get my dad?'

'Sure kid, what's the matter?'

'I'm stuck.'

'Well, that's Hungarian food for you. You want to get some broccoli, mate.'

Menuetto Da Capo – Senza Ritornello

Providence may be as fake as a fire-snorting wongy-bird, which is in itself a good enough reason for hating it, but it saved Haydn's sanity under intolerable circumstances for an artist. Fate had imprisoned him in Esterházy Palace, where it was uncommonly hard to do as one liked. Haydn would have considered Fate an unchristian term and always preferred to use the word Providence, because he believed events were guided by the hand of God.

The doctrine of recurrence, that is to say the transmigration of souls, or if you prefer, reincarnation, is another a fire-snorting wongy-bird. That didn't stop Satma devoting her life to it. If you believe in Providence or Fate or Karma or even Luck you might as well go around with a sign in your hat saying 'I have given up on rationality'.

Providence had, so far, been absent from Edward's repertoire. Was it Providence that made him forget that he had put their passports under his pillow, or was it Providence that had arranged it that there were only three of them? However, he knew all about the abdication of will. Although he refused to wear the hat, Edward clutched at a fatalistic prop to help him through the senseless vacuity of grief. Since thinking brought on pain, he made the minimum number of decisions required to get through each day. He went through his life on the basis that the decision to get up at all was the precursor to an inevitable series of subsequent events that followed on ineluctably.

The absence of free will in his daily dealings was a comfort to him since he wanted to withdraw himself entirely. Perhaps he had unwittingly submitted himself to Providence.

He was watching Sally sleeping, curled across three chairs. As he took off his jacket and placed it over her as a blanket, he overheard a conversation behind him about tragically premature death. He recognised the voices as being those of Satma and Professor Kirchel. Though he considered himself egoless, Edward jumped to the conclusion that they were talking about him, as Satma asked: 'What did the poor old dear say? Was he utterly broken?'

The speakers still hadn't seen Edward, who was bent over Sally stroking her hair, but Edward was ever more convinced that they were discussing his predicament when he heard Kirchel say: 'I think I can recall his response. He said "I was quite beside myself for a long while because of this death and could not believe that so irreplaceable a person could be so rapidly despatched to the other world". I think they were his exact words.'

Edward did not think they were his exact words, though it was exactly what he thought – he only doubted that he could have expressed it so well. Professor Kirchel was unable to resist adding improvements to his bald expression of loss. He rose like a startled pheasant and squawked: 'Why are you talking about me?'

'We weren't,' asserted Satma.

Discretion now being impossible, Edward had to fall back on valour. 'Yes you were. I heard you. Everyone is constantly talking about me. I wish you would at least do it in German so I wouldn't have to listen.'

'We were talking about Mozart,' corrected Professor Kirchel, and Satma preened her cravat.

By the time Kevin got back to the Sala Terrena he found that the orchestra was already seated and the audience were also beginning to settle. He spotted the English kleptomaniac sitting alone trying to behave normally, with his jacket covering something on the chair beside him – probably his stash of stolen swag. Kevin was about to place the casket on a pietra dura side table with ormulu legs, when Professor Kirchel rushed over.

'I recognise that container!' he cried. 'I held it in these very hands when I was but a boy. Of course, at that time it contained the skull of Joseph Haydn.'

'Well it doesn't any more, mate.'

The best Kevin could claim was that it contained the guttural outpourings of a reincarnation of Mozart. Actually, all he did was jiggle it at Kirchel's eye level to give him a good look at some part-digested Hungarian food.

'The Society of the Friends of Music might be interested,' Professor Kirchel said. 'Shall I take it from you for safe keeping?'

'No worries, Prof,' said Kevin cheerily, glad to be rid of it. He handed the box to the professor, who took it back to the hallway.

Having consummated this satisfactory exchange, Kevin made his way to his cubby-hole to dim the lights. Professor Kirchel carefully placed the object beneath the seat next to Edward.

'Wouldn't you rather sit next to your wife?' asked Edward.

'Oh no, I can't stand being near her at concerts,' said the professor, furtively glancing about. 'She crosses her legs and waves her foot about like she's the conductor – and she's not even in time with the music. Arrg! She is not very musical – it is a pain for me to say. She wouldn't know if she was listening to Verklarte Nacht or a concerto for vacuum cleaner!'

'Really?'

'Oh yes, she loves to sit beneath the chandelier and look up at the tiny lights. Imagine! How simple. That is when she is not complaining about me forcing her to listen to difficult music. I sometimes think that if you could take the acrimony and recrimination out of her conversation she would be . . .'

'Silent?'

'Quite so, but I could forgive her all that, if she wasn't tone deaf.'

'I feel for you,' Edward said implausibly.

Whenever he aired his marital complaints, Kirchel failed to mention the cause of them: his past infidelities with female students and underlings for which his wife was exacting a prolonged and relentless revenge. 'It must have been different for you, with *your* wife being so musical. You have known music all the time in your house, I imagine.'

'Not really, living with a musician must be very different to living with a music lover. She never liked to have music playing on the radio. I am sure this was not her intention, but living with her only encouraged me to neglect my own musical interests.'

'Are you a musician then?'

'As I confessed to you this morning, I played the viola, which apparently doesn't qualify me.'

'Ah yes, the viola. Do you know what we call it in German?'

'Yes, it's bratsche, isn't it?'

'And do you know why we call it a bratsche?'

'Is that the sound it makes when you sit on it?'

Edward's recollected joke did not transmit itself to Kirchel, but some impulse made Edward try out another joke on the musicologist: 'What's the difference between a viola and a coffin?'

Kirchel seemed to be attentive. He was certainly silent.

'The dead person is on the inside of a coffin.'

Kirchel sighed and almost broke into a chuckle. After a while, Edward realised he had been amused by the train of his own thoughts and had not been listening. At last the professor came to a conclusion: 'Like Haydn, I have only one ambition, which is to outlive my gaoler. A long marriage is a terrible thing, Edward – you are lucky to have been spared it.' Before Edward could react to the outrageous insensitivity of this statement, Kirchel continued: 'The best thing to be said for Haydn's marriage was that he seldom saw his wife. Their relationship was entirely financial; he paid her a stipend to stay away. She called herself a widow and befriended other aggrieved women to form a vicious circle.'

Edward was still pondering the assertion that a long marriage can be worse than one terminated by death, when a distant movement caught his eyes and looking up he saw Anjali standing up and waving at someone across the room. Determined though he was not to fall into the trap of thinking it was him she was waving at, he thought it was him. Despite having seen comedians stumble over this very misunderstanding, he behaved exactly like them in a situation that is guaranteed to get a predictable laugh when the camera pulls back to reveal a much better looking man seated behind the clown.

In this case, Edward was actually the person the beautiful woman was gesticulating to across the crowded room. This doesn't prevent him also behaving like a clown, as he went on to demonstrate by stumbling across innumerable knees and murmuring apologies to each pair. Edward reached Anjali, imagining that all eyes were on him, which they were not. He tried to act naturally, and failed, understandably when you consider that it is a contradiction in terms.

'Yes! Hello, Anjali!' he said heavily, hoping he had got the name right but hiding his doubt by adding pompously: 'About our thing earlier I hope you don't think I meant it.'

'You sounded sincere.'

'I don't want you to think that I go around offering to murder people just because they have views that are different from mine. I hope I didn't scare you.'

'I'm not made of porcelain. I wouldn't last long with Satma if I was.'

'Good. It's just that Sally misses her mother and she's so terribly vulnerable.'

'I wanted to tell you something about her.'

'About Sally? Has she been pestering you?'

'No, about her mother. I have just seen her.' She looked at his perplexed and dozy expression with pity. 'I have just seen your wife.'

'What?' Edward exaggerated his breathlessness from the exertions of crossing a rococo ballroom at speed. He looked as if he had spun several gavottes. 'I don't understand . . .' he added self-evidently.

'Your wife – Jemima.'

'Pamela,' corrected Edward. 'Jemima is a bloody duck.'

He had clung to the principal that you don't discuss wives (even dead ones) when talking to other women (especially pretty ones). This was not a furtive plan; it was simply a matter of keeping the paths clear.

'She was a violinist, yes?'

Edward nodded.

'Sally has told me all about her. She was very beautiful. But I know that, as I have just seen her with my own eyes. She was my first ghost, and such a pretty one. She died very young,' added Anjali, harmlessly.

Hearing these words, Edward couldn't hold back the irritation he felt that this – the first gentle look from the beautiful eyes of Anjali, a look that really warmed his emotions, was accompanied by such a cruel reminder. He was not sufficiently hypocritical to use the sympathy of women as a stepping-stone to seduction. If he had been, he could have had his pick of Pamela's friends, who had paid him comfort visits after her death, their sympathetic instincts inflamed. Edward became the object of more female interest than he had ever experienced before thanks to the allure of bereavement. So many pairs of empathetic eyes, kind offers of support, little encouraging pinches and hugs and jutting proffered breasts.

They went away having shed tears and shared hugs but with a diminished view of his worthiness as a mate for their departed friend. Not that any of them had been trying to do anything more than take him out for a test drive.

The recollection of some of these insensitive encounters contributed to Edward's antagonised response, when Anjali said: 'I have just seen her. She has appeared in a room of the palace. It must have been her; she was playing something on the violin. Perhaps it was a message.'

'Oh, right, what was she playing? "Come Into the Garden Maud"? "Unchained Melody"? The theme from *Ghostbusters*?'

'You're not taking me seriously,' said Anjali, shocked.

'And you are mocking me, I think. As if I would fall for a haunted-house story!'

'I tell you, she was there in the east wing. That part of the palace is closed to the public, the rooms are all empty.'

'What were *you* doing there?'

'I was lost.'

'Well, I am certainly not going on a ghost hunt.'

'Don't be so sceptical. Surely you want to find out for yourself? What if it *is* a message?'

'Return to sender!' thundered Edward. 'This is your revenge for what I said earlier. And to think that I was worried that I might look a fool, when you hold such a worthless stock of ideas.'

When he said this he knew, as any banker must, that stocks hold value precisely in so far as people believe in them.

'But what if she has come back?'

'People DON'T COME BACK.'

'In our tradition . . .'

'And leave my daughter alone from now on, do you hear?'

'Come on, you talk as if I have been inducting her into a cult; samsara is an ancient and venerable belief.'

'That you're not prepared to die for.'

Silence fell between them. Anjali had discovered that reintroducing ghosts to deranged widowers was a dangerous pursuit. Her struggle to find a dignified exit was ended by a disembodied cough. It was Dr Dietrich.

'Tonight's performance will commence very shortly,' she whispered. 'Please return to your seats so that the performance may begin.'

Anjali went back to rejoin her friend and said nothing. They were in an intermediary phase between speaking and not speaking to one another. Meanwhile, Edward made his way back to the empty seat between those occupied by Sally's recumbent form and the one playing host to Professor Kirchel's music-loving rump. He tried to settle himself after the shocks his mind had just received.

'Been checking on your other child?' asked Kirchel.

Edward couldn't lie, but he chuckled and said: 'Neverending.' Then, in an attempt to get back to smaller talk, he asked: 'Did Haydn have many children?'

Almost at once he realised the magnitude of his mistake: Kirchel was determined to pursue his favourite theme:

'Haydn had no children at all – leaving him free to be Papa to so many others. Looking for the cause of his childless condition it would probably be better to point to the fact that he maintained a very distant relationship with his wife, several leagues distant in fact, rather than speculate on medical matters. However, it is an extraordinary fact (as Dr Dietrich would say) that at a young age he was actually offered the chance to be neutered.

'Haydn's musical life began as a boy soprano in the cathedral in Vienna. It was suggested that he could extend his early success indefinitely by means of an operation: to put it bluntly, castration. He would then have had a lucrative singing career ahead of him and no children. His brain came to the rescue of his nether organs and he had a lucrative career without singing – and also without children.'

'That is very strange,' said Edward. 'I am glad my children didn't have to hear it though – the stuff about the severed head was bad enough.'

'Haydn's father, that gentle wheelwright whose house we visited earlier today, heard of the proposed operation and rushed to Vienna to prevent it being carried out. He arrived at Haydn's lodgings after a difficult journey unaware of whether or not he was too late. Well, you can imagine: the rustic father, already discomforted by the smart surroundings, the polished floors, the cleanliness. The poor fellow began to make awkward inquiries into his boy's health without mentioning any specifics, too mortified to utter the words.'

Edward laughed warmly.

'At the end of his long life Haydn told this story with great affection for his father, and indeed I know of no greater concern for a male parent than this.'

'Lakshman would probably say he was simply maximising the number of his grandchildren.'

'Yes, well Haydn held on to his orchids but nothing ever came of them. As I said, that is why he was able to be Papa to so many. I sometimes think I might have been a better father myself if I hadn't had any children.'

This was another statement that would require some effort to unravel. Instead, Edward asked: 'Do you have children?'

'Yes, but they are not friends of music,' sighed the professor.

What could this mean? Were they still allowed to visit? wondered Edward. Kirchel's son (it turned out in the subsequent conversation) was an engineer and his daughter was in pharmaceuticals. These facts could have signified almost anything: the boy could be a garage mechanic and the girl a drug addict.

'You must be very proud of them,' probed Edward. Professor Kirchel sighed again, unwilling to reveal that his children had not forgiven him for his repeated betrayals of their mother.

'That reminds me,' Edward went on briskly, 'this morning Sally was asking about Haydn's mother. Dr Dietrich didn't know much, save that she died young, but I couldn't very well tell that to Sally. Was she musical at all?'

'She was fond of music and a dulcet singer in her way. It is true she was not spared to witness Haydn's rising fame. More than one intimate of Haydn in his old age declared that he still knew by heart all the simple airs which she had been wont to lilt about the house.'

'That is very comforting.'

Tucking Sally's sleepy foot under the vented skirt of his corduroy jacket, Edward wondered if she would recollect in her old age the sounds of her mother practising the violin in the next room. He could never get that sound out of his mind, and often thought he heard fragments of it in the night.

Whilst Dr Dietrich stood at the front of the audience to make her important announcement, Teresa and Tomek were waiting outside the Sala Terrena so that they could make their regal entrance and take their places in the two great gilded chairs upholstered with imperial motifs. As they waited, Tomek began rummaging under Tessa's skirts, seeking those parts to which his hands had not long previously enjoyed unrestricted access. 'Lets do it again.'

'There isn't time. Fingers off!'

'I won't last as long the third time, honestly, just a quick one whilst that old bag is talking.'

Teresa and Tomek hurriedly engaged in their final bout. They ran through it in a brisk tempo, to reinforce the memory of the first time in their minds. It was not the same; it was neither worse nor better, but it rounded off their erotic dance with a reinforcement of the initial idea, thrusting home what splendid filthy acts they were committing again and again into the memory.

'Am I better than Kevin?'

Teresa laughed.

'Tell the truth – am I?'

'To tell the truth – Kevin doesn't really do it for me, never has.'

Rather than triumphant, Tomek was disappointed. 'That spoils the whole thing.'

'What do you mean?'

'I wanted to beat him, but if he's a dud, it is like outsmarting a kid – there's no real fun in it.'

Teresa could not reconcile this with his attitude to punching people, where he clearly had no objection to taking an unfair advantage over an older and frailer opponent, and his uncompromising seduction technique. 'You are little better than a rapist, Tomek.'

Tomek only grunted.

'And a thief.'

A lower grunt.

'And you are a murderer too.'

'What do you mean?'

'Bernhard Croek is dead.'

'I hardly touched him.'

'Never mind; he had it coming.'

'The punch?'

'No, idiot, the stroke.'

Dr Dietrich's announcement was prolonged, because she had some sad news to pass on: 'There has, very regrettably been a death among us.'

Edward rose up from his seat in protest. 'This is intolerable! My private life has become a public entertainment.'

There was an astonished murmur. It slowly registered with Edward that he was not, in fact, the centre of attention, or at least he wouldn't be if he sat down, which he did, blushing deeply and apologising.

So here you are, old chum, going insane, Edward's critical commentator concluded. *There's no need to rush it, though.*

Now everybody seemed to know his private thoughts. Quite possibly they *were* his thoughts. Half of them seemed to know things about him that he didn't know himself – except they kept getting his wife's name wrong.

'As I was about to say,' Dr Dietrich continued, 'our old friend Bernhardt Croek has passed away peacefully.'

'He's croaked!' whispered Satma.

'Really Sati! Is nothing sacred?'

Actually it was a sacred belief of Satma's that Bernhardt was more than ready to move on. She had never met a soul who had less reason to remain in this world.

'Plus, it means I was right, the death I foretold has happened.'

'Oh good! So we can all relax now, is that right? Nothing else can go wrong?'

Dr Dietrich had not finished her announcement. 'We shall be performing this Farewell Symphony in his memory. Bernhardt Croek will be sorely missed.'

'By Herman Fraenkl and nobody else,' added Tomek, offstage right.

Edward turned to Professor Kirchel. 'You would think they had enough practice to put on a little concert without the whole thing going tits-up.'

'Titsup? What is this word? I am not familiar with it.'

'It's a banking term.'

'Oh I see.' Kirchel was storing this in his cranial Berlitz.

Dr Dietrich told the audience that the performance would commence *subito* or, in German, *sofort*, or if you prefer it in English and are not too fussy, momentarily. But it takes more than bunching people together and sitting them down in gold upholstered chairs to make an attentive audience. Some of them found that the conversations they had been having held far more interest than performances of old symphonies; others were troubled by the unstable behaviour of the rococo decorations and wanted to curl up and sleep. This was a problem because audiences are terribly important; without them performers would be redundant and composers deluded. Imagine a world where everyone is talking and no one is listening. That shouldn't be too hard, which only goes to show how precious listeners are.

Outside the palace, Bernhardt's body was being taken slowly down the long driveway in the back of an ambulance. There was no need for haste or the disturbance of a siren.

James and Rosie were probably going to miss the concert. She had been wandering in the palace grounds when she heard her husband's voice calling out her name and she called back. He ran to her and found her, and what greetings they shared ought to remain a mystery between man and wife. She was currently lying on her back on the grass enjoying experiences she had never had before with her husband, partly because it would never occur to him to lie her down on her back on some damp grass. The effects of the magic mushrooms were wearing off but she had not yet returned to this world from the realms of euphoria.

You may adjust yourself, the complex dance is finally over. Haydn has shown us that music can resume at the beginning; all the composer has to do is write the words *da capo* on the score and the whole thing starts again. But life is not quite like that: you can't go *da capo* in life, which is lived *senza ritornelli*. You can only go back to the head *in your head*. And yet, without the ability to relive the past in our minds, how unbearable life would be.

Without repeat marks, music would be an ever-changing noise that made no sense to the listener. It would be as nearly meaningless as a life lived without memory.

That twice-told tale, the minuet and trio, eventually became a decorous relic and was replaced as the third movement of a symphony by the far louder and simpler Scherzo, which lived up to its jocular name (*scherzo* being Italian for joke). Haydn's jokes were not so explicit, as we shall shortly see.

IV

SENSE OF FUN

Presto

The raised scroll of Sophie's violin fell onto an emphatic downbeat and the music began. There was no conductor, but all Haydn symphonies benefit from the absence of a baton-twirler, this one in particular. The musicians set to work thwacking out the vigorous first subject and silenced all conversation. The expanse of listening heads silently ingested their musical nourishment. Edward stretched out his neck and tilted his head up at the ceiling of the Sala Terrana where he saw his own initial being decorously abducted by gangs of angels. If only. He felt a morsel of blatterteig stuck in his teeth, and loosened it with the tip of his introspective tongue. Dewy grass clippings clung to his shoes. Please lovely angel, come and take me away . . .

To say that his mind wandered would be to promote the same fallacy as the movement of the mind out of the body in a state of unconsciousness, or the transit of the soul out of the body after death, but there is no better way of describing it. His thoughts were taken away from the music, just not by angels.

Edward's buttocks, though endowed with amply sufficient cushioning in themselves, found that theirs was not a princely throne. Indeed, it was not anything of authentic derivation; it was a reproduction that had been knocked up in a factory in Eastern Europe, and despite its apricot hued upholstery and gold paint it did not offer a luxurious welcome to the seat of the user, owing to the use of cheap stuffing and the absence of lumbar support. It was the ache in his buttocks that distracted Edward and derailed him from Haydn's musical train of thought.

He was taken back to that dreamless night he had spent in hospital, in a leatherette armchair with wings, so that the lolling head can be supported. They had even given him a tiny pillow but it kept slipping off, obeying some mutual repulsion of man-made fibres, and during the endless night in which he was tormented with discomfort, she had passed away. He could never forgive himself for paying attention to his little aches and pains at such a time. He could never forgive that chair, and the one he was currently sitting in was scarcely more deserving of clemency. Beside him, Professor Kirchel sat in a blissful state of ease; he seemed to be unaffected by the discomfort brought on by upholsterers from hell, or shame from somewhere else. He had the self-satisfied air of the Enlightenment.

Those eighteenth-century princes were tougher than you might think: Prince Nikolaus sat through hours of this, thought Edward. Perhaps the fact that the whole elaborate concoction extolled his gracious existence made it more tolerable.

Edward tried reading the programme to distract himself:

> Haydn's symphonies are littered with musical jokes, so many jokes that his detractors called him a musical prankster. The Farewell Symphony, however, is a joke with serious intent.

He looked up at the return of the 'thwacking-as-usual' theme Kirchel had spoken of. He listened attentively for almost three minutes when an unpleasant gastric odour wafted into his consciousness. His senses were being made aware of the presence of Haydn's head-box that was hidden under Professor Kirchel's seat, though understandably the rational part of Edward's brain did not immediately deduce this. How could he suspect that a respected Viennese musicologist had taken to concealing boxes full of vomit under his chair? Edward simply attributed the origin to Professor Kirchel himself.

Edward read on doggedly, emptily, queasily:

> The difference between the music of Haydn and those of later revolutionaries such as Beethoven is the difference

> between joking that you have a bomb in your suitcase and actually having a bomb in your suitcase. Whilst Beethoven roared like a lion, Haydn roared like a nightingale, making subversive jokes whilst the ancien regime was still in power, which took more courage than to thunder imprecations on it after it had fallen.

It was no good. The music, though full of vigour, could not compete with events occurring in the tiny stadium that was Edward's brain, and he heard no more of it. He was digesting a piece of data that would take some time, possibly a whole symphony worth, to compute. He had just been told his dead wife had appeared in ghostly form to a pretty woman he was seeking to impress.

Defensive thoughts whiff-whaffed through his mind – he hadn't been flirting with her. No one could ever accuse Edward of flirtatiousness, but even *he* saw the futility of trying to explain this to a wife, especially a dead one. The more he urged himself to believe that he had no interest in beauteous Anjali, the more his conscience suffered. So, she just happened to be the most attractive woman on the tour, did she? He could hardly claim he hadn't noticed. She was probably the most beautiful thing currently in Austria or Hungary and wasn't he here to see the sights? Hell, that wouldn't convince anyone. She was good with Sally, who had been through a lot. *Oh don't give me that, chum. You are on the hunt for a replacement mother.*

Am I going to be persecuted by these quibbling objections every time I speak to a woman? He knew that such an argument would be unlikely to assuage Pamela's ghost. Pamela's ghost! There was no such thing. And yet – what if she really had come back to him, incredible as it may seem? Hadn't he spent nights crying out 'my darling, come back to me' to the empty pillow beside his?

Supposing for the moment that by some miracle she *had* come back: and like a prince refusing to hear a petition for clemency he had refused to see her. How stuck-up can you get? His own wife had taken the trouble to return from the dead and he stood her up. He rejected her out of rational prejudice. What sort of grieving widower was he?

As the music of the recapitulation was filling the air around Satma, she tried to cheer herself up by recalling her previous visit to Esterházy in an earlier lifetime. She told herself a merry tale of Mozart's visit to his mentor, imagined them playing quartets together, but it was not so much fun without Anjali. Even though her friend was as psychically inert as a rock, Satma's gift needed her. Like the clash of a stream with a boulder, Anjali made her unstoppable imagination run on more wildly.

As soon as the first movement came to an end, releasing a fusillade of coughs that popped into the air harmlessly, Edward got up once again from his seat, leaving Sally sleeping across the three chairs, with Jemima as a pillow and his corduroy jacket over her legs. The people seated in the row behind made justified aspersions about the English *Jack-in-der-box*. Making for the exit, where the *Ausgang* sign was happily illuminating its message that there was a way out, he apologised for disturbing the other members of the audience as he bashed their knees, but he was somewhat careless, knowing that he had to be quick and they all thought he was a lunatic anyway.

Owing to the enormity of the curtains that had been drawn in front of the glass doors and the stiffness of the latch mechanism, Edward's furtive exit drew the attention of at least half the audience. Otherwise it was successful – the door gave way and he stumbled out.

Tomasino (or Sophie, rather) heard the distant clatter and paused the raised scroll of her violin in mid up-beat before commencing the second movement. Edward heard the opening notes as he tried to close the door silently.

Satma whispered: 'Wasn't that your future husband running out of the room, Anjali?'

'Shhh, don't be an uber-bitch.'

'Do you think he is feeling unwell at all? Perhaps he is just a little hot, dear,' suggested Satma.

Anjali leaned in to whisper to her friend: 'He's probably gone to look for his wife.'

'You told him that you saw her then?' Satma hissed.

Anjali nodded.

'Was that a good idea?'

The cool air was an aid to clear thinking and Edward began to think that – quite clearly – he had no idea which way to go, and experienced one of the drawbacks of symmetry in architecture; the façade extended to all four compass-points with equal certitude. Anjali had said something about seeing the ghost in the east wing, so all he had to do was find the east wing and look for his dead wife. To do this Edward began counting stars, looking for the Great Bear in the night sky. *This palace is so huge you need an astrolabe to navigate your way around, old chum. It's lucky for you the stars are out.* The dots of light in the sky seemed to form a perfect dome, the universe nodding along with him as he orientated himself, located the fixed star and began the arm movements that were an unfortunate necessity if he ever had to work out whether east was to his left or right. Assured of himself at last, he strode off and rounded a pilastered corner. His plan was to circumnavigate three sides of the palace in order to re-enter at the far end and work his way back in a methodical spook-sweep.

Preparing for a spectral encounter, he was in danger of spooking himself. He stumbled across a dark lawn and stopped when he heard some strange cries. These cries suggested a woman crying out in pain. Out here in the countryside he thought it could be a vixen calling her cubs in the night. He had just reassured himself that it must have been a fox when the female screech articulated a cry that sounded like a drawn-out 'yes'.

As he swirled his head the stars seemed to rotate. He got the sense of the whole firmament freewheeling round him. He was becoming as ridiculous as those Indian women. Forcing himself to think scientifically, he analysed the phenomenon he had perceived: you can only see as far as you can see, no matter which direction you look, so the stars seems to form a dome around your head. Nature fools us into thinking we are the centre of things.

It was ridiculous, but he preferred to be ridiculous. Right now he didn't want a universe that was fully explained, he just wanted one that contained Pamela. Within ourselves the timeless, fateful stars burn. If this was Lakshman's intelligent universe, what could account for the emptiness and stupidity of his portion of it? Only the black hole left by her absence. He had continued to exist in an inexcusably dull way. He was dust.

Edward was not just angry with the universe. If he *did* encounter her ghost he would no doubt be angry with Pamela too. *Can you actually remember, old chum, when you stopped crying over her and started crying over yourself?* The accusation heard in Edward's head was pitiless. *The only emotion you are capable of feeling is self-pity.* That, Edward knew, was not quite true. He also felt guilt and panic.

'And love!' he cried out. 'I still love her!'

A cold droplet of sweat trickled down Edward's spine, as if a trail of starlight had got in at the neck of his shirt. Perhaps it would bring a fleck of universal intelligence with it. He remembered the words written on a card attached to one of the wreaths. It ran: *'No one is truly dead until they are no longer loved.'* This assertion appeared to grant continued life to Pamela, since she was still loved by him. It was supposed to be comforting. As he walked on round the perimeter of the palace the consequences for him were less hopeful when he thought about it along these lines: owing to her absence she is unable to love me. *Owing to her absence.* What a stupid way to put it. Nevermind, continue. And so? And so I am no longer loved, *owing to her absence*, yes, owing to her absence, and therefore, following the logic of the statement, she is not the dead one.

I am. I am a dead viola player.

He had reached a glass door, very like the one that opened into the Display Room where Hamish was still locked in the lavatory. Knowing the aristocratic obsession with having two of everything, matching and symmetrical, no doubt he was exactly parallel to Hamish, but he did not know yet whether, when he forced open the door, it would respond with a shrill alert. He found that the door offered feeble resistance to his intruding shoulder and had been left with the alarm deactivated. His first attempt at breaking and entering was progressing smoothly so far.

'Sati, you look terrible. Are you sure you have completely finished being sick?' observed Anjali when the orchestra drew the slow movement to a suspirating close. A less imaginative person than Satma might perhaps have attributed the tension in her stomach to the aftermath of a vigorous purge, but for her it was a foresight of yet more imminent disasters. Satma was almost crushed by another wave of psychic vibrations. Since she wasn't fully speaking to Anjali, she merely sighed, 'Do you have a mint?'

Anjali handed her a stick of chewing gum that Dr Dietrich had pressed on her earlier. The music began again and Satma's sleepy eyes widened as the spearmint fumes travelled up her sinuses. Eyes watering, Satma stiffened her spine for the disaster yet to come.

Edward began walking through rooms very like the ones they passed along earlier, except that those ones had been over-furnished and over-lit by Kevin's masterfully discrete but penetrating spots. These ones were empty and dark, lit only by starlight through the windows. Edward entered one of the rooms carefully, kicked a paint pot and stumbled into a stepladder. As he struggled to remain upright he became entangled in the dustsheet that the decorator had left draped over the ladder. As the ladder crashed to the floor, Edward, now entirely cloaked in the white sheet, kept himself from falling by staggering with arms outstretched.

Once he had regained his equilibrium the absurdity of his situation struck him. He certainly had spooked himself; here he was acting the ghost: A fool on a fool's errand. Then a further thought occurred to him. It couldn't be! Was that woman really so simple as to believe a Halloween prop like that was the ghost of Pamela? The idea was so ridiculous he expelled a loud guffaw of laughter that would probably have been heard in the Sala Terrena, if not in the realms beyond.

In that stately hall the orchestra was working its way through the turns of the minuet and trio. Tomek, on the point of falling asleep, was roused by Teresa's elbow digging into his ribs, since she knew instinctively that he would be a loud baritone snorer, and she had to prevent him performing an unwelcome solo. Only vigorous use of the elbow could counteract the soporific effect of a minuet and trio after so much wine and lewd exercise.

Edward returned towards the sound of the minuet when it was going round *da capo senza ritornello*, and found that he was approaching the Sala Terrena from the back of the hall, which gave him a chance to see if he was still capable of discretion. When he heard the music stop, he stepped forward and flung himself next to Lakshman, who was (as usual) sitting alone. Whenever anyone approached him, the old physicist's face would break into warm a smile, revealing his white uneven teeth, but his welcoming nature had not prevented his solitude and may even have helped to cause it. To Edward, he was at this moment as welcome a sight as a true friend met at a pretentious wedding. With the customary gestures, Edward gained permission to seat himself beside the physicist.

'Come, sit, you have missed most of it. You have been looking for someone?'

'Yes,' admitted Edward.

'Your children, I suppose.'

'No, I know where they are. I've just been on a ghost hunt.'

'Really. Did you find one?'

'Yes, and I'm quite cured now. Do you believe in ghosts?'

'Of course not.'

'Neither do I.'

The final movement got underway. They listened to the music and Edward began to feel better. Haydn knew how to dispel bad humour with sound. The spasmodically merry final movement began briskly, and gathered energy as it went. Just exactly what Prince Nikolaus would expect to finish off a soirée musicale going with a swing. The music reached a passage that sounded very much as if it were coming towards the final bars of the symphony, when the fine-spirited jollity broke off on an unexpected chord.

Adagio

At last it was time to find out why this Farewell Symphony was so called. The presto section came to a sudden halt just when you would expect the second theme to be introduced, but there was no second theme, instead there was a pause of indeterminate rhythmical length. After this fermata the music resumed in the wrong key and in a new time signature. Even the most preoccupied ones in the Sala were jolted from their thoughts and exchanged inquiring looks of recognition that something strange had happened; you may be able to slip the key-change past them, but the fact that the tempo had become stuck in traffic was impossible to miss. The music crept along at an adagio, as you will have already gathered from the title of this final section.

This adagio did not create one of those new-age ambient moods intended to decelerate the workings of the mind – ideally to a complete halt. The pulse may have been slowed but there remained semiquavers of persistent thought flittering about. Edward was thinking lucidly for the first time in a while.

The wheels had not quite come off this symphony, though the horses had certainly been unhitched and the cart had lost all momentum. It did not so much grind to a standstill – that would make an ungracious noise, being a musical carriage and not a real one – rather, the symphony dissolves *a la cortega di Cinderella* into nothing, leaving the Prince behind . . . you might say like a pumpkin, as the mice scuttle away at the tolling of the fairytale clock.

It began with the wind players prominent, displaying various kinds of virtuosity, and then they stood up to leave, quite literally, for this is a symphony that comes with stage directions: the players are instructed to get up, snuff out their candles (which in our modern interpretation meant switching off the artificial candles on their stands) and tiptoe out of the room as the music continues without them.

As soon as he saw the oboist and the second horn quit their places, Edward knew at once that one of Haydn's celebrated jokes was underway. Tomek, our mock-up of a prince, over-acted his part, gawping at the tails of the retreating musicians. At the successive departure of each musician the audience listened more attentively to the remaining players in their dwindling pool of light.

In this prolonged farewell, the double bass lingered with an unusually long solo, which in itself was of comic value, for that musical armoire is intrinsically laughable. Tonight's contrabasso could not help being dwarfed by his instrument; he resembled a squat millionaire with a leggy blonde – and yet he carried on playing, oblivious to the absurdity of a midget taking the part of Romeo. That double bass outstaying its welcome was a caricature in sound of Prince Nikolaus, as certainly as if Haydn had scored that part for the baryton.

Then, having churned and chuntered for a while, the bassist departed, trying not to clatter as he carried his oversized bride off the stage, and what remained was a string quartet playing on in the twilight. In this way, Papa let the all-powerful Prince know, if he cared to interpret it, that his mind was not really in the palace, that it was, in reality, far away, swapping ideas with other musical minds.

The cellist departed and soon after the viola did too, which left just two muted violins duetting like two birds at dusk, circling each other, searching for a place to perch, their lines crossing over one another, swapping the tune back and forth between them, never landing on a downbeat until at last they settled on a delicate cadence, hopping down thence to another, lower one.

Finally, Tomasino blew out the last candle, bowed to the Prince, and retreated. Had this silent communication been relayed between Herman Fraenkl playing the Prince and Bernhardt Croek as the perpetrator of the jest, no doubt the significance of it would have been eloquently conveyed in gesture and expression. Tomek rather overdid the astonishment and the rubbing of eyes, which was surprising when you think how he could express the subtlest nuances when they were at the end of a length of string. The puppet's exquisite gestures drew all finesse out of the puppeteer.

The word *farewell* has so often been used to convey sentimentality, a synthetic substitute for emotion, but Haydn's message was as unsentimental as an eviction order. Hadyn's Farewell Symphony was the most refined withdrawal of labour in history. The fact that it was successful might disguise how brave it had been, because the Prince's employees were also his subjects, and to even suggest that they had any function other than to please their God-appointed master would have been unthinkable. The symphony was a revolutionary act cunningly disguised by sentimentality. It was a courteous notice to down tools; it was at the same time a gentle reminder of its maker's intellectual freedom.

Edward, who felt terribly oppressed most of the time, realised that this is how you free yourself from oppression; you just walk away from it. As the final notes played, he imagined a pastoral landscape painted by a great master: at the centre of the canvas was the figure of a woman, whose face, since her beautiful profile would be spoiled with too heavy a brushstroke, was delineated in the faintest pencil line. The delicate profile faded, and there was silence.

Since music is a temporal medium, perhaps it would be better to compare the close of this symphony to a four-course meal, which after satisfying the appetite ends with an unexpected fifth course in the form of a weightless dish into which the chef has poured all his talent without apparently adding any other ingredients apart from lightly whisked air – an *amuse bouche* that has the power to quell reality.

When you listen to the final notes, it takes your most rapt attention; it is essential to keep absolutely still for the birdlike notes to land on your shoulder. Or, to put it within our culinary formula, you must listen with all the care and attention required to clean out the dish of the tiniest morsel. Then, with the music finished, you sit in a suspended moment. There are no musicians left. They have gone. Of course, something is going to break the spell, particularly if the performance is marred by the presence of a conductor, waving his baton at nothing, standing in full view like an over-attentive waiter. If the audience is unsophisticated, applause inevitably will break into this silence and destroy the static moment, as when the waiter pulls away your plate too soon. For the rest of the evening – no, perhaps for the rest of your life – you will try to recapture that moment with the frustration of someone struggling to recall a broken dream. It was at just such a moment, when an assembly of a hundred were paused in one thought, that a theoretical physicist like Lakshman might hope to come up with a breakthrough of understanding.

On this occasion, the universe wobbled in the cottony embrace of an inexorably growing, proliferating silence . . . until the spell was inelegantly broken by Kevin.

Kevin had fallen asleep in his secret chambre-de-valet, which he liked to think was the nerve centre of the whole show. He was quite wrong about this, for the controlling mind behind the production resided under Teresa's wig, and not within these perplexing scribbles of wiring, despite their resemblance to neural systems. The most they could claim was a few simple motor functions and primitive sensory inputs. In other words, it was at best a reptilian brain, despite occupying most of the space in the room. It was so primitive it couldn't even dream, and even lizards do that. And so did Kevin, whose dreams need not concern us as he dozed in his chair with his feet up on the console and an empty pilsner bottle on the floor beside him.

Kevin was the proud creator of this electronic brain and frequently boasted of its accomplishments, oblivious to its limitations. It was able to sense that an infrared beam had been broken, signalling that someone had stepped in front of a display and it would respond by throwing some halogen light on the object. It could tell if a door had been opened – or at least it would have been able to if Kevin hadn't switched off this function in order to take the short cut to the puppet theatre. Had he not performed that casual lobotomy the tiny lizard brain would certainly have detected the plume of smoke that now rose up from the mixing desk and began to fill the little room. After a sufficient density of smoke had been achieved to disturb his dreams, Kevin awoke with a spluttering cough and staggered to his feet. He summed up the urgency of the situation with an unformed exclamation that began with f –, though he could not bring himself to utter the word *fire*. Then he opened the door that was camouflaged as part of the panelling, and in doing so allowed the ingress of a gust of oxygen that almost instantaneously made the situation worse.

Kevin was not just responsible for this emergency by his negligence – he was the progenitor of it as well. I have already recorded how Sophia, the music student forced into the costume of Tomasino in order to play first violin in the Esterházy Orchestra, had made use of the delay to the concert to practise for her finals recital, and how she had found it necessary to remove the restrictive clothing of an eighteenth-century male and play in her under-things, and that whilst she had taken every effort to ensure her privacy, she had been observed by Kevin over his extensive system of closed circuit cameras: these innocent events were the sources of the disaster that had been foreseen by Satma.

He had been enjoying Sophia's near-naked performance when the only part of Kevin that could never be described as lazy, his sperm, sought consummation in the mixing desk. Sperm being a good conductor of electricity as well as of other things, it only needed one lucky individual to cause a short circuit and create a spark. The circuit board smouldered into life, and began to give off the smell of burning plastic and dust, with just a hint of boiled spunk.

Choking and blinking, Kevin staggered from the doorway that broke open the ornate decorative wall of the Sala Terrena, and forgetting to shut the door behind him, dashed into the dimness and muttering of the concert hall pulling swags of beige smoke in his wake. To those who saw his sudden appearance from an apparently solid wall he must have seemed an alarming supernatural apparition. Teresa saw his clumsy entrance with irritation rather than alarm. How like Kevin to spoil things – probably one light bulb had gone out and now he was acting as though there was an emergency.

Kevin was indeed acting like there was an emergency, with justification. Once he had refilled his lungs with clean air, he shouted as loud as he could. 'Out! Now! Out, out!' Then astutely in German he cried 'Ausgang!'

The AUSGANG signs were not flashing and there was no siren or alarm to corroborate the words of this hysterical New Zealander, but given his performance no one cared to doubt his words. There was a terrible hubbub of voices and scrapings of reproduction chair legs on newly varnished parquet.

'What the hell are you doing, Kevin?' demanded Teresa when she reached him.

'Tess, we have to get everyone out. We're on fire.'

'Where is it?'

'In there.'

Teresa slammed the little partition door shut, but it was too late, she was enclosing an orange maelstrom of fire, and the walls were already hot, smoke oozing through the cracks of the panelling.

'Why isn't the alarm sounding?'

'I switched it off.'

'Well switch it back on.'

'I can't, the switch is on fire.'

Obliged to perform the function of the fire bell, Teresa began to whoop and wave her arms. With cries of *Aus!* and *Shoo!* she quickly made herself understood, and the audience got to their feet and began to clump together as people in an emergency tend to do. Teresa and Kevin split the audience, and drew them out through the two most obvious means of exit. If you could see the palace from the air it would look as though it was expelling humans at both ends, like a patient with severe food poisoning. Some spewed out onto the south terrace and some were evacuated through the rear entrance and ran down the steps.

Edward was an exception to the general parting and departing, he had to rescue his children and neither of them was easy to locate. He decided to get Sally out first and then go and find Hamish, and began to push against the general outward flow from the back of the hall to the middle of the room, where Sally was. He lost sight of her among the bodies pushing against him. Explosive noises emanated from Kevin's control room as another piece of his equipment blew its state-of-the-art gasket. At every bang the seriousness of the threat was reconfirmed. The mass-anxiety was rising towards panic level.

The members of the orchestra were in their rehearsal room when they heard the tumult. This was not the kind of departure envisioned by Papa Haydn: musicians fleeing for their lives and a palace in flames. Yet they fled with their instruments and began to count themselves lucky to have survived – and then they began to count one another to see if any one of their orchestra was missing. Then they began to discuss whether this would affect their chances of getting paid.

As soon as she had got the people out and down the steps, Teresa Martz pulled out her phone and called the fire brigade. Meanwhile, Dr Dietrich, who had come out through the other exit, was also on the phone urgently summoning Carl to the rescue. Nothing like this had happened on a Euphony Escorted Tour before.

Lubricating her throat with a double dose of lozenges, Dr Dietrich made the following announcement: 'Would the Euphony Escorted Tour group members muster here, please. Members of the Esterházy Orchestra and other personnel should assemble on the other side of the path so numbers can be taken. We will endeavour to take you back to your homes and hotels in Vienna in good time,' she croaked, straining her unamplified voice. 'I have a list of the people on the trip. My colleague is checking that the performers are all safe. If you could all co-operate by standing in line and not wandering about so I can see who is here.' She said the same thing in German, and pulled out a sheet of EET-headed notepaper (recognisable for the over-sized treble clef) and began ticking names off the passenger list.

It was difficult for the evacuees to stand in line as instructed and not wander about, since they were still absorbing the novelty of being tumbled out of a burning palace into the cold of a Hungarian night. Urgently working her way down the names, and cross-referring with Teresa Martz, Dr Dietrich announced the definitive list of persons missing or dead, bringing a tragic end to what was intended to be an evening's harmless entertainment.

If, like me, you prefer happy endings, you will be relieved to hear that the final pages of this book will not consist of a score-sheet of the dead. And so in contrary motion to the ending of Haydn's Farewell Symphony, my players shall return to the performance platform, one by one. To encourage my readers to pursue the narrative to the end I will not spoil the suspension in the cadence by thumping down with the tonic chord before we have had an opportunity to discover the various ways they have come back to that safe key from their troublesome modulations.

National stereotypes being rather tenacious, you may not be surprised that the Germans filed out of the exit in an orderly manner, and were all found to be present and correct. Having established that happy fact, they lined themselves up in rows three deep, with the women one end and the men the other. This seemed an odd way in which to muster, but their segregation was explained when they broke into song. They gave the opening chorus from the Creation, the oratorio for which Haydn modestly gave the credit to a power above. It was an unexpected choice of repertoire, given the amount of destruction taking place nearby. Presumably they hoped to raise morale by it. 'And the Spirit of God mov'd upon the face of the waters,' they sang, 'and God said "let there be light," and there was light.'

The rest of the survivors were still performing a representation of chaos. It was dark, no flames were visible from outside, and they had to find their way by following the sound of Dr Dietrich's failing voice. The Duchess of Poundland, though some might say her demise would not be much regretted, was first to be welcomed to safety. In fact she was one of the first out. Even the fleet-footed Lakshman was unable to push ahead of her. Dr Dietrich complimented her on her vigour and asked whence it came.

'From terror; sheer *frightful* terror,' replied the panting arthritic.

Lakshman appeared out of the gloom to register his survival of the danger. His name received a tick beside it, but he was not congratulated for his part in maintaining the total quantity of intelligence in the universe.

'Don't wander off, please,' said Dr Dietrich.

He stood alone, as usual, in his ill-deserved friendless state. Deprived of the academic arena in which to shine, he was terribly easy to ignore.

The Pratts were officially missing, but no one volunteered to go in search of them.

'They will turn up, I expect,' shrugged Dr Dietrich.

'And if they don't?'

'Then I won't have to hear how this catastrophe has held back their conception schedule.' Dr Dietrich gave another shrug as she fished her cigarettes from her bag. She had a smoker's face, a special pattern of wrinkles that gave her the look, when drawing hard on a filter tip, of a veteran jockey squinting at the finishing post.

Further evacuees began to trickle home like also-ran horses staggering to the line. Anjali and Satma received two ticks beside their names. Professor and Frau Kirchel got just one. Since Professor Kirchel had been avoiding his wife all day, he was unable to testify to her whereabouts at the time of the alarm. 'Where could she be?' he fussed. 'There were only two exits and we all assembled here in the big D, so. . . .'

'It's all right, Professor, your wife is fine,' said Dr Dietrich.

'You have been talking rubbish all day, why should I believe you now?' snapped the professor. A great crash broke out as the roof timbers collapsed and the Sala Terrena made no further attempt at putting up a brave façade. At the same moment, Professor Kirchel was on his knees panting 'I am too old to live alone.'

Dr Dietrich shouted with all the power of her chronically damaged lungs: 'Professor Kirchel! Your wife wasn't in the palace at all – she was in the coach all along. Professor, she's alive!

'I know when one is dead and when one lives,' groaned the old musicologist. 'She's dead as earth.'

'Have it your way,' Dr Dietrich said rather mechanically, as she tried to light another cigarette and found her disposable lighter had finally given up. She flicked the trigger in frustration and then threw the lighter aside, a little abashed at her failure to conjure flame when behind her an entire palace was on fire.

To Lakshman, who had scampered over, Professor Kirchel looked like a man who had just crashed through from a parallel universe. If so, he had landed egg-shaped on the grass and Lakshman looked down at the fallen professor and experienced for the first time the sensation of towering over someone and the rare sensation of not knowing what to say. The imperious voice of the Duchess of Poundland carried itself to his ears on a gust of Neusiedlian wind. 'I can't stand this much longer,' she roared.

Lakshman turned to her and asked, 'What can't you stand? The fact that his wife is in there burning to death?'

'I couldn't care less about his *flammable* wife – I can't stand waiting any longer, I'm famished.' She opened her Poundland bag and withdrew a slightly dented pastry.

'Why don't you go and see if anyone else needs something to eat?'

'Would you like something?'

'No thanks, I'm not hungry.'

Irritated by the little man, the Duchess strode with Churchillian steps, holding her bulging Poundland bag forward. She began telling everybody not to make such a fuss, and, in doing so, she was wondrously relieved of her infirmities.

'You must eat!' she cried, even though most of them were unable to think of their stomachs in such a crisis. Determinedly, she foisted her stale croissants, cakes, ham and other comestibles she had stolen from the buffet tables, a theft that now looked much more like famine relief. Food was a great comfort to her, and so was spreading edible comfort to others.

The flames had taken hold now, gathering together until they seemed to be burning in unison, or at least a full tutti, putting on a grand finale. With the palace burning down ostentatiously behind them, the tiny black figures, ousted so brusquely from their seats, sought each other in the dark, avoiding the little Verboten signs implanted to admonish (or failing that to trip up) trespassers on the lawn, as all the while they were being upstaged by a gloriously wasteful bonfire.

For the evicted audience waiting in the cold for the coach to collect them, the death throes of the palace seemed to take an inordinately long time. If any of them felt guilty that was only to be expected. The empty palace had persisted in a stable condition until aroused by dreams of remembrance triggered by their arrival. It was their presence that had brought on this fatal fever. As they watched the historical edifice disintegrate, whilst listening to the Germans singing the Creation Mass, they agreed that if Napoleon had really wanted to rid Europe of its aristocratic vermin, this would have been a good way of doing it. He had an ideal opportunity to burn the place down around the time of Haydn's funeral. But he harboured ambitions to be the biggest parasite of them all, and destroying a palace would diminish the extent of his victory and lessen the valuable loot he had won.

It was the Duchess of Poundland's loot that was being distributed now. She even retraced her steps and tried to tempt the stricken Professor Kirchel with an iced fancy. He took it without knowing what it was.

Satma, replenished with food, was in a kind of sublime ecstasy. The roaring flames reflected in her eyes and she said in a deep thrilling voice: 'I saw all this before! I knew this was going to happen!'

'Why didn't you get us all out a bit earlier, then?' asked Kirchel reproachfully. 'You might have saved my wife.'

'Perhaps your wife had a very tiny aura.'

But what had become of our wayward hero? The duties of parenthood had prevented Edward from making his way directly to the exit. First he scrambled over to where Sally was sleeping across three seats. She had been woken by the cries of alarm and was standing on her chair when her daddy reached her. Edward picked her up and carried her in his arms to the back of the clutch of people filing out of the doors. She was still wrapped in his corduroy jacket but in her drowsy condition she dropped her toy duck, making Jemima a probable fatality in the fire.

Edward ran to the crowd of dark figures carrying Sally in his arms. He had to leave her somewhere safe and go back for Hamish. The figures were indistinct, but he heard some raised female voices in Hindi and staggered towards them.

Satma and Anjali's voices were raised in an altercation which had begun as a murmur in the darkness. It was started, as all such tiffs were, by Satma telling Anjali what to do. 'You have to tell them about the woman you saw playing the violin, Anjali.'

'I can't, Satma, it would be absurd. She was a ghost.'

Satma smiled dryly; Anjali's own smile began to wilt. 'You don't believe me do you?'

'Anjali, you say you saw a ghost. I'm not saying you didn't or even that you just made it up – whether to impress me or compete against me – I'm just saying go and tell Dr Dietrich or that other one with the wig.'

Anjali understood that there was more to this. 'It really got to you that I saw a ghost and you didn't! You can't stand it that she came to me and not you!'

'Oh yes? As though any ghost would waste their time haunting you! You haven't the charisma to attract spirits, you are too insignificant.'

Satma's cruelty was understandable when you consider that she had suddenly realised that the disaster she had foreseen had come about – the loss of Anjali's love. Her response was, as far as Anjali was concerned, a typical over-reaction. Though ill equipped to deal with this sort of attack, she had no idea how to retreat either, so she stood still, passively awaiting the next blow. This was the point at which Edward arrived and poured Sally into her arms.

'Anjali, look after Sally for me, could you? I've got to go back inside.'

'What? Are you mad?' barked Satma.

There was no reply, Edward was gone. He ran off towards the burning building.

'Now look what you've done, Anjali. You told him his wife was in that building and now he's going to get killed looking for her.'

Despite the portentous reputation Satma had for augury, Anjali knew at this moment she was all bluff. However, she could see that Sally was frightened and told her to be a brave girl.

'I could be a brave girl, if I had Jemima with me,' said Sally. 'But she's in there.'

'Jemima is your mother isn't she?' said the all-comprehending Satma, as Sally sobbed for her puddleduck. Anjali had a terrible fear that this fire would result in Sally being an orphan. She held Sally's hand very tight and went over to Dr Dietrich and explained the emergency.

'Did your father come out of the building?'

'Yes.'

'Thank goodness.'

'But he went back in.'

'What? Is he mad?'

Heads nodded to confirm this assertion. Sally stuck up for him. 'He went in to get Hamish.'

'Hamish, yes, he's on the list as well.'

'He's my brother, he went to do a number two.'

'What? He went inside a burning building to use the lavatory?'

'No, he was already started before it caught fire – he takes a very long time, Doctor.'

Dr Dietrich went a little way off to phone for an ambulance. This left Anjali and Teresa together. Anjali had no choice but to broach the subject of the ghostly violinist. 'I thought I should mention something: there may have been someone else in the palace,' she began hesitantly.

Teresa Mertz had counted the orchestra and come to the correct total of sixteen. She told Anjali that she should return to stand with the others. Then she jolted – of course! Kevin! 'Has anyone seen Kevin?' she cried.

'Right behind you, Tess,' said Kevin, with a grin on his face. Instead of the outpouring of relief and love that he had a right to expect, he received an outpouring of fury, possibly caused by the same anxiety. 'Don't do that to me you great fool!' she said punching him hard in the stomach.

Anjali thought this was a rough way for the concert organiser to treat one of her underlings who had just escaped death, but was ready to forgive the wig woman on the grounds that perhaps she was still in character as Princess Maria. Teresa offered another more down-to-earth explanation: 'It's all right, he's my boyfriend.'

Something made Teresa think of her agricultural prince. 'Kevin, you must go and find Tomek.'

'You're as subtle as a flying mallet, Tess; that's my greatest work going up in flames over there, and you want me to go in and get myself killed looking for your new buddy. I hope he roasts.'

'There may be someone else,' said Anjali again. 'Someone else is missing.'

Anjali explained how she had seen a girl playing a violin, but added, timidly, defiantly, that she thought it might have been a ghost. Teresa was typically practical in her response: 'I don't see why I should worry about the death of a ghost – should I? That must have already happened, surely? I mean I can put the ghost down on my list if you like. Do you know whose ghost it was?'

'It was my mummy's ghost,' said Sally, who had not been noticed for a while, clinging to Anjali's salwar.

Teresa saw the agony in this little girl's face and, despite her many other pressing duties, bent to speak with her.

'What's your mother's name, darling?'

'Pamela.'

Teresa began to look down the list for a Pamela.

'The thing is,' simpered Anjali, 'I saw her playing the violin in an empty room in the east wing.'

Kevin was suddenly laughing. 'Come with me,' he said. 'I'll introduce you to your ghost.' He led her over to where Tomasino was standing with Stephan and the oboist, still holding their instruments, since there had been no time to put them back into their cases, and of course still dressed in their eighteenth-century gear, the uniform of the Esterházy Orchestra. 'Here is your phantom fiddler.'

Feeling Kevin's tap on the shoulder Sophia turned and held out her hand. When Anjali touched it she felt a sudden pulse through her fingers.

'There – very much alive as you see, thank Christ!'

'No! The violinist I saw was a girl,' said Anjali.

'So is Signor Tomasino,' whispered Kevin – 'or rather, signorita!' His voice flecked with the illicit thrill of remembered pleasure. 'Underneath those clothes Sophie is a woman just like you. I know that for a fact.'

Sophie removed her wig and handed it to Kevin. 'You can throw this on the fire. I won't be needing it any more,' she said, shaking her blonde hair loose.

Kevin didn't know what to do with the empty wig, so he took it away with him. The blush on his face was probably caused by the warmth of the flames that were growing more intense all the time. He couldn't approach the palace to throw the wig onto the pyre so he furtively stuffed it into his pocket.

'I'm glad you're not a ghost, though,' said Sally sweetly when he had left.

'That's very nice of you to say so. I am too. Being a ghost is not much fun I think.'

'Hamish says there's no such thing as ghosts,' added Sally. 'He's my big brother.'

'Well, your brother is probably right.'

Anjali heard Satma calling for her and left Sally in the care of Sophie to go and see what she was bellowing about now. She was laughing. 'It seems that your ghost has been unmasked, Anjali. How disappointing for you,' she mocked.

To her surprise, Anjali was uncowed. 'Satma, you may prefer the company of spirits but I am glad she wasn't a ghost. I am not even sure I like ghosts at all. I think I prefer living people.'

Satma gave a shudder as though something was passing through her.

'Sati, I don't care which life are you leading, or if you're stuck in your previous one, but I've decided to live in this world from now on. I'm not going back with you.'

'I know.'

Concern for Sally gave Anjali the immediate excuse to go back to Sophie and the other musicians. Satma understood precisely what this was about. The conflagration had given everyone a chance to change their allegiances – it was not a revolution, but it was a brief moment of anarchy – an interregnum – that allowed some realignment of relationships. So, as she watched Anjali join the charming Sophie and the other musicians, she said nothing.

I don't belong with them, she thought gloomily. I've got a tin ear for music anyway. This was true: Satma's inheritance of Mozart's soul hadn't advanced her own musical talent, whereas Anjali was adept at the keyboard, a very eighteenth-century accomplishment.

Tessa's concern for Tomek, was threatening to embarrass her, when a crude folk song, ripped off loudly in Hungarian with more gusto than élan, alerted her to the approach of her ruffian lover, who was looking even stockier than usual in a theatrical cape.

'What's that you're wearing Tomek?'

'It's curtains,' he declared dramatically, swirling round in the light of the conflagration to show off the gold crests embroidered on a field of dark velvet. 'They should have burned it down in 1793,' roared the grinning Tomek. 'Still, better late than never.' Striding across the lawn with his arms full of puppets and a bottle in each hand, he resembled a medieval painting in which crowds of penitents are enfolded in the Virgin's gowns. The heads of the slack-stringed puppets were humbly bowed, but Tomek himself was triumphant.

'I see you have rescued some victims from the fire,' said Teresa. 'Were they in any danger – down in that cave?'

'Now listen, my dear, these puppets were lost in the flames, as far as you or anyone else knows, am I right?'

Teresa did not make any objection to this testimony.

'I am their rightful owner.' Tomek clung to the puppets as to booty won fair and square. 'I brought them to life.'

'Yes, you can have them, Tomek, I don't see why not.'

Teresa, who was now wigless, but otherwise still in costume, now noticed Kevin's absence. 'Oh shit! That silly boy has gone back to rescue *you*, Tomek.'

Tomek laughed. This was a good joke.

'You have to go after him.'

'What would be the point, Madama? As you see, I don't need rescuing.'

'Yes but *he* might – now.'

Teresa recognised from his shrug that it was idle to suppose that she could motivate Tomek into such an act of nobility.

Kevin had not gone inside to look for Tomek. Only a lunatic would think of going back into the burning palace. Kevin looked open-mouthed at the palace in which he had spent the last nine months supervising the laying of innumerable cables and directing the placement of millions of fake candles – the palace – along with all its contents – was now being exothermically converted into gas and ash. All his efforts to bring the palace to life with light were being literally outshone, and he had guessed the probable cause. Despite the pointless wastage, he couldn't help feeling a gratifying sense of his own potency that amounted to pride. 'I made that!' he thought. 'I made those huge flames, taller than me. That's my blaze.'

It was truly Kevin's masterpiece. He thrust his stone-washed groin forward as he shielded his eyes from the radiating heat. He wriggled his hips, repressing the urge to do a full-blown fire dance, his body taken over by excitement. Then he punched the air and cried: 'Whose the Daddy NOW!!'

Another person who was enjoying the pyrotechnical display was

Rosie, who lay on her back in the damp grass watching the sparks spin-wheeling above her as the palace sprouted orange feathers from both wings and seemed about to take off like a phoenix. However, she managed to see all these things without realising that the palace was on fire. She attributed them to some new-found vigour acquired by her husband.

Anyone who thinks that burning alive a constipated boy before he has had a chance to see anything of the world or even wipe his own arse constitutes a fitting climax to our evening has got the wrong idea of the comic spirit. Let them read other writers work wherein children are sacrificed for the sake of action. I shall not let even one boy, no matter how dumpy and unprepossessing he may be, suffer for my narrative. Is it not enough that I have made him humourless and rather badly toilet trained? Do I have to fry him too? I have put an entire palace to the flames and that should be enough. In exchange for the life of this unlovely boy I will grant that not one scrap of Esterházy will be salvageable from the conflagration.

Edward did not think twice about braving the flames in order rescue his boy, and he certainly did not wait to get his bearings by consulting the stars. When he broke into the nearest door and saw the flames devouring the decorators' rags and dustsheets, he knew at once that he had entered the wrong wing. He ran back out and crossed the large courtyard at a run, and came to the opposite wing. This was it, the Display Room itself. He recognised the headless Sheila as he fumbled with the handle of the door.

The mannequin was not going to revolve or oscillate or anything, because she was on fire, within her case, the electric motor having blown out. When the door finally gave, she fell forwards against the glass and he had to jump sideways to avoid her.

The room he was now in, though some distance from the source of the blaze, was filling with smoke. Edward didn't like to think how little time he had. He banged on the toilet door with his fists and cried out his son's name.

Unfortunately, rescuing Hamish was not made any easier by Hamish himself.

'What do you want, Dad?'

'You've got to get out of there.'

'I told you to go away, I'm not ready.'

'Don't you realise? The fire engines are coming.'

'Is this another of your stupid jokes, Dad? First it was aeroplanes now it's fire engines.'

'No, Hamish, the palace is on fire.'

'Dad, you must think I'm a total idiot.'

'How much proof do you want? Asphixiation?'

'If it is true, how come the alarm's not ringing then?'

'You want an alarm?' Edward caught sight of a small red glass-fronted box mounted on the wall. A metal clapper hung on a chain from its side. He broke the glass, and there was no responding alarm. Then, in rising desperation, he detached a fire extinguisher from the wall and used it to break the glass of the nearest display cabinet. Instantly the room was filled with a painfully loud ringing, and the baryton toppled off its stand and was about to fall to the floor when Edward caught it.

The shrill confirmation of the burglar alarm brought Hamish out of his hiding place. The moment he opened the toilet door Edward grabbed him by the arm and dragged him towards the exit, which by now was hidden behind a sheet of flame. The intense heat had blistered the pretty paintwork and the gold leaf was melting off the rococo sconces, and, having scorched the 200-year-old dust behind this painted skin, the flames had now set to work on attacking the skeletal timberwork.

'We can't get through,' said Hamish. 'I'm scared I won't do it.'

'Don't worry, Hamish, I've got a fire extinguisher!' screamed Edward. He held the baryton to the burning door in the manner of a fire extinguisher and only then realised that true to its nature as a baryton it wasn't going to be of any practical use. There was no time to figure out how he had made the switch. They ran headlong through the wall of flames.

The headless Sheila was lying across the exit spitting sparks.

'Kick her out of the way, Dad!'

Edward and Hamish staggered away from the sources of heat and danger, and didn't stop until they reached the grass. Looking back they saw how close it had been.

'Where are we, Dad?'

'We're safe,' gasped Edward, leaning against the flank of a sleeping bulldozer.

The smoke rose endlessly upward into the dark sky, taking flecks of molten gold leaf with it and obscuring the stars to which they looked for guidance. Lost as mariners cast adrift, they floated about, taking in lungfuls of air. It was up to them to find their way back, guided by the fateful stars that burned within them. They almost tripped over a pair of recumbent figures and the apologies and glimpses of rapidly adjusted pastel clothing revealed that they had found the Pratts.

'What do you take us for?' barked the man. 'There's room for just the two of us. Go and find your own spot . . .'

Edward simply gestured behind him, by way of explanation.

'Oh my goodness!' exclaimed Pratt. 'The palace is on fire.'

'That's right. You must have been too occupied to notice.'

Edward and Hamish returned to the safety of the group, singed and smoking gently. Now, with no human occupants inside, the fire can finish off the physical destruction of Nikolaus the Magnificent's fairy castle, until nothing of it but the memories remain, except for one misshapen object that Edward was carrying under his arm.

Edward saw the figure of Anjali, unmistakable from its elegant draperies. She was coming towards him, as though into his arms – a vision that he would have treated with deep suspicion, even if it had occurred in a dream. She was being pulled towards him, her hand held tightly in the grip of Sally's fearsome little fingers. Sweat lubricated the join and whilst Sally ran to her father, Anjali trudged behind in the capacity of an unpaid babysitter.

'It wasn't Mummy's ghost Daddy!' said Sally amid numerous sooty kisses. 'It was someone else.'

'That's a relief.'

Sally flung her arms around her father and instantly felt something unfamiliar about his customary girth.

'What's that big lump, Daddy?'

Edward trusted Hamish to stand unaided and revealed the fact that he was holding a baryton. 'Don't you want to give your big brother a hug too?'

'He smells like burnt sausages,' said Sally, as she wrapped Hamish in her hands without making too much contact.

'Why on earth did you want to save that dreadful thing?' asked Anjali. 'I mean the musical instrument,' she added hastily.

A complicated answer slowly formed itself in Edward's head, something about how it was a symbol of something that has got stuck, whilst time went on ahead, but he couldn't put it into words, particularly not to her, so instead he shrugged his shoulders and said with his best attempt at insouciance: 'I thought I might just take it up.'

'You know, you are a very strange man, but you have such nice children, you must be doing something right.'

'Goodbye Anjali. I have been an utter fool. I am sorry.' And with uncharacteristic candour he added: 'I was clumsy because you're just so beautiful and I saw you laughing at me this morning.'

'Laughing?' said Anjali. 'I don't think I could have been . . .'

'Oh yes. When I was looking for the passports in my bag you were looking down from the coach and mocking me.'

'Oh, then! Satma was telling me a dirty joke about Mozart's magic flute.'

'I have been trying all day to mend that ridiculous first impression, when in fact I hadn't made one at all.'

'Oh don't worry, you have now. Goodbye Edward, you are a good father. I hope you find happiness. Next time you meet a woman you like the look of, try not to threaten to murder her on the first evening.'

To his surprise, Anjali did not get onto the coach to join Satma. He watched her slim figure float away to be greeted by the young musicians, and then moving off with Stephan's arm over her shoulder and Sophie's hand in hers. He could see their silhouettes, identified by the violin swinging at Sophie's elbow and the cello mounted on Stephan's hip.

Edward had mixed feelings when he saw the palace collapsing in on itself. It would be rebuilt if it was profitable, and if it wasn't, then what was there to be sad about? Once again the place reminded him of work. Some banks go up in flames, and the remaining ones attribute their survival to some imagined merit.

Dr Dietrich had received a call from Carl, the driver of the Travego, and gathered that he would be here soon to take them all away from this evening.

All the while, the wind blew across Lake Neusiedl with its customary briskness. It swept over the surrounding landscape chilling the evacuated humans whilst simultaneously fanning the flames in the building where they had left their coats. The severity of this wind had always ruled this land with cold tyranny, but never before had it operated with such neat cruelty.

Three fire engines had arrived and even the firemen refused to enter the burning building, preferring to moisten it with great spurts of liquid pumped up from Lake Neusiedl. But we need not concern ourselves with their efforts, which were utterly ineffectual.

The rumble of yet more heavyweight diesel engineering was assurance that the coach was at last approaching up the long drive; Dr Dietrich could hear its crescendo. She went to fetch Professor Kirchel and found him still on the ground. He gave off howls of despair, which was disconcerting, especially since he didn't really howl, he said the word *howl*. 'Howl howl howl!' he said, in a painfully drawn-out way. You could not imagine a more piteous display of loss. Bernhardt would have been proud that his peculiar brand of histrionic self-pity was being continued after his death.

'Come with me, Professor, the coach is coming,' said Dr Dietrich. I don't know if her kindly act was not mixed with eager anticipation of witnessing the remedy for grief that was about to be administered when the coach arrived.

A roar of approval from the audience greeted the Travego's reappearance. They were shipwrecked on that wide oval lawn and a rescue vessel had at last arrived. The relaxation of the valves was followed by the slow sweep of the doors opening, and a figure that made its way down the steely steps, descending with great care, as though onto alien territory. 'What is it?' asked the woman in perfect German (which was not surprising since it was Frau Kirchel herself).

Hearing her voice, the forlorn professor uncurled and staggered upright. 'You have come back to me!' he gasped, recovering with a start from his brief widowhood.

'You idiot,' said Kirchel's wife.

The smoke-stained refugees began to mount the Mercedes. And now our attention is caught by the approach of the young couple from a far distant lawn. They were walking hand-in-hand. James had lost his spats and Rosie was smiling, dishevelled and pregnant.

All had been accounted for on Dr Dietrich's list. The Germans stopped singing Haydn's oratorio and cheerfully joined the rest.

'That was very nice music,' said Satma, getting onto the coach alone. 'Are you a professional choir?'

'No, we are amateurs. We are visiting Vienna for the choral festival.'

'I was wrong about you too,' said Satma humbly. 'I told my friend that you were wife-swappers.'

There was a shared laugh when this comment was translated into German and passed around the group.

'What's so funny?'

'Actually, you were right. Would you care to join us?'

The Duchess of Poundland demanded to know where the *financial* man in corduroy thought he was. She needed him to elevate her into the vehicle. Edward came dutifully forwards.

'Where have you been? Now that little man and that *frock-coated* woman have got the best seats.'

'I'm sorry, I had to go back for something.'

'Mooning around looking for ghosts? We've all had enough of your *phantom* wife.'

'So everyone *has* been talking about me, I knew it.'

'Well, if you will insist on making a *frantic* exhibition of yourself . . .'

With his hands proffered in the correct spacing to give an even thrust to each buttock, Edward heaved, and the great lady rose into the coach. As Edward wiped his palms together in a symbolic gesture of achievement, the surrounding crowd laughed and some of them actually applauded him. Edward bowed, acknowledging their acclamation, and then, when he saw that he had left two black handprints of soot on the grand ascending buttocks, bowed again with silent laughter.

Carl took one look at Edward and shook his head. He spoke to Dr Dietrich and she explained to Edward: 'I am sorry, but he will not allow you onto the coach in that condition. It's the upholstery.'

Edward had not seen himself but he assumed he was perhaps a little sooty.

'You are completely black with it,' remarked Dr Dietrich.

'What am I to do then?'

'If you could just stand aside, so the others may get on board...'

So Edward retreated, baffled. Slowly he gathered himself sufficiently to defend himself. 'Excuse me,' he said, turning to Dr Dietrich.

'What is it now?'

'Do you think I could have my bag?'

Dr Dietrich sighed wearily and called Carl down from his seat, respectfully apologising for putting him to so much trouble. Edward stood aside as Carl opened the luggage hold. When the bag was thrust at him, Edward wondered what he had done to offend the driver. Carl was seething at the intended outrage to his upholstery that had only been averted by his watchfulness.

Edward did not protest at this maltreatment because he was more concerned with getting warm clothing for his children. Once he had done so, he realised that, being denied access to the coach, they would be stranded in Esterházy all night.

'You can come back with me,' said a voice.

It was Teresa. Edward had not spoken to her before, though he knew her as Princess Maria. He introduced himself and apologised for the soot.

'Never mind, my car is an old banger anyway. Kevin! Come here!'

Kevin heard his name being called and sloped up alongside. 'What do you want now, for crying out loud?'

'Get on the coach.'

'What for Tess?'

'To make room, of course.'

'Are you saying we're no longer an item, Tess?'

'Item? Kevin, we were never an *item*. The word item sounds like something on a wedding present list.'

'We both know *that* was never going to happen, Tess. It's useless going on about it.'

'Yes, well, now you *can* be useful. Carl has refused to allow one of our guests onto the coach because he would leave soot stains on the upholstery, so I have offered to give him a lift back in my car. I am assuming that you can make the journey back to Vienna without leaving any stains, Kevin.'

When Kevin saw that Edward was putting something away in a large empty holdall, he seized the chance to counter-attack: 'I told you he was a thief! Look, Tess, he's got that barrytron. He's stashing it away in his bag.'

'He rescued it from the flames – he'll probably get a medal from the Society of the Friends of Music.' Teresa guided her guests towards her car, turning her back on Kevin, who now knew how it felt to be a disfavoured courtier.

The children shared the back seat of Teresa's old Passat and Edward took the passenger seat. 'Are you sure about this? It's very kind . . .'

'It's the least I could do, since you are the hero of the night!'

'Hero? I tried to put the fire out with a musical instrument.'

'Yes, but you rescued your boy.'

'What shall I do with it now? Do you want it?'

'What use is it without a palace to put it in? Why don't you learn to play? It would be nice for you to have some music around the house. It's the perfect instrument for the non-musician.

Edward was about to mention that he had once been a musician, but refrained, remembering the viola jokes. The baryton would suit him. The only reason it was not the butt of jokes like the viola was because no one had heard of it. 'I suppose it might be interesting, so long as I only play it in private.'

'Keep the memory alive,' said Teresa.

With Hamish and Sally sleeping in the back seat, they drove through the night back to Vienna.

As the thirty-two valves of the Mercedes Travego sparked up once again, and the last human beings to experience Nikolaus Esterházy's fairyland prepared to commence their long drive back to their various hotels in Vienna, we must wave this symphony farewell.

The deepest sigh came not from the pneumatics, not from Carl, who would have a terrible job getting the smell of bonfires out of his top-grade upholstery, not even from his smoke-stained passengers, but from Tomek.

Sitting on the grass in front of the smouldering palace, with his puppets around him, he watched the coach depart, and a sudden whimsy taking him, he made Columbine sit up and wave goodbye. Then Arlechino leapt up and the two marionette lovers danced a pleasant minuet.

At once, the words that he had painstakingly learned in both English and German came back to Tomek. It was his only line of speech, which he was supposed to utter once the applause had died down at the end of the concert, to round off the evening. They were the words spoken by Prince Nikolaus the Magnificent at the end of the performance and showed the good grace with which the Prince conceded to his Kapellmeister's symphonic farewell. As the English version had it:

'Now that they have all gone – it is time that we must too.'

To this day the Palace of Esterhazy
stands unsinged and magnificent in Fertod, Hungary,
and no one should be put off visiting it
by the lies told in this book.